CYBERBOOKS

Also by Ben Bova
published by Tor Books

As on a Darkling Plain
The Astral Mirror
Battle Station
Colony
Escape Plus
The Kinsman Saga
The Multiple Man
Orion
Out of the Sun
Peacekeepers
Privateers
Prometheans
The Starcrossed
Test of Fire
Vengeance of Orion
Voyagers II: The Alien Within
The Winds of Altair

Edited by Ben Bova
The Best of the Nebulas

CYBERBOOKS

Ben Bova

A Tom Doherty Associates Book
New York

To Ginny and John, Eldene and Bill:
shipmates and treasured friends.
And to Barbara and the Rock.

This is a work of fiction. All the characters and events
portrayed in this book are fictitious, and any resemblance to real
people or events is purely coincidental.

CYBERBOOKS

A TOR BOOK
Published by Tom Doherty Associates, Inc.
49 West 24 Street
New York, NY 10010

Library of Congress Cataloging-in-Publication Data

Bova, Ben, 1932—
    Cyberbooks.

    "A TOR book"—P. iv.
    I. Title.
PS3552.084C9   1989   813'.54   88-33476

ISBN: 0-312-93181-6

First edition: May 1989
0 9 8 7 6 5 4 3 2 1

SPRING,
Book I

MURDER ONE ━━━━━━

THE first murder took place in a driving April rainstorm, at the corner of Twenty-first Street and Gramercy Park West.

Mrs. Agatha Marple, eighty-three years of age, came tottering uncertainly down the brownstone steps of her town house, the wind tugging at her ancient red umbrella. She had telephoned for a taxi to take her downtown to meet her nephew for lunch, as she had every Monday afternoon for the past fourteen years.

The Yellow Cab was waiting at the curb, its driver imperturbably watching the old lady struggle with the wind and her umbrella from the dry comfort of his armored seat behind the bulletproof partition that separated him from the potential homicidal maniacs who were his customers. The meter was humming to itself, a sound that counterbalanced nicely the drumming of rain on the cab's roof; the fare was already well past ten dollars. He had punched the destination into the cab's guidance computer: Webb Press, just off Washington Square. A lousy five-minute drive; the computer, estimating the traffic at this time of day and the

3

weather conditions, predicted the fare would be no more than forty-nine fifty.

Briefly he thought about taking the old bat for the scenic tour along the river; plenty of traffic there to slow them down and run up the meter. Manny at the garage had bypassed the automated alarm systems in all the cab's meters, so the fares never knew when the drivers deviated from the computer's optimum guidance calculations. But this old bitch was too smart for that; she would refuse to pay and insist on complaining to the hack bureau on the two-way. He had driven her before, and she was no fool, despite her age. She was a lousy tipper, too.

She finally got to the cab and tried to close the umbrella and open the door at the same time. The driver grinned to himself. One of his little revenges on the human race: keep the doors locked until *after* they try to get in. They break their fingernails, at least. One guy sprained his wrist so bad he had to go to the hospital.

Finally the cabbie pecked the touchpad that unlocked the right rear door. It flew open and nearly knocked the old broad on her backside. A gust of wet wind flapped her gray old raincoat.

"Hey, c'mon, you're gettin' rain inside my cab," the driver hollered into his intercom microphone.

Before the old lady could reply, a man in a dark blue trenchcoat and matching fedora pulled down low over his face splashed through the curbside puddles and grabbed for the door.

"I'm in a hurry," he muttered, trying to push the old woman out of the taxi's doorway.

"How dare you!" cried Mrs. Marple, with righteous anger.

"Go find a garbage can to pick in," snarled the man, and he twisted Mrs. Marple's hand off the door handle.

She yelped with pain, then swatted at the man with her umbrella, ineffectually. The man blocked her feeble swing, yanked the umbrella out of her grasp, and knocked her to the pavement. She lay there in a puddle, rain pelting her, gasping for breath.

The man raised her red umbrella high over his head, grasping it in both his gloved hands. The old woman's eyes went wide, her mouth opened to scream but no sound came out. Then the man drove the umbrella smashingly into her chest like someone would pound a stake through a vampire's heart.

The old lady twitched once and then lay still, the umbrella sticking out of her withered chest like a sword. The man looked down at her, nodded once as if satisfied with his work, and then stalked away into the gray windswept rain.

True to the finest traditions of New York's hack drivers, the cabbie put his taxi in gear and drove away, leaving the old woman dead on the sidewalk. He never said a word about the incident to anyone.

ONE

I T was a Hemingway kind of day: clean and bright and fine, sky achingly blue, sun warm enough to make a man sweat. A good day for facing the bulls or hunting rhino.

Carl Lewis was doing neither. In the air-conditioned comfort of the Amtrak Levitrain, he was fast asleep and dreaming of books that sang to their readers.

The noise of the train plunging into a long, dark tunnel startled him from his drowse. He had begun the ride that morning in Boston feeling excited, eager. But as the train glided almost silently along the New England countryside, levitated on its magnetic guideway, the warm sunshine of May streaming through the coach's window combined with the slight swaying motion almost hypnotically. Carl dozed off, only to be startled awake by the sudden roar of entering the tunnel.

His ears popped. The ride had seemed dreamily slow when it started, but now that he was actually approaching Penn Station it suddenly felt as if things were happening too fast. Carl felt a faint inner unease, a mounting nervousness, butterflies trembling in his middle. He put it down to the excitement of starting a new job, maybe a whole new career.

Now, as the train roared through the dark tunnel and his ears hurt with the change in air pressure, Carl realized that what he felt was not mere excitement. It was apprehension. Anxiety. Damned close to outright fear. He stared at the reflection of his face in the train window: clear of eye, firm of jaw, sandy hair neatly combed, crisp new shirt with its blue MIT necktie painted down its front, proper tweed jacket with the leather elbow patches. He looked exactly as a brilliant young software composer should look. Yet he felt like a scared little kid.

The darkness of the tunnel changed abruptly to the glaring lights of the station. The train glided toward a crowded platform, then screeched horrifyingly down the last few hundred yards of its journey on old-fashioned steel wheels that struck blazing sparks against old-fashioned steel rails. A lurch, a blinking of the light strips along the ceiling, and the train came to a halt.

With the hesitancy known only to New Englanders visiting Manhattan for the first time, Carl Lewis slid his garment bag from the rack over his seat and swung his courier case onto his shoulder. The other passengers pushed past him, muttering and grumbling their way off the train. They shoved Carl this way and that until he felt like a tumbleweed caught in a cattle stampede.

Welcome to New York, he said to himself as the stream of detraining passengers dumped him impersonally, indignantly, demeaningly, on the concrete platform.

The station was so big that Carl felt as if he had shrunk to the size of an insect. People elbowed and stamped their way through the throngs milling around; the huge cavern buzzed like a beehive. Carl felt tension in the air, the supercharged crackling high-stress electricity of the Big Apple. Panhandlers in their traditional grubby rags shambled along, each of them displaying the official city begging permit badge. Grimy bag ladies screamed insults at the empty air. Teenaged thugs in military fatigues eyed the crowds like predators looking for easy prey. Religious zealots in saffron robes, in severe black suits and string ties, even in mock space suits complete with bubble helmets, sought alms and converts. Mostly alms. Police robots stood immobile, like fat little blue fireplugs, while the tides of noisy, smelly, angry, scampering humanity flowed in every direction at once. The noise was a bedlam of a million individual voices acting out their private dramas. The station crackled with fierce, hostile anxiety.

Carl took a deep breath, clutched his garment bag tighter, and clamped his arm closely over the courier case hanging from his shoulder. He avoided other people's eyes almost as well as a native Manhattanite, and threaded his way through the throngs toward the taxi stand outside, successfully evading the evangelists, the beggars, the would-be muggers, and the flowing tide of perfectly ordinary citizens who would knock him down and mash him flat under their scurrying shoes if he so much as missed a single step.

There were no cabs, only a curbside line of complaining jostling men and women waiting for taxis. A robot dispatcher, not unlike the robot cops inside the station, stood impassively at the head of the line. While the police robots were blue, the taxi dispatcher's aluminum skin was anodized yellow, faded and chipped, spattered here and there with mud and other substances Carl preferred not to think about.

Every few minutes a taxi swerved around the corner on two wheels and pulled up to the dispatcher's post with a squeal of brakes. One person would get in and the line would inch forward. Finally Carl was at the head of the line.

"I beg your pardon, sir. Are you going uptown or downtown?" asked the man behind Carl.

"Uh, uptown—no, downtown." Carl had to think about Manhattan's geography.

"Excellent! Would you mind if I shared a cab with you? I'm late for an important appointment. I'll pay the entire fare."

The man was tiny, much shorter than Carl, and quite slim. He was the kind of delicate middle-aged man for whom the word *dapper* had been coined. He wore a conservative silver-gray business suit; the tie painted down the front of his shirt looked hand done and expensive. He was carrying a blue trenchcoat over one arm despite the gloriously sunny spring morning. Silver-gray hair clipped short, a toothy smile that seemed a bit forced on his round, wrinkled face. Prominent ears, watery brownish eyes. He appeared harmless enough.

The big brown eyes were pleading silently. Carl did not know how to refuse. "Uh, yeah, sure, okay."

"Oh, thank you! I'm late already." The man glanced at his wristwatch, then stared down the street as if he could make a cab appear by sheer willpower.

A taxi finally did come, and they both got into it.

"Bunker Books," said Carl.

The taxi driver said something that sounded like Chinese. Or maybe Sanskrit.

"Fifth Avenue and Eighth Street," said Carl's companion, very slowly and loudly. "The Synthoil Tower."

The cabbie muttered to himself and punched the address into his dashboard computer. The electronic map on the taxi's control board showed a route in bright green that seemed direct enough. Carl sat back and tried to relax.

But that was impossible. He was sitting in a Manhattan taxicab with a total stranger who obviously knew the city well. Carl looked out the window on his side of the cab. The sheer emotional energy level out there in the streets was incredible. Manhattan *vibrated*. It hummed and crackled with tension and excitement. It made Boston seem like a placid country retreat. Hordes of people swarmed along the sidewalks and streamed across every intersection. Taxis by the hundreds weaved through the traffic like an endless yellow snake, writhing and coiling around the big blue steam buses that huffed and chuffed along the broad avenue.

The women walking along the sidewalks were very different from Boston women. Their clothes were the absolutely latest style, tiny hip-hugging skirts and high leather boots, leather motorcycle jackets heavy with chains and lovingly contrived sweat stains. Most of the women wore their biker helmets with the visor down, a protection against mugging and smog as well as the latest fashion. The helmets had radios built into them, Carl guessed from the small whip antennas bobbing up from them. A few women went boldly bareheaded, exposing their long hair and lovely faces to Carl's rapt gaze.

The cab stopped for a red light and a swarm of earnest-looking men and women boiled out of the crowd on the sidewalk to begin washing the windshield, polishing the grillwork, waxing the fenders. Strangely, they wore well-pressed business suits and starched formal shirts with corporate logos on their painted ties. The taxi driver screamed at them through his closed windows, but they ignored his Asian imprecations and, just as the light turned green again, affixed a green sticker to the lower left-hand corner of the windshield.

"Unemployed executives," explained Carl's companion, "thrown out of work by automation in their offices."

"Washing cars at street corners?" Carl marvelled.

"It's a form of unemployment benefit. The city allows them to earn money this way, rather than paying them a dole. They each get a franchise at a specific street corner, and the cabbie must pay their charge or lose his license."

Carl shook his head in wonderment. In Boston you just stood in line all day for a welfare check.

"Bunker Books," mused his companion. "What a coincidence."

Carl turned his attention to the gray-haired man sitting beside him.

"Imagine the statistical chance that two people standing next to one another in line waiting for a taxi would have the same destination," the dapper older man said.

"You're going to Bunker Books, too?" Carl could not hide his surprise.

"To the same address," said the older man. "My destination is in the same building: the Synthoil Tower." He glanced worriedly at the gleaming gold band of his wristwatch. "And if we don't get through this traffic I am going to be late for a very important appointment.''

The taxi driver apparently could hear their every word despite the bulletproof partition between him and the rear seat. He hunched over his wheel, muttering in some foreign language, and lurched the cab across an intersection despite a clearly red traffic light and the shrill whistling of a brown-uniformed auxiliary traffic policewoman. They swerved around an oncoming delivery truck and scattered half a dozen pedestrians scampering across the intersection. Carl and his companion were tossed against one another on the backseat. The man's blue trenchcoat slid to the filthy floor of the cab with an odd thunking sound.

''Who's your appointment with?'' Carl asked, inwardly surprised at questioning a total stranger so brazenly—and with poor grammar, at that.

The older man seemed unperturbed by either gaffe as he retrieved his trenchcoat. ''Tarantula Enterprises, Limited. Among other things, Tarantula owns Webb Press, a competitor of Bunker's, I should think.''

Carl shrugged. ''I don't know much about the publishing business. . . .''

''Ahh. You must be a writer.''

''Nosir. I'm a software composer.''

The rabbity older man made a puzzled frown. ''You're in the clothing business?''

''I'm a computer engineer. I design software programs.''

''Computers! That *is* interesting. Is Bunker revamping its inventory control system? Or its royalty accounting system?''

With a shake of his head, Carl replied, ''Something completely different.''

''Oh?''

In all of Carl's many telephone conversations with his one friend at Bunker Books a single point had been emphasized over and over. *Tell no one about this project,* the woman had whispered urgently. Whispered, as though they were standing in a crowded room rather than speaking through a scrambled, private, secure fiberoptic link. *If word about this gets out to the industry—don't say a word to anybody!*

"It's, uh, got to do with the editorial side of the business," he generalized.

"I see," said his companion, smiling toothily. "A computer program to replace editors. Not a very difficult task, I should imagine."

Stung to his professional core, Carl replied before he could think of what he was saying, "Nothing like that! There've been editing programs for twenty years, just about. Using a computer to edit manuscripts is easy. You don't need a human being to edit a manuscript."

"So? And what you are going to do is difficult?"

"Nobody's done it before."

"But you will succeed where others have failed?"

"Nobody's even tried to do this before," Carl said, with some pride.

"I wonder what it could be?"

Carl forced himself to remain silent, despite the voice inside his head urging him to reach into the courier case lying on the seat between them and pull out the marvel that he was bringing to Bunker Books. A slim case of plastic and metal, about the size of a paperback novel. With a display screen on its face that could show any page of any book in the history of printing. The first prototype of the electronic book. Carl's very own invention. His offspring, the pride of his genius.

The taxi lurched around a corner, then stopped so hard that Carl was thrown almost against the heavy steel-and-glass partition. His companion seemed to hold his place better, almost as if he had braced himself in advance. His trenchcoat flopped over Carl's courier bag with a heavy thunking sound that was lost in the squeal of the taxi's brakes.

"Synthoil Tower," announced the cab driver. "That's eighty-two even, with th' tip."

True to his word, the dapper gray-haired man slid his credit card into the slot in the bulletproof partition, patted Carl's arm briefly by way of farewell, then scampered to the imposing glass-and-bronze doors of the Synthoil building. It took a few moments for Carl to gather his two bags and extricate himself from the backseat of the taxi. The cabbie drummed his fingers on his steering wheel impatiently. As soon as Carl was clear of the cab, the driver pulled away from the curb, the rear door swinging shut with a heavy slam.

Carl gaped at the rapidly disappearing taxi. For a wild instant a flash of panic surged through him. Clutching at his courier case, though, he felt the comforting solidity of his prototype. It was still there, safely inside his case.

So he thought.

Reader's Report

Title: *The Terror from Beyond Hell*

Author: Sheldon Stoker

Category: Blockbuster horror

Reader: Priscilla Alice Symmonds

Synopsis: What's to synopsize? Still yet another trashy piece of horror that will sell a million copies hardcover. Stoker is *awful*, but he sells books.

Recommendation: Hold our noses and buy it.

TWO

LORI Tashkajian's almond-shaped eyes were filled with tears. She was sitting at her desk in the cubbyhole that passed for an editor's office at Bunker Books, staring out the half window at the slowly disappearing view of the stately Chrysler Building.

Her tiny office was awash with paper. Manuscripts lay everywhere, some of them stacked in professional gray cartons with the printed labels of literary agents affixed to them, others in battered cardboard boxes that had once contained shoes or typing paper or even children's toys. Still others sat unboxed, thick wads of paper bound by sturdy elastic bands. Everywhere. On Lori's desk, stuffing the bookshelves along the cheap plastic partition that divided the window and separated her cubicle from the next, strewn across the floor between the partition and gray metal desk, piled high along the window ledge.

One of management's strict edicts at Bunker Books was that editors were not allowed to read on the job. "Reading is done by readers," said the faded memo tacked to the wall above Lori's desk. "Readers are paid to read. Editors are paid to package books that readers have read. If an editor finds it necessary to read a manuscript, it is the editor's responsibility to do the reading on her or his own time. Office hours are much too valuable to be wasted in reading manuscripts.''

Not that she had time for reading, anyway. Lori ignored all the piled-up manuscripts and, sighing, watched the construction crew weld another I-beam into the steel skeleton that was growing like Jack's beanstalk between her window and her view of the distinctive art-deco spike of the Chrysler Building. In another week they would blot out the view altogether. The one beautiful thing in her daily grind was being taken away from her, inches at a time, erased from her sight even while she watched. Coming to New York had been a mistake. Her glamorous life in the publishing industry was a dead end; there were no men she would consider dating more than once; and now they were even taking the Chrysler Building away from her.

She was a strikingly comely young woman, with the finely chiselled aquiline nose, the flaring cheekbones, the full lips, the dark almond eyes and lustrous black hair of distant romantic desert lands. Her figure was a trifle lush for modern New York tastes, a touch too much bosom and hips for the vassals of Seventh Avenue and their cadaverous models. Her life was a constant struggle against junk food. Instead of this week's fashionable biker image, which would have made her look even more padded than she was naturally, Lori wore a simple sweater and denim skirt.

She sighed again, deeply. There was nothing left except the novel, and no one would publish it. Unless . . .

The novel. It was a work of pure art, and therefore would be totally rejected by the editorial board. Unless she could gain a position of power for herself. If only Carl . . .

The desk phone chimed. Lori blinked away her tears and said softly, "Answer answer." The command to the phone had to be given twice, as a precaution against setting off its voice-actuated computer during the course of a normal conversation.

"A Mr. Lewis to see you," said the phone. "He claims he

has an appointment.'' Whoever had programmed the communications computer had built in the hard-nosed suspicion of the true
New Yorker. Even its voice sounded nasty and nasal.

"Show him in," commanded Lori. Softly. On second thought
she added, "No, wait. I'll come out and get him."

Carl could be the answer to all her problems. He was brilliant.
His invention could propel Bunker Books to the top of the industry. And, having dated him more than once in Boston, Lori
was willing to try for more. But Carl would never find his way
through this rabbit warren of offices and corridors, Lori told
herself as she made the three steps it took to get through the only
clear path between her desk and her door. Carl could design
electronic software that made MIT professors blink with pleasured
surprise, but he got lost trying to cross the street. She hurried
down the narrow corridor toward the reception area.

Sure enough, Carl stood blinking uncertainly at the first cross-
hallway, trying to figure out the computer display screen on the
wall that supposedly showed even the most obtuse visitor the
precise directions to the office he or she was seeking. True to his
engineering nature, Carl was peering at the wall fixture with its
complex code of colored paths rather than asking any of the people
scurrying along the corridors.

He looked exactly as she remembered him: tall, trim, handsome
in a boyish sort of way. He carried a garment bag and a smaller
one both slung over the same shoulder, rumpling his tweed jacket
unmercifully and making him look like an ill-clothed hunchback.

"Carl! Hi!"

He looked up toward Lori, blinked, and his smile of recognition
sent a thrill through her.

"Hi yourself," he replied, just as he had in the old days when
they had both been students: he at MIT and she at Boston University.

Carl put out his right hand toward her, and Lori took it in hers.
Instead of a businesslike handshake she stepped close enough to
peck at his cheek in the traditional gushy, phony manner of the
publishing industry. But the heavy bags started to slip off Carl's

shoulder and somehow wrapped themselves around her. Lori found herself pressed against Carl, and the traditional peck became a full, warm-blooded kiss on his lips. Definitely not phony, at least on her part.

Somebody snickered. She heard a wolf whistle from down the hall. As they untangled, she saw that Carl's face was red as a May Day banner. She felt flustered herself.

"I . . . I'm sorry," Carl stammered, trying to straighten out the twisted shoulder straps of his bags.

Lori smiled and said nothing. She took him by the free arm and led him back toward her office.

"Did you bring it?" she asked as they strode down the corridor. It was barely wide enough for the two of them to pass through side by side. Lori had to press close to his tweed-sleeved arm.

He nodded. "It's right here."

"Wonderful."

As she pushed open the door to her cubbyhole, Lori's heart sank. It was such a tiny office, so shabby, so sloppy with all those damned manuscripts all over the place, schedules and cover proofs tacked to the walls. It seemed even smaller with Carl in it; he looked like a giant wading through a sea of paper.

But he said, "Wow, you've got an office all to yourself!"

"It's a little on the small side," she replied.

"I'm still sharing that telephone booth with Thompson and two freshmen."

Lori had not the slightest doubt that Carl was being sincere. There was not a dissembling bone in his body, she knew. That was his strength. And his weakness. She would have to protect him from the sharks and snakes, she knew.

"You can hang your garment bag on the back of the door," Lori told him as she picked a double armload of manuscripts off the only other chair in the office and plopped them onto the window ledge, atop the six dozen already there. What the hell, she thought. I can't see much out of the window now anyway.

"We don't have much time before the meeting starts," she said as she slid behind her desk and sat down.

"Meeting?" Carl felt alarmed. "What meeting? I thought—"

"The editorial board meeting. It's mandatory for all the editors. Every Tuesday and Thursday. Be there on time, or else. One of the silly rules around here."

Carl muttered, "I'm going to have to show this to your entire board of editors?"

Lori moved her shoulders in a semishrug that somehow stirred Carl's blood. He had not seen her in nearly two years; until just now he had not realized how much he had missed her.

"I wanted you to show it to me first," she was saying, "and then we'd go in and show the Boss. But now it's time for the drippy meeting, and I _have_ to attend."

"It's my own fault," said Carl. "The train was late, and it took me longer to get a cab than I thought it would. I should have taken an earlier train."

"Can you show me how it works? Real quick, before the meeting starts?"

"Sure." Carl took the emptied chair and unzipped his courier case. From it he pulled a gray oblong box, about five inches by nine and less than an inch thick. Its front was almost entirely a dark display screen. There was a row of fingertip-sized touchpads beneath the screen.

"This is just the prototype," Carl said almost apologetically. "The production model will be slightly smaller, around four by seven, just about the size of a regular paperback book."

Lori nodded and reached out her hands to take the electronic book from its inventor.

The phone chimed. "Editorial board meeting starts in one minute," said the snappish computer voice. "All editors are required to attend."

With a sigh, Lori said, "Come on, you can show the whole editorial board."

"This'll only take a few seconds."

"I can't be late for the meeting. They count it against you when your next salary review comes up."

"They take attendance and mark you tardy?"

"You bet!"

Stuffing his invention back in the black case and getting to his feet, Carl said, "Sounds like kindergarten."

With a rueful smile, Lori agreed, "What do you mean, 'sounds like'?"

Twenty floors higher in the Synthoil Tower sprawled the offices of Webb Press, a wholly owned subsidiary of Tarantula Enterprises (Ltd.). The reception area was larger than the entire set of grubby editorial cubicles down at Bunker Books. Sweeping picture windows looked out on the majestic panorama of lower Manhattan: the financial district, the twin Trade Towers, the magnificent new Disneydome that covered most of what had once been the slums and tenements of the Lower East Side. Farther away stood the Statue of Liberty and the sparkling harbor.

Harold D. Lapin sat patiently on one of the many deep soft leather chairs arranged tastefully across the richly soft silk carpeting of the reception area. His blue trenchcoat lay neatly folded across the chair's gleaming chrome arm. Being the man he was, Lapin's interest was focused not on the stunningly beautiful redhaired receptionist sitting behind her glass desk, microskirted legs demurely crossed, nor even on the splendid view to be seen through the picture windows. Rather, he studied the intricate floral pattern of the heavy drapes that framed the windows, mentally tracing a path from the ceiling to the floor that did not cross a flower, leaf, or stem.

"Mr. Lapin?" came the dulcet tones of the receptionist.

He turned in his chair to look at her, and she smiled a practiced smile that suggested much and revealed nothing.

"Mr. Hawks will see you now."

As she spoke, a door to one side of her desk slid open soundlessly and an equally lovely woman appeared there. She nodded slightly. Like the receptionist she was red of hair, gorgeous of face and figure, and dressed in the microskirt and tailored blouse that seemed to be something of a uniform at Webb Press.

Lapin followed the young woman wordlessly along broad quiet corridors lined with exquisite paintings and an occasional fine small bronze on a pedestal. All the doors along the corridor were tightly closed; the brass nameplates on them were small, discreet, tasteful.

Power exuded from those doors. Lapin could feel it. There was money here, much money, and the power to do great things.

At the end of the corridor was a double door of solid oak bearing an equally simple nameplate: P. Curtis Hawks. Idly wondering what the "P." stood for, and why Hawks preferred his second name to his first, Lapin allowed himself to be ushered through the double doors, past a phalanx of desks and secretaries (all red-haired), into an inner anteroom where still another gorgeous red-haired young woman smiled up at him and gestured silently toward the unmarked door beyond her airport-sized desk.

Are they all mute? Lapin wondered. Does Hawks clone them, all these redheads?

The unmarked door opened of itself and Lapin stepped through. The sanctum sanctorum inside was somewhat smaller than he had imagined it would be, merely the size of a bus terminal or a minor cathedral. It was splendidly panelled in teak, however, and its floor-length windows opened onto a handsome terrace that looked out on the East River, the Brooklyn condo complex, and the slender grace of the Verrazano-Narrows Bridge. A massive teak desk took up one end of the room, its broad clean top supported by four carved elephants with real ivory tusks. The other corners of the huge office contained, respectively, a conference table that could seat twelve, an electronics center that rivalled anything in Cape Canaveral, and a billiard table with an ornate Tiffany lamp hanging above it.

Hawks was standing by the French windows, fists clenched together behind his back, with the morning sun streaming in so boldly that it made Lapin's eyes water to gaze upon the president of Webb Press.

"Well?" Hawks snapped, without turning to face his visitor.

Squinting somewhat painfully, Lapin said, "Mission accomplished, sir." He had been told by the man who had hired him that Hawks preferred military idioms.

Hawks spun around and clapped his hands together with a loud smack. "Good! Let's see what you got."

P. Curtis Hawks was a short, chubby man in his late fifties. His curly red hair was obviously a toupee, to Lapin's refined eye. Hawks's face was round, puffy-cheeked, with eyes so small and set so deep beneath menacing russet brows that Lapin could not tell what color they were. The man had a plastic pacifier clamped between his teeth; it was colored brown and shaped like a cigar butt. He wore a sky-blue suit tailored to suggest a military uniform: epaulets, decorative ribbons over the left breast pocket, trousers creased to a razor's edge. Yet he did not look military; he looked like a beach ball that had been unexpectedly drafted.

Hawks gestured to the electronics center. Lapin placed his trenchcoat neatly on the back of one of the six chrome chairs there, and slid an oblong black box from the coat's inner pocket.

"You know how to work a scanner?" Hawks growled. His voice was like a diesel engine's heavy rumbling, yet there was a trace of a whine in it.

"Yessir, of course," said Lapin. Without sitting, he slid his black box into a slot on the console, then studied the control keyboard for a brief moment.

Hawks paced back and forth and chewed on his pacifier. "Three-D X rays," he muttered. "Do you realize that with this one hologram we'll be able to save the corporation the trouble of buying out those assholes at Bunker Books?"

Tapping commands into the console, Lapin replied absently, "I had no idea so much was at stake." Then he found himself adding, "Sir."

"There's billions involved here. Billions."

The display screen before the two standing men glowed to life, and a three-dimensional picture took form.

"What in hell is *that*?" Hawks shouted.

Lapin gasped in sudden fear. Hanging in midair before his

horrified eyes was a miniature three-dimensional picture of what appeared to be the rear axle of a New York taxicab, overlain with vague blurs of other things.

"You shitfaced asshole!" Hawks screamed. "You used too much power! The X rays went right through his goddamned device and took a picture of the goddamn cab's axle! I'll have you broken for this!"

THE WRITER

THE Writer eagerly pawed through the mail box hanging at a precarious tilt from the door of his rusted, dilapidated mobile home. It was not a *very* mobile home; so far as he knew, it had not moved an inch off the cinderblocks on which it rested since years before he had bought it, and that had been almost a decade ago.

Automatically ducking his head to get through the low doorway, he let the screen door slam as he riffled through the day's mail. Four bills that he could not pay, six catalogues advertising goods he could not afford, and a franked envelope bearing the signature of his congresswoman, who was being opposed in the upcoming primaries by the owner of a chain of hardware stores.

Nothing from Bunker Books! Exasperated, the Writer tossed all the envelopes and catalogues onto his narrow bunk, which was still a mess of twisted sheets from his thrashing, tossing sleeplessness the night before.

Six months! They've had the manuscript for six months now. He had checked off the days on the greasy calendar hanging above the sink. The pile of dirty dishes nearly obscured it, but the red _x_'s on the calendar showed how the days had marched, one after another, without a word from Bunker Books.

All the magazine articles he had studiously read in the town library said that the longer a publishing house held on to a manuscript, the more likely they were to eventually buy it. It meant that the manuscript had been liked by the first reader and passed on to the more important editors. They, of course, were so busy that you couldn't expect them to sit right down and read your manuscript. They were flooded with hundreds of manuscripts; thousands, more likely. It took time to get to the one that you had sent in.

But six months? The Writer had sent follow-up letters, servilely addressed to "First Reader" and "Editor for New Manuscripts." No response whatsoever. On one daring night, emboldened by several beers at Jumping Joe's Bar, he sent an urgent, demanding telegram to the Editor-in-Chief. It was never answered, either.

As he sat in the only unbroken chair in the cramped living room area and turned on the noontime news, the Writer felt close to despair. For all he knew, the manuscript had never even gotten to Bunker Books. Some wiseguy in the post office might have dumped it in a sewer, figuring it was too heavy to carry. He'd heard plenty of stories like that, especially around Christmastime.

On the TV screen the solemn yet bravely smiling face of the network anchorman was replaced by a scene somewhere in the Middle East. The U.S. secretary of state was back there, trying to get the Arabs and Jews to stop shooting at each other. Fat chance, thought the Writer.

But something the secretary of state said to the reporters caught his attention. "We must do everything we can do to bring about a satisfactory solution to the problem. No matter how slim the chances, we must not shrink from doing everything we can do."

It was as if the TV screen had gone blank after that. The Writer saw no more, heard no more. He stared off into a distant, personal infinity. He must do everything he can do, no matter how slim the chances.

Absolutely right! Instead of going to the fridge and pulling out a frozen dinner, the Writer stalked out the front door of the mobile home and got into his battered old GMota hatchback. He gunned the engine and drove out to the throughway heading north. Toward New York. They would probably fire him, back at the garbage recycling plant, when he didn't show up for work that night. The bill collectors would probably grab his mobile home and all its contents. So what? He was heading for New York, for Bunker Books, for his rendezvous with destiny.

He was already more than a hundred miles north when the tornado ripped through town. Suddenly his ex-home became *very* mobile and wound up in the bottom of the bay, seven miles from its original site. Police dredged the bay for three days without finding his body.

THREE ███████████████████

AS he sat in the stuffy conference room, Carl
thought he had somehow fallen down a rabbit hole or plunged
into another dimension. Here he was with the greatest invention
to hit the publishing world since Gutenberg, and the people
around the conference table were ignoring him completely. The
table looked cheap, hard-used. Carl ran a fingertip across its top:
wood-grained Formica.

As one of the female editors droned on endlessly, Carl leaned
toward Lori, sitting next to him. "They're talking about *books*,"
he whispered.

With a small grin she whispered back, "Of course, silly. This
is the editorial board meeting."

"But what about my presentation?"

Lori's eyes flicked to the empty chair at the head of the table.
"Not until the Boss comes in."

"The boss isn't here?"

"Not yet."

Carl sank back in his chair. It creaked. Or is it my spine? he
wondered. The chair was old and stiff and uncomfortable. He

was sitting at the foot of the table, farthest from the conference room's only door, squeezed in beside Lori. The Formica table top was scratched and chipped, he noticed. The walls of the windowless conference room bore faded color prints from the covers of old Bunker books.

Eight other editors sat slumped in various attitudes of boredom and frustration. Four men, four women, plus the male editor-in-chief, a pudgy little fellow with a dirty white T-shirt showing beneath his unzipped leather jacket, a fashionable two-day growth of beard on his round little chinny-chin-chin, pop eyes, and thick oily lips. He reminded Carl of a scaly fish. The editors all were dressed in ultramodish biker's black leathers with chains and studs, except for Lori in her simple golden-yellow sweater and midcalf denim skirt. A burst of sunshine in the midst of all the black gloom.

Editorial bored meeting, Carl said to himself. Then, with a mental shrug of his cerebral shoulders, he decided to pay attention to what the editors were saying. Maybe he could learn something about how the publishing business worked. It beat chewing his fingernails waiting for his moment to speak.

The editor sitting next to the chief, an enormous mountain of flesh, was droning like a Tibetan lama in a semitrance about Sheldon Stoker's latest horror novel. Her name was Maryann Quigly, and she gave every appearance of loathing her job.

"It's the same old tripe," she said in a voice that sounded totally exhausted, as if just the effort of getting up in the morning and dragging her bloated body to this meeting had almost overwhelmed her. "Blood, devil-worship, blood, supernatural doings, blood, and more blood. It's awful."

"But it sells," said Ashley Elton, the bone-thin, nasal-voiced editor sitting across the table from the lugubrious Ms. Quigly. Ashley Elton was not her real name: she had been born Rebecca Simkowitz, but felt that her parents should have given her a name that sounded more literary. Hence Ashley Elton. She was an intense, beady-eyed toothache of a woman with the pale pinched face and smudged black eye makeup of a Hollywood vampire. The living dead, Carl thought.

"Sure it sells," Maryann Quigly agreed, barely squeezing the words past her heavy-eyed torpor.

The editor-in-chief shook his wattles. "Stoker writes crap, all right, but it's *commercial* crap. It keeps this company afloat. If we ever lose him we all go pounding the pavements looking for new jobs."

Quigly sighed a long, pained, wheezing sigh.

"What'd we give him as an advance for his last book?" asked the editor-in-chief.

"One million dollars." Quigly drew out the words to such length that it took almost a full minute to say it.

"Offer him the same for this one."

"His agent will want more," snapped Ashley Elton (nee Simkowitz).

"Murray Swift," muttered the editor-in-chief. "Yep, he'll hold us up for a million two, at least." Turning back to Quigly, he instructed, "Offer a million even. Give us more room for negotiating."

One by one, the editors presented books that they thought the company should publish. Each presentation was made exactly the same way. The editor would give the book's title and author, and then a brief description of the category it fit into. Thus:

Jack Drain, the young ball of fire who sported a small Van Dyke on his receding chin, proposed *Taurus XII: The Return of the Bull.* "It's by Billy Bee Bozo, same as the other eleven in the series. Fantasy adventure, set in a distant age when men battled evil with swords and courage."

"And all the weemen have beeg breasts," said Concetta Las Vagas, the company's Affirmative Action "two-fer," being both Hispanic and female. There were those in Bunker Books who claimed she should be a "three-fer," since her skin was quite dark as well. There were also those who claimed that Concetta's idea of Affirmative Action was to say *"Sí, sí,"* to any postpubertal male. The standard line among the office gossips was that a man could get lucky in Las Vagas.

"Look who's talking about beeg breasts," mimicked Mark

Martin, who wore a pale lemon silk T-shirt beneath his biker's leather jacket, and a tastefully tiny diamond on his left nostril.

Drain frowned across the table at Las Vagas. "There are women warriors in this one. Bozo's not as much of a male chauvinist as he used to be."

"There go his sales," somebody mumbled.

Ted Gunn, sitting next to Drain, perked up on his chair. Although he wore leathers and metal studs just like the rest of the editors, he gave off an aura of restless energy that announced he was a Young Man Headed for the Top. He was the only one in the conference room who smoked; his place at the table was fenced in by a massive stainless-steel ashtray smudged with a layer of gray ash and six crushed butts, and a pair of electronic air purifiers that sucked the smoke out of the air so efficiently that they could snatch up notepaper and even loose change.

"What have sales been like for the *Taurus* series lately?" Gunn asked.

Drain said, "Good. Damned good." But it sounded weak, defensive.

"Haven't his sales been dropping with every new book?"

"Not much."

"But if a series is effective," Gunn said, suddenly the sharp young MBA on the prowl, "his sales should be going up, not down."

That started a long, wrangling argument about the marketing department, the art director's choice of cover artists, the hard winter in the Midwest, and several other subjects that mystified Carl. What could all that have to do with the sales of books? Why didn't they all have pocket computers, so they could punch up the sales figures and have them in hard numbers right before their eyes?

Carl shook his head in bewilderment.

With great reluctance, P. Curtis Hawks entered the private elevator that ran from his spacious office to the penthouse suite of the Synthoil Tower. Lapin had been ushered away in the grip of two burly security men to learn the lessons of failure. Now Hawks had to report that failure to the Old Man.

Once he had enjoyed talking with the Old Man, gleaning the secret techniques of power and persuasion that had built Tarantula Enterprises into one of the world's largest multinational corporations. But ever since the takeover battle had started, the Old Man had seemed to recede from reality, to slide into a private world that was almost childlike. Senility, thought Hawks. Just when we need him most, his mind turns to Silly Putty.

He whacked the only button on the elevator's control board four times before the doors could close, like a true New Yorker, impatient, urgent, demanding. The doors swished shut and he felt the heavy acceleration of upward thrust. Years ago, when he had first become president of Tarantula's publishing subsidiary, whenever Hawks entered this elevator he had pictured himself as an astronaut blasting off to orbit. I could have been an astronaut, he told himself. If only I could have passed algebra in high school.

The ride was all too swift. Hawks felt a moment of lightness as the elevator slowed to a stop. ("Zero gravity," he used to say to himself. "We have achieved orbit.") The doors slid smoothly open. The office of Weldon W. Weldon, president and chief executive officer of Tarantula Enterprises (Ltd.) lay before him.

It was a jungle. The office had been turned into a tropical greenhouse. Or maybe a zoo. All sorts of lushly flowering shrubs were growing out of huge ceramic pots dotting the vast expanse of the Old Man's office. Palm trees brushed their fronds against the ceiling. Raucous birds jeered from perches in the greenery, and Hawks heard a new sound—a hooting kind of howl that must have been a monkey or baboon or some equally noisome animal. Vines trailed along the incredibly expensive Persian carpeting. Hawks wrinkled his nose at the clashing, cloying scents of the jungle. For god's sake, look at the stains on the carpeting! Those goddamn birds!

There were snakes in those bushes, too, he knew. Poisonous snakes. The Old Man said he needed them for protection. Ever since the takeover struggle had started, he had become more and more paranoid. Said he was training them to guard him and attack strangers.

Wishing he had brought a machete, Hawks made his perilous way slowly through the Old Man's personal jungle. The heat and humidity were intolerable. Hawks's expensive silk suit was already soaked with perspiration. It dripped off the end of his pudgy nose and trickled along his belly and legs. His skull steamed under his toupee. He felt as if he were melting.

The old bastard changes the layout every day, he fumed to himself. One of these days I'm going to need a native guide to find his goddamned desk.

After nearly ten minutes of stalking around potted orchids and stepping over twisted vines (and hoping they were not snakes lying in wait), Hawks ducked under a low palm bole, turned a corner, and there in a clearing was the Old Man. Watering a row of Venus flytraps with a seltzer bottle.

Weldon W. Weldon sat in his powered chair, in his usual undertaker's black suit, a heavy plaid blanket tucked over his lap, blissfully spritzing the Venus flytraps. His back was to the approaching Hawks. A line from Shakespeare sprang into Hawks's mind: "Now might I do it, Pat."

Hawks had never understood who Pat was, and why he had no lines to speak in the scene. But he understood opportunity when he saw it. I could come up behind him, whisk the blanket off his lap, and smother him with it. Nobody would know, and I would be elected to replace him, Hawks told himself.

Then he saw the jaguar lying indolently in the corner by the picture windows. Its burning eyes were fastened on Hawks, and there was no chain attached to its emerald-studded collar. Hawks was not certain that anyone could train a snake to attack on command, but he had no doubts whatsoever about the jaguar. He swallowed his ambition. It tasted like bile. The sleek cat purred like the rumble of a heavy truck.

The president and chief executive officer of Tarantula Enterprises (Ltd.) spun his powered chair around to face Hawks. Weldon was old, stooped, wrinkled, totally bald, and confined to his powered chair since his massive coronary more than a year earlier. The coronary, of course, had come in the midst of Tarantula's battle to avoid an unfriendly takeover by Etna Industries, a multinational corporation headquartered in Sicily and reputed to be a wholly owned Mafia subsidiary. A decidedly unfriendly takeover bid. The struggle was still going on, the battlefields were the stock exchanges of New York, London, and Rome, the law courts of Washington and Palermo. This war had already cost Weldon his health. Maybe his sanity.

And there was no end in sight. The swarthy little men from Sicily had great persistence. And long memories. Hawks could *feel* the brooding Sicilians hovering over them, like dark angels of death, waiting for the chance to grab Tarantula in their rapacious claws.

"You didn't get it," the Old Man snapped. His voice was as sharp and scratchy as an icepick scraping along a chalk board.

"Not exactly," said Hawks from around his pacifier. His tone was meekly servile. He hated himself for it, but somehow in the face of the Old Man he always felt like a naughty little kid. Worse: an incompetent little kid.

"And what do you mean by that?" Weldon laid his seltzer bottle on the blanket across his lap and drove the chair over to his desk. Its electric motor barely buzzed, it was so quiet. The once immaculate expanse of Philippine mahogany was now a miniature forest of unidentifiable potted plants. Hawks had to sit at just the right angle to see his boss through a clearing in the greenery.

"The man we hired to copy the device used too strong an X-ray dose," Hawks confessed, feeling sheepish.

"And? And?"

"The hologram contains a complete three-dimensional picture of the device, but it's a very weak image. Blurred. Very difficult to make out any details."

Weldon snorted. His wizened old face frowned at Hawks. "I see," he sneered. "If I want a perfect three-D image of a taxicab's rear axle, you can get it for me. But not the device we're after."

Hawks felt a shudder of fright burn through him. He's bugged my office! He's been listening to everything that I do!

Pointing a crooked, shaking finger at Hawks, the old man commanded, "You get the best people in NASA, or the air force, or wherever to work on that fudged hologram. I want to see that device!"

Hawks swallowed again. Hard. "Yessir."

"And get somebody who knows what he's doing to make another copy of it. Steal the damned thing if you have to!"

"Right away, sir."

Weldon's frown relaxed slightly. He almost smiled, a ghastly sight. "Now listen, son," he said, suddenly amiable. "Don't you understand how important this device is? It's going to revolutionize the publishing industry."

"But publishing is such a small part of Tarantula," Hawks heard himself object. "Why bother . . ."

He stopped himself because the old man's smile faded into a grimace.

"How many times do I have to tell you," Weldon said sharply, "that publishing is the keystone to all of Tarantula's business lines? Control publishing and you control people's minds, their attitudes. Books and magazines and newspapers tell people what to think, how to vote, where to spend their money. How many idiots do you know who let the *Times* book reviews decide for them what's good reading and what isn't?"

"But what about TV?" Hawks asked, unfazed by the non sequitur. "And even radio . . ."

The old man snarled at him, making the jaguar's ears perk up. "Television? Are you serious?" He cackled. "Those Twinkies and egomaniacs get their ideas and their information from books and magazines and newspapers! Don't you understand that yet? Why do you think I put you in charge of our publishing subsidiary? Because I thought you were incompetent?"

That was exactly why Hawks thought he had been made president of Webb Press. But he remained silent as Weldon continued:

"Sure, Webb runs in the red every year. It's a good tax shelter for us; the more money Webb loses, the less taxes we pay. But the books Webb publishes are important to the rest of Tarantula. The magazines and newspapers even more so.''

Hawks nodded to show he understood. He did not agree, of course, but if the Old Man thought publishing was that important, he was not going to argue.

"This device," Weldon went on, "this electronic book doo-hickey . . . it's the wave of the future. We've got to have it!''

"But—"

"Don't you understand?'' Weldon's eyes began to shine, he seemed to vibrate with inner energy. "With electronic books we can undercut all the other publishers. We can corner the entire publishing industry!''

"Do you really think so?'' Hawks felt entirely dubious. Clearly the Old Man's trolley was derailed.

Weldon's eyes were glowing now. His arms stretched out to encompass the world. Hawks almost thought he was going to rise out of his chair and walk.

"First we take over publishing here in the States," he said, his voice deep, powerful. "But that's just the spring freshet that precedes the flood. From the States we go to Japan. From Japan to Europe. Soon all the world will be ours! One publishing house, telling the whole world what to think!''

The Old Man sank back in his chair, panting with the exertion of his dynamic vision.

"I . . . I think I understand," Hawks murmured. And he almost did.

"This young engineer—what's his name?''

"Carl Lewis, sir.''

"We've got to have his invention. One way or the other, we've got to have it!''

"I've already taken steps in that direction, sir.''

Weldon scowled at him. "Such as?''

Feeling pleased as a puppy laying his master's slippers before the great man's feet, Hawks said, "I have arranged for one of our editors to be hired away from us by Bunker Books.''

The Old Man's scowl melted into a crooked grin. "A spy in their camp, eh?"

"A Mata Hari, in fact."

"Ms. Dean, isn't it? Very attractive woman. Very formidable."

Again Hawks shuddered inwardly. He *has* bugged my office. He knows everything I'm doing.

"Well, if you don't have anything else to tell me, get on with your work. Get me that electronic book." Weldon made a shooing motion with his long-fingered, liver-spotted hands.

Hawks got up from his chair, dreading the trek through the Old Man's jungle. There were a lot of snakes between him and the elevator.

"Oh, one little thing more," the Old Man said, with a slight cackling that might have been laughter. "There's going to be a few changes at Webb. I've hired a new assistant for you."

Hawks turned back to face Weldon. He had to stand on tiptoe to see over the plants on his desk. "An assistant?" His voice nearly cracked with anxiety.

"Yes. A corporate systems engineer. What we used to call an efficiency expert in the old days."

"Corporate . . ." Hawks knew what the title meant: hatchet man.

"Gunther Axhelm." Weldon's wrinkled face was grinning evilly. "You may have heard of him."

Hawks's knees turned to water. Heard of him? Who hadn't heard of Axhelm the Axe, the man who single-handedly reduced General Motors to a museum with a staff of six, the man who fired four thousand management employees of AT&T in a single afternoon and drove Du Pont out of business altogether. He was coming to Webb! Might as well get in line for unemployment compensation now, before the rush.

"Don't get scared," the Old Man said, almost kindly.

"Scared? Me?"

"You're white as an albino in shock, son."

Hawks tried to control the fluttering of his heart. "Well, Axhelm's got quite a reputation. . . ."

"Nothing for you to worry about, son. I promise you. Just give him a free hand. It'll all work out for the best."

"Yessir."

"And get that electronic book for me! I want it in our hands. I want this brilliant young inventor on our team—or out of the picture altogether. Do you understand me?"

"Certainly, sir." Hawks saw the diamond-hard glint in the Old Man's eyes and decided that he would rather face the snakes.

Weldon W. Weldon watched his protégé slink away through the jungle foliage. "Brain the size of a walnut," he muttered to himself. "But he follows orders, like a good Nazi."

With a sigh, Weldon poked a bony finger at the floral design on one of the ceramic pots atop his desk. The plants were all plastic, beautiful fakes. The pot's curved surface turned milky, then steadied into a three-dimensional image of Tarantula's corporate organization chart.

Tapping a few more places here and there among the flower pots, Weldon got the display to show the distribution of stockholders in Tarantula. Although he himself was the largest individual stockholder, he only owned twelve percent of the company. There were others out there, selling out to the Sicilians.

It was a complicated situation. Tarantula was supposedly an independent corporation. But Synthoil Inc. owned a majority of the stock, and Tarantula was in fact controlled by that Houston-based corporation. Yet sizable chunks of stock were owned by other companies, too, such as Mozarella Bank & Trust—an obvious Mafia front.

The old man shook his head tiredly. The stockholders meeting coming up this November will determine the fate of the corporation, and I'm not even sure who the hell owns the company!

Reader's Report

Title: *Midway Diary*

Author: Ron Clanker (Capt., U.S.N., [Ret.])

Category: WWII historical fiction

Reader: Elizabeth Jane Rose

Synopsis: Tells the story of the Battle of Midway from the point of view of a young navy officer serving aboard a U.S. ship. He is in love with a Japanese-American woman who lives in Hawaii, which causes no end of troubles because we are at war with Japan at the time. I don't know much about WWII (I was an English major, of course), but his writing is vivid and there's not too much blood and machismo. The novel is really very romantic and sensitive in spite of all the war stuff.

Recommendation: Should be considered seriously by the editorial board.

FOUR

After two hours, Carl finally began to under-
stand the way the editorial board worked, although it didn't seem
to make any sense.

He had thought, from the little Lori had told him, that the
purpose of the meeting was to decide which books Bunker would
publish, out of all the manuscripts the editors had received since
the last meeting. One by one, each editor seated around the
conference table described a book manuscript that he or she believed should be published. The editor usually started with the
author's name and a brief listing of the author's previous books.
Then the editor spoke glowingly of the book's subject matter:
"This one is *hot!*" was a typical remark. "A diet that allows
you to eat all the chocolate you want!"

Not a word was said about the quality of the writing, nor of
the ideas or philosophies the writers were writing about. The
editors talked about each manuscript's category (whatever that
was) and the author's track record. Are they talking about writers
or racehorses? Carl wondered. After the first hour he decided that
the editors viewed their writers as horses. Or worse.

That much he understood. But what followed confused Carl, at first. For no matter how enthusiastically a book was described by the editor presenting it, the rest of the editors seemed to go right to work to destroy it.

"His last two novels were duds," one of the other editors would say.

Or, "I can just picture the sales force trying to sell *that* in the Middle West."

"He's out of his category; he doesn't have a track record with mysteries."

"It's just another diet book. Even if it does work it'll get lost on the shelves."

Slowly it dawned on Carl that the real purpose of the editorial board meeting was not to decide which books Bunker would publish. It was to decide which they would *not* publish. He felt like a child watching a great aerial battle in which every plane in the sky would inevitably, inexorably, be shot down.

Except for the Sheldon Stoker horror novel, which everyone agreed was so terrible that it would sell millions of copies. Carl began to wonder how Thackeray or Graves or Hawthorne would get through an editorial board meeting. Not to mention Hesse or Hugo or Tolstoy. Not that he had read the works of those masters, of course; but he had seen dramatizations of their novels on public television.

As the second hour dragged on into the third, and Carl's stomach began to make anticipatory noises about lunch, the Moment of Truth moved down the table and finally arrived at Lori's chair.

"Well, Ms. Tashkajian," asked the editor-in-chief, "what priceless work of art do you have for us today?" Carl thought the mouth-breathing bastard was being awfully sarcastic.

Lori forced a smile, though, from her seat at the foot of the table and began to speak glowingly about a novel titled *Midway Diary*.

"But it's a first novel!" gasped Ted Gunn, once he realized that the author had written nothing earlier. "The guy's got no track record at all! How's the sales force going to tell how many copies he ought to sell if he's never had a book out there before?''

"It's a good novel," said Lori.

"Goods we get at a fabric store," giggled Gina Lucasta, who sat just to Lori's left. She was one notch above Lori in seniority, and she was not about to let the lowliest member of the editorial board move past her. She had started with the company as a receptionist, but her surly way with visitors, her propensity to cut off telephone calls at the switchboard, and her apparent inability to get even the simplest message to its intended recipient resulted in her being promoted to the editorial staff, where, it was felt by management, she could not do so much damage to the company.

Lori answered softly, "This novel has romance for the women and war action for men. Properly promoted, it could become a best-seller."

"By a first-timer?" Ted Gunn scoffed. "Do you know the last time a totally unknown writer made it to the best-seller list?"

"That was when the publishing house recognized that the book had terrific potential and backed it to the hilt," Lori said sweetly.

"It's a historical novel?" asked the editor-in-chief.

"World War Two."

"What page does the rape scene come on?"

Lori shook her head. "There isn't any rape scene. It's more romantic than a bodice ripper."

"A historical novel without a rape scene in it? Who'd buy it?"

Lori bit her lips and did not reply. Ashley Elton started to say, "Most women are offended by that kind of violence. Just because—''

But at that moment the door swung open and the Boss stepped into the room.

All the editors stood up. Kee-ripes, thought Carl as he reluctantly got to his feet, this is worse than kindergarten. But he realized that his buttocks had gone numb from sitting so long on the uncomfortable chair. It felt good to be off his backside.

The relief lasted only a moment. The Boss nodded a tight-lipped hello to the editorial board, cast a slightly raised eyebrow at Carl, and took the chair at the head of the table. The editor-in-chief held the chair for her as she daintily sat down.

The Boss was a slim blond woman of an age that Carl was hopelessly unable to fathom. More than thirty, less than sixty; that was all he could estimate. Her skin was glowing and flawless, like the finest porcelain. Her hair was cut short, almost boyish, but as impeccably coiffed as a TV ad. Although she obeyed the dictates of current fashion and wore a biker-type suit, it was all of pure white leather, both jacket and slacks, with a slightly frilly white blouse beneath. Where the others wore metal chains or studs, the Boss wore gold. Gold necklaces, several chains, and heavy gold bracelets on both wrists. Carl could not see (and probably would not have noticed, even if he had been close enough to see) the cold, hard glint of her eyes. They were the tawny fierce eyes of an eagle; they missed nothing, especially opportunities for making money.

The editor-in-chief, whose appearance looked even grubbier next to this saintly vision of white and gold, said to the Boss, "We're almost finished, Mrs. Bunker, but if you want us to review everything for you . . ."

"That won't be necessary," said Mrs. Bunker in a tiny china doll's voice that everyone strained to hear. "I have a few announcements to make."

Carl sensed tension crackle across the conference table. Several of the editors actually drew back in their chairs, as if trying to avoid some invisible sniper's bullet that was heading their way.

"First, the rumors that our company will be bought out by some multinational corporation are strictly rumors. Mr. Bunker has no intention of selling his company to anyone."

They relaxed so hard that Carl could feel the breeze of their sighs gusting past him at close to Mach 1.

"Second, our son P. T. Junior has graduated with honors from the Wharton School of Business—"

A round of "Ahhs" and clapping interrupted her. When it died down, Mrs. Bunker continued. "And will join the company as a special assistant to the publisher. You can expect him to attend the next editorial board meeting."

The congratulatory vibrations in the air vanished like the smoke from a birthday cake's candles.

"Third, we have been fortunate enough to obtain the services of one of the top editors in the business, Scarlet Dean. She has accepted our offer and will start here on Monday." The Boss allowed a satisfied smile to bend her lips slightly.

"She's leaving Webb Press?" asked one of the editors.

"But she was the head of their romance and inspirational lines!"

"I invited her to lunch a few weeks ago," said Mrs. Bunker, "and"—her smile broadened—"made her an offer she couldn't refuse."

"Wonderful!"

"Just what we needed!"

"A real coup!"

The congratulations buzzed around the table; everyone seemed anxious to get their word in. All except the editor-in-chief, who looked slightly puzzled.

Once the acclamations died down, Mrs. Bunker turned to the man and said softly, "I'm afraid we can't have two editors-in-chief, Max."

The man's stubbly jaw flapped several times, like a flounder gasping on the hard planks of a dock, but no sounds came out.

"I'd appreciate it if you'd clear out your office by the end of the day," said the Boss with the sweetness of a Borgia princess.

The man slumped back in his chair, his face white and lifeless, his eyes round and vacant. The rest of the editors looked away, as if fearing to be touched by his hollow-eyed stare. Carl felt hollow himself; he had never seen a public execution before.

Mrs. Bunker looked down the table, toward Carl. "Now then, Lori. Is this the young genius who's going to transform the publishing industry?"

With a visible swallow to clear her throat, Lori nodded and

said, "This is Carl Lewis, assistant professor of software design at the Massachusetts Institute of Technology. He's brought us the prototype of the device that will become as important to the world as the printing press was."

"Let's see it," said the Boss with a slight smile. It looked to Carl as if she was amused by Lori's grandiose claim.

Carl got to his feet once again. As he unzipped his courier case he began to explain, "The concept of the electronic book is nothing new; people have been predicting it for years. What *is* new is that"—he pulled his invention out and held it up for them all to see—"here it is!"

Total disinterest. The editors did not react at all. It was if he had pulled out a bologna sandwich or a copy of the postal service's zip code guide. Nothing. Carl could not see Lori's beaming face, of course, because she was sitting beside him. And he did not know Mrs. Bunker well enough to detect the gold-seeking glitter in her eyes and the tiny, furtive dart of her tongue across her lower lip. The just fired editor-in-chief, of course, simply sat there like a dead fish, his mouth gaping open, his eyes staring at nothing.

Somewhat grimly, Carl went on with his prepared presentation. "More than ninety percent of a publisher's costs stem from moving megatonnages of paper across the country, from the paper mills to the printers, from the printers to the warehouses, from the warehouses to the wholesalers, from the wholesalers to the retail outlets."

Mrs. Bunker nodded slightly.

"I contend that publishers are in the information business, not the wood pulp and chemical industry. What you want to get into the hands of your readers is *information*—which does not necessarily have to be in the form of ink marks on paper."

Holding his device up for them all to see, Carl said, "This is an electronic book. It does away with the need for paper and ink."

"How does it work?" Lori prompted brightly in the silence of the rest of the editors.

Placing his device on the scarred top of the conference table, Carl explained, "Instead of printing books on paper, you 'print' them on miniature electro-optic wafers, like the diskettes used in computers, only smaller. This device in my hand allows you to read the book. The screen here shows you a full page. It can show illustrations as well as printed material; in fact, the quality of the pictures can be made better than anything you can achieve with the printed page."

"Can you show us?" Mrs. Bunker asked.

"Sure," replied Carl. "I've programmed one of my favorite children's books onto a wafer. It's called *Rain Makes Applesauce.* . . ."

Carl reached into his bag again and pulled out the tiny electro-optic wafer. It was barely the size of a postage stamp. "A wafer this size, incidentally, can hold more than a thousand pages of text."

Still no response whatsoever from the assembled editors. A few of them, however, glanced sideways toward the Boss, waiting to see her reaction and then follow suit.

Carl slid the electro-optic wafer into his device with the tap of a forefinger. "These touchpads work just about the same as a videocassette recorder's controls: start, stop, fast forward, reverse. You can also punch in a specific page number and the screen will go right to that page."

Holding the slim oblong box up so that they all could see its screen, Carl tapped the "start" button. Nothing happened.

"Shouldn't do that," he muttered, frowning. Carl touched it again. Still nothing appeared on the screen.

Suddenly perspiring, Carl pressed frantically on each of the touchpads in turn. The screen remained stubbornly blank.

Now the editors reacted. They laughed uproariously. They guffawed. All except the former editor-in-chief, who still sat there with his mouth hanging open and his eyes staring as sightlessly as a flounder on ice in a fish store display.

MURDER TWO ━━━━━

REX Wolfe was walking his dog along Riverside Drive, pooper-scooper dutifully clutched in one hand, the leash attached to the toy terrier in his other. They made an incongruous pair, the fleshily ponderous yet utterly dignified old man and the nervously twitchy little dog. Wolfe was impeccably garbed in the old style: a hand-tailored pinstripe suit with vest, off-white classic shirt with a real collar, and a rep tie that he had knotted flawlessly himself.

Traffic along the drive was its usual hopeless snarl, taxis and trucks and buses honking impatiently, drivers screaming filthy admonitions at one another. Wolfe sighed an immense sigh. In all his long years he could not remember it otherwise. When the city had finally prohibited private automobiles from entering Manhattan, it had been hailed as the solution to the traffic problem. It was not. It simply made room for more trucks. And buses. The number of taxis remained constant, thanks to the political clout of the cabbies, but their fares skyrocketed.

The dog yapped scrappily at the traffic zooming by as Wolfe waited patiently for the traffic light to change. "Quiet, Archie," said Wolfe as a middle-aged matron stared distastefully at the dog.

But secretly Wolfe felt the dog was right: the drivers needed someone to set them straight.

He crossed the drive, with the little dog tugging at its leash. They looked like a tiny scooter towing an immense dirigible.

Once inside Riverside Park, Wolfe allowed the dog to run loose. But he kept an eye on the animal as he ambled slowly northward, toward the ancient graffiti-covered edifice of Grant's Tomb. The dog, for its part, never wandered too far from its master as it scurried from lamppost to bench to wall to bush, sniffing out who had been around the old haunts lately.

"Ulysses S. Grant," Wolfe muttered to himself as he approached the pile of Victorian stonework. One of the great examples of the old Peter Principle. A hard-drinking farm boy who rose to command in the U.S. Army during the Civil War and literally saved the Union, only to be elected president, a task that was clearly beyond his powers. Promoted one step too far, elevated to the level of his incompetence. It was an old story, but a sad one still the same.

And now the final indignity. A tomb forgotten by everyone except the graffitists who regularly spattered it with their semiliterate proclamations of self: Gavilan 103; Shifty; The Bronx Avengers. What could possibly be worth avenging in the Bronx? Wolfe asked himself.

The only reply he got was a tremendous blow to the back of his head. Wolfe felt himself lifted off his feet, then hitting the concrete walk facedown with the crunching thud of breaking bones. There was no pain, only stunned surprise. Another enormous blow to his ribs rolled him over partially onto one side. Standing above him, silhouetted against the late afternoon sunlight, was a figure in some sort of a trenchcoat with a baseball bat raised above his head in both hands.

The ultimate fate of the native New Yorker, Wolfe thought. Mugged and murdered.

The bat crashed down again and everything went black.

FIVE

CARL Lewis sat broodingly hunched over his second beer in the noisy dark bar at the street level of the Synthoil Tower. Lori Tashkajian sat next to him in the cramped little booth, nursing a glass of white wine; the bench on the other side of the table held Carl's two bags. The bar was crowded with men and women at the end of the working day, starting to unwind from their tensions, the young ones looking for friends and possible mates for the evening; the older ones fortifying themselves before the rush to the homeward-bound trains and their more-or-less permanent mates.

"I just don't understand how it could have malfunctioned," Carl mumbled for approximately the seventy-fourth time in the past hour.

He had spent the afternoon in Lori's office, desperately examining his failed electro-optic book reader.

"It was fried," he repeated to Lori. "Darned near melted. Like somebody had put it in a microwave oven, or an X-ray machine."

"Maybe the airport security . . ."

"I came in by train, remember?" Carl said.

"Oh, yeah, that's right." Lori sipped at her wine, then suggested, "Maybe they have a security X ray on the train?"

Carl shook his head. "If they did they wouldn't keep it a secret. And even if they did, it wouldn't be powerful enough to fry electro-optical circuitry."

"Can you fix it?" Lori asked.

"Sure."

"How quickly?"

He shrugged. "A day, two days. I'll have to replace most of the components, but that shouldn't be too tough."

"Can you do it overnight?"

"Overnight? Why?"

Lori grasped Carl's arm in both her hands. "We've got to get this across to the Boss before she comes to the conclusion that the idea's a dud."

Frowning unhappily, Carl said, "She's already come to that conclusion."

"No! While you were poking into your little machine in my office, I spent the afternoon in *her* office, pleading with her to give you another chance."

"You did?"

"She's willing to listen," said Lori, "but she certainly isn't enthusiastic."

"Can you blame her?" Carl felt seething anger in his guts, and something worse: self-disgust. How could I let this happen? My one big chance . . .

Yet Lori's face, in the dimness of the shadowy bar, was bright and eager. "We've got to get her before she cools off altogether. A lot of people are always bringing her ideas; there's a lot of pressure on her constantly. We've got to strike right away."

"Okay, but overnight—I don't know if I can do it that quick. I have to go back to my lab. . . ."

"Can't you do it here?"

"I need the components. And the tools."

"Gee," said Lori, "we're right next to NYU. Don't you think they'd have the stuff you need?"

"Maybe. But how do I get it? I don't know anybody there."

Lori pressed her lips together and turned to scan the crowded bar. "I hope he's still . . . yes! There he is."

Without another word she slid out of the booth, wormed her way through the crowd at the "meat market" of unattached singles jammed around the bar, and came out towing a wiry-looking man of about thirty-five or forty. He had a slightly puzzled grin on his face.

Sliding onto the booth's other bench, he pushed Carl's bags into a squashed mess. He had a thick mop of reddish hair that looked like a rusty Brillo pad, long lean arms that ended in oversized hands with long fingers that looked almost like talons. He held big mugs brimming with beer, one in each clawlike hand.

"Saves time going for refills," he said in answer to Carl's questioning gaze.

"Carl, this is Ralph Malzone; Ralph, Carl Lewis."

"I heard about your fiasco." Malzone said it jovially, as if he had heard and seen plenty of other fiascos, and even participated in a few of his own.

He released the beer mugs and reached across the table to shake Carl's hand. His grip was strong. And wet. He had a long, lopsided, lantern-jawed grinning face that seemed honest and intelligent. Carl immediately liked him, despite his opening line.

"Ralph is our director of sales," Lori said. "And our resident electronics whiz. Whenever a computer or anything else complicated breaks down, Ralph can fix it for us."

The wiry guy seemed to blush. "Yeah, but from what I hear, your gadget is way out of my league."

"Do you know where I might find a good electronics lab at NYU?" Carl asked.

"Nope. But maybe I could get you into one at my old alma mater, Columbia."

"I didn't know you were a Columbia graduate," Lori said, sounding surprised.

"Electrical engineering, '91," Malzone said amiably. "Then I went back three years ago and got the mandatory MBA. Only way to get promoted."

"How did you get into the publishing business?" Carl wondered aloud. "And sales, at that."

"Long story. You really don't want to hear it." He raised one of the mugs to his lips and drained half of it in a gulp.

"Can you really get Carl into a lab where he can fix his . . . his . . ."

"It's an electro-optical reader," said Carl.

Malzone knocked off the rest of the beer in mug number one and thunked it down on the table. "You're going to have to get a sexier name for the thing, pal. And, yeah, I can get you into the lab. I think. Lemme make a phone call."

He slid out of the booth with the graceful agility of a trained athlete.

Lori glanced at her wristwatch. "I'll have to be going in a few minutes," she said.

"Going? You're not coming along with me?"

"I'd love to, but I can't. I've got my other job to get to."

"Other job?" Carl felt stupid, hearing himself echo her words.

With a sad little smile Lori explained, "You don't think an editor's salary pays for living in New York, do you?"

"I . . ." Carl shrugged and waved his hands feebly.

"All the editors who live in the city have second jobs. It's either that or live in Yonkers or out on the Island someplace. Or New Jersey." She shuddered. "And then you have to get up before dawn and spend half the day travelling to and from your office."

Carl held himself back from replying. But he thought, I'm going to change all that. The electronic book is just the beginning. I'm going to revolutionize the whole business world, all of it. I'm going to put an end to senseless commuting and make the world safe for trees.

"Maryann Quigly weaves baskets and sells them to anybody she sink her hooks into," Lori was explaining. "Didn't you notice them all over the offices upstairs? And Mr. Perkins, the editor-in-chief—uh, the former editor-in-chief—he writes book reviews under several noms de plume and teaches literary criticism at the Old New School."

"What's going to happen to him now that he's lost his position at Bunker Books?" Carl wondered.

"Who? Perkins?" asked Malzone, pushing himself into the other side of the booth, two fresh beer mugs in his hands.

Both Carl and Lori nodded.

"That's all taken care of," Malzone said jovially. "He's landed a job at S&M as head of their juvenile line."

Lori gasped. "I thought Susan Mangrove . . ."

"She's out. They bounced her yesterday. Found out she had a four-year-old niece in Schenectady."

"No!"

"What's wrong with that?" Carl asked.

"She was a children's book editor," answered Ralph with glee. "One of the requirements of a children's book editor is that he, she, or it has never seen or dealt with a child. Ironclad rule."

"Don't listen to him," Lori snapped. Then, to Ralph, she asked, "So what's Susan going to do?"

"She's moving over to take Alex Knox's place at Ballantrye."

"Knox is gone?"

"Yep. He starts Monday as head of Webb's romance and inspirational line."

"Replacing Scarlet Dean."

"Who's taking Max's job, that's right," said Malzone.

Carl's head was spinning, and not from the beer. "It sounds like musical chairs."

"It is," Malzone said. "The average lifetime of an editor in this business is about two years. Some last longer than that, but a lot of 'em don't even hang in that long."

"Two years? Is that all?"

Malzone laughed. "Long enough. It takes roughly two years for the accounting department to figure out that the books the editor is putting out don't sell. Accounting sends word to management, and the poor dufo gets tossed out."

"That's not exactly true," Lori said.

"Close enough. Meanwhile, over at the competition's office across the street, they've just found out that one of their editors has been putting out books for the past two years that don't sell. So they deep-six him. The two unemployed editors switch places. Each one goes to work at the other's old office, where they'll be safe for another two years. And the two publicity departments put out media releases praising their new hire as the genius who's going to lead them out of the wilderness."

"You mean they'll keep on publishing books that don't sell?" asked Carl.

"Not exactly," Lori said.

"Exactly!" Malzone said with some fervor.

"But why does the publishing house keep on putting out books that don't sell?"

"Simple," replied Malzone, almost jovially. "The books are picked by the editors."

Lori started to protest. "Now wait . . ."

Halting her with a lopsided grin, Malzone went on, "The publishing community is like a small town. We all work in the same neighborhood, pretty much. Eat in the same restaurants. Editors move back and forth from one company to another. They all share pretty much the same values, have the same outlook on life." With sudden intensity, he added, "And the editors all publish the same sorts of books, the books that interest *them*."

Lori frowned slightly but said nothing.

"The editors all live in the New York area," Malzone continued. "They all work in a small neighborhood of Manhattan. They think that New York is America. And they publish books that look good in New York, but sink like lead turds once they cross the Hudson."

"They don't sell well?" Carl asked.

"Most books don't sell at all," said Malzone. "Ask the man who's stuck with the job of selling them."

Lori said, "Only a small percentage of the books published earn back the money originally invested in them. Most of them lose money."

"But how can an industry stay in business that way?" Carl asked. He felt genuinely perplexed.

Malzone laughed and quaffed down a huge gulp of beer. "Damned if I know, pal. Damned if I know."

Lori looked at her wristwatch again. "I've really got to go. See you tomorrow, Carl. In my office. Early as you can make it."

Carl got up to let her out of the booth. She reached up and bussed his cheek. He felt confused; did not know how to react, what to do.

"Uh . . . you didn't tell me what your second job is," he mumbled.

Lori smiled sweetly. "Same as it was when we met."

"Belly dancing?" Carl blurted.

Lifting one hand before her face in imitation of a veil, Lori said, "I am Yasmin, the Armenian Dervish. But only from nine to midnight, three nights a week."

Purchase Requisition 98021

Title of Work: *The Terror from Beyond Hell*
Author: Sheldon Stoker
Agent: Murray Swift
Editor: Scarlet Dean (upon arrival)
Contract terms: To be negotiated; offering will be same terms as
   Stoker's last book
Advance: To be negotiated; offering $1,000,000.00

Purchase Requisition 98022

Title of Work: *Midway Diary*
Author: Ron Clanker (Capt., U.S.N., [Ret.])
Agent: none
Editor: L. Tashkajian
Contract terms: Standard, all rights retained by Bunker Books
Advance: Minimum, $5,000, returnable

SIX

LONG after the end of the business day, P. Curtis Hawks remained in his office, sitting glumly at his desk, staring out the wide windows as Manhattan turned on its lights to greet the encroaching night.

Bugged my office, he kept repeating to himself as he chewed ceaselessly on his plastic cigar butt. The Old Man has bugged my office. My office. Bugged.

There were wheels within wheels here, he realized. The Old Man, up there in the dotty jungle he had turned his office into, was playing crazy, senile games. Hawks remembered from history when other great tyrants had gone mad: Ivan the Terrible, Hitler, Stalin—they had all gone on paranoid sprees of suspicion and wholesale murder. Even within the publishing industry right here in New York, Kordman and Dyson and even Wanly had all gone nuts toward the end; each one of them pulled their own houses down on top of them.

Weldon was clearly cracking up. One minute he wants to buy out Bunker, the next he doesn't. Then he wants this kid Lewis's invention copied, or stolen, or the guy himself snatched away from Bunker. It's crazy.

Why is the Old Man behaving this way? Hawks asked himself for the thousandth time that evening. Some electronic gadget that shows books on its screen can't be that important. Something else is going on; something he hasn't told me about.

Then it hit him, with the clarity and bone-chilling certainty of absolute truth. *He knows about the warehouse!* Hawks blanched with terror. *He knows about the warehouse!* There was no other explanation for it. The Old Man was toying with him, like a grinning Cheshire cat playing with a very tiny, very terrified mouse.

With a shaking hand, Hawks reached for the telephone. But as soon as his fingers touched the instrument he yanked them away as if they had been scorched by molten lava.

He's bugging my office. Damnation! He's probably tracing all my phone and computer traffic, too.

Pull yourself together, he commanded himself fiercely. You can't let yourself go to pieces. This is life or death, man! It's him against me! Hawks shifted the plastic cigar butt from one side of his mouth to the other.

He's out to get me. Just because of that goddamned warehouse the old bastard is after my ass. Hawks grunted with the realization of it. Despite years of the Old Man's calling him ''son'' and grooming him to take over the top slot at Tarantula, Hawks could not escape the conclusion that the only thing he was at the very top of was Weldon W. Weldon's personal hit list. One little mistake. That's all it takes in this business.

Well, two can play at that game, by god. If the senile old bastard wants to do away with me, I've got to do away with him first.

But how? he asked himself. There's nobody in the whole corporation that you can trust. Anybody might be a spy for the Old Man. You'll have to get outside help.

Which meant going to New Jersey and having a talk with the Beast from the East.

* * *

". . . so I'm sitting there, just a skinny kid right out of the navy, it's my first job . . ."

Ralph Malzone was talking while Carl bent over the exposed innards of his electro-optical reader. They sat side by side at a laboratory bench strewn with tools, wires, and flea-sized electronic components. Both men wore disposable white lab coats and silly-looking hats made of paper. This was a clean-room facility, and they even had to put paper booties over their shoes before Malzone's friend would reluctantly allow them in.

Carl had a surgeon's magnifiers clamped over his eyes and a pair of ultrasensitive micromanipulators in his white-gloved hands as he operated on his failed machine, trying to bring the dead back to life.

Malzone was passing the time by recounting his early adventures as a route salesman for a magazine distribution company.

"So I'm sitting there in what passes for a waiting room, a crummy hallway piled high with old magazines waiting for the shredder. Just this one rickety bench; I think he stole it from a kids' playground. All of a sudden, from inside the guy's office I hear him holler, 'Nobody's gonna give *me* a fuckin' ultimatum!' And then a pistol shot!"

"Jeez," muttered Carl.

"Yeah. And this salesman comes whizzing out of the office like his pants are on fire. The owner walks out after him with a smoking Smith & Wesson in his hand!"

Carl grunted. He had just dropped an electro-optical chip out of the micromanipulator's tiny fingers. Malzone took it as a comment on his unfolding story.

"Now remember, *I* had been sent there to give him an ultimatum, too. The sonofabitch hadn't been paying any of his bills for months. So there he is, the smoking gun in his hand and fire in his eyes. And he sees me sitting there, just about to crap in my pants."

"Uh-huh." Carl picked up the chip and deftly inserted it where it belonged, at last.

" 'Whaddaya you want?' he asks me, waving the gun in my general direction. Before I can answer, he says, 'You're the new kid from General, ain'tcha?' I sort of nod, and he tucks the gun in his pants and says, 'Come on, kid, I'll show you what this business is all about.' He takes me to the bar next door and we spend the rest of the afternoon drinking beer.''

Without looking up at him, Carl asked, "Did he ever pay you what he owed?''

"Oh sure, eventually. He got to be one of the best customers on my route.''

"That's good,'' said Carl.

Malzone's lanky face frowned slightly, but from behind his magnifiers Carl could no more see the expression on his face than a myopic dolphin could see the carvings of Mt. Rushmore. Malzone sank into silence. The two men were alone in the electronics lab. It was well after midnight. Silent and dim in the corridors beyond the lab's long windows. Silent and dim inside the clean room, too, except for the pool of intense light Carl had focused onto his work area from a swing-neck lamp.

The older man studied Carl intently as he worked. His stories about his youthful adventures in the sales end of the publishing business had been a way to pass the time, and to hide the terrible smoldering jealousy he felt burning in his guts. For wiry, grinning, gregarious Ralph Malzone was secretly, totally, hopelessly in love with Lori. He had never told her how he felt. He had never even worked up the courage to ask her for a date. But as he watched Carl working on electronic circuitry that was far beyond his own knowledge, Ralph realized that this guy was Lori's own age and they had known each other in Boston, before Lori had come to New York, before he had met her and fallen so hard for her. He heard someone sigh like a moonstruck moose. Himself.

"Maybe I should go out and get us a coupla beers,'' Malzone suggested.

"Not for me. Anyway, I think it's just about finished.''

"Yeah?'' The older man brightened.

Carl held his breath as he inserted the final filament lead. "Yeah," he said in a shaky whisper. "Yeah, I think that's it."

He straightened up painfully, his spine suddenly telling him that he had spent too many hours bent over his labor. Taking off the magnifiers, Carl blinked several times, then rubbed his eyes.

"Will it work now?" Malzone asked.

"It should."

Still, Carl's hands trembled slightly as he snapped the cover shut on the oblong case and turned it over so that its screen glinted in the lamp's powerful light.

He touched the first keypad with his index finger. The screen sprang to life instantly, glowing with color to reveal the title page of *Rain Makes Applesauce*.

Carl let out the breath he had not realized he'd been holding in. It worked. It worked!

He picked up the glowing box and offered it to Malzone, grinning. It looked much smaller in the sales manager's long-fingered, big-knuckled hands.

"What do I do?" Malzone asked.

"Just touch the green button to move ahead a page. Hold it down and it will riffle through the pages for you until you take your finger off. Then it'll stop. If you want a specific page, tap in the number on the little keyboard on the right."

Malzone spent several minutes paging back and forth. Looking over his shoulder, Carl saw that the screen was working fine: everything in clear focus. The illustrations looked beautifully sharp.

"Nice gadget," Malzone said at last, handing it back to Carl.

"Is that all you can say?"

Malzone hunched his shoulders. "It's an electronic way of looking at a book. Like a pocket TV, only you can see books with it instead of TV programs. Might make a nice fad gift for the Christmas season."

"But it's a lot more than that!" Carl said fervently. "This is going to replace books printed on paper! This is the biggest breakthrough since the printing press!"

"Nahhh." Malzone shook his head, his russet brows knitted. "It's a nice idea, but it's not going to replace books. Who'd buy a machine that's got to cost at least a hundred bucks when you can buy a hardcover book for fifty? And a paperback for less than ten?"

"Who would buy a hardcover or a paperback," Carl retorted, "when an electronic book will cost pennies?"

Malzone grunted, just as if someone had whacked him in the gut with a pool cue.

"Pennies?"

"Sure, the reader—this device, here—is going to cost more than a half-dozen books. But once you own one you can get your books electronically. Over the phone, if you like. The most expensive books there are will cost less than a dollar!"

"Now wait a minute. You mean . . ."

"No paper!" Carl exulted. "You don't have to chop down trees and make paper and haul tons of the stuff to the printing presses and then haul the printed books to the stores. You move electrons and photons instead of paper! It's cheap and efficient."

For a long moment Malzone said nothing. Then he sighed a very heavy sigh. "You're saying that a publisher won't need printers, paper, ink, wholesalers, route salesmen, district managers, truck drivers—not even bookstores?"

"The whole thing can be done electronically," Carl enthused. "Shop for books by TV. Buy them over the phone. Transmit them anywhere on Earth almost instantaneously, straight to the customer."

Malzone glanced around the shadows of the clean room uneasily. In a near whisper he told Carl, "Jesus Christ, kid, you're going to get both of us killed."

And deep within his innermost primitive self he thought, Maybe I ought to knock you off myself and save us both a lot of misery.

Typical Editor's Day	**Typical Editor's Day**
(Scheduled)	*(Actual)*

9:00 A.M.: Arrive in office.	9:00 A.M.: Gobble breakfast.
9:05 A.M.: Read mail. Answer memos.	9:05 A.M.: Catch train to office.
10:30 A.M.: Production meeting.	10:30 A.M.: Arrive office (tell them train was late).
11:30 A.M.: Editorial board meeting.	10:35 A.M. Production meeting (argue with managing editor and art director).
	11:15 A.M.: Coffee break.
	11:30 A.M.: Editorial board meeting.
12:30–1:30 P.M.: Lunch.	
	2:00 P.M.: Go to lunch (editorial board meeting ran late).
1:35 P.M.: Review readers' reports.	
4:00 P.M.: Answer mail, phone calls.	4:24 P.M.: Back from lunch with author and agent (cocktails, two bottles of wine plus brandy afterwards).
5:00 P.M.: Leave for home, bringing manuscripts to read.	4:30–5:00 P.M.: Aspirin and Maalox.
	5:00–6:30 P.M.: Catch up on office gossip.
	6:30–7:30 P.M.: Drinks with the gang (why try to fight the rush hour?).

Typical Editor's Day

(Actual)

7:40 P.M.: Take train home (the Battle of Lexington Ave.).

8:45 P.M.: Fall asleep over TV dinner.

11:30 P.M.–12:30 A.M.: *The Tonight Show Starring Johnny Carson II.*

SEVEN

THE following morning, a bleary-eyed Carl Lewis sat before Mrs. Alba Blanca Bunker, the publisher of Bunker Books. Her husband, of course, was sole owner of the company—almost. A few shares of stock were scattered here and there, but the controlling interest was firmly in the hands of Pandro T. Bunker, his wife, and his only son, P. T. Jr.

The Boss sat behind her petite desk, with Junior at his mother's side, a crafty little smile on his narrow-eyed face. Mrs. Bunker was, as usual, dressed entirely in white. Her office was all in white as well: the dainty Louis-Something-or-Other furniture was bleached white, the carpeting looked like softly tufted white angora wool, the walls and ceiling were white cream. Carl had once been trapped in a sudden blizzard in the (where else?) White Mountains years earlier, and the effect of the Boss's office was much the same. Whiteout. Almost snowblind.

But warmer. Much warmer. Golden sunlight streamed through the windows of the corner office. And Mrs. Bunker was smiling pleasantly as she tapped away at Carl's invention, happily reading *Rain Makes Applesauce* from beginning to end.

Absolute silence reigned. Not even the crackle of a page being turned, of course. Carl watched the almost childlike expression on Mrs. Bunker's face as she read through the delightful book and studied its fascinating illustrations. Junior peered over her shoulder now and then, but mostly he seemed to be staring at Carl as if trying to size him up. Carl felt that uncomfortable sensation a man gets when he's confronted by a determined haberdashery salesman.

Lori sat beside him, close enough almost to touch. Their chairs were delicate, graceful, yet surprisingly comfortable.

The suit Mrs. Bunker was wearing seemed identical to the one she wore the previous day, to Carl. Her jewelry was different, however, although still all gold. Junior wore jeans and a ragged biker's T-shirt, complete with artificial sweat and grease stains. Its front bore a Bunker Books logo. Lori was in a simple wide-yoked light tan dress that showed her smooth shoulders to advantage.

Carl felt distinctly grubby. He had grabbed a few hours' sleep in the hotel room that Bunker had provided, and then climbed back into the same slacks and tweed jacket he had worn the day before. Except for one change of underwear and shirt, that was all the clothes he had brought with him.

Mrs. Bunker finished *Rain Makes Applesauce* at last, and put Carl's reader down on the immaculate surface of her little desk.

"It's a beautiful book," she said. "I noticed from the copyright date that it's almost fifty years old. Is it in the public domain yet? Can we reprint it?"

Surprised by her question, Carl stammered, "Gosh, I . . . it never occurred to me that you would want . . ."

"That's not really why we're here, Mrs. Bee," said Lori with equal amounts of politeness and firmness in her voice.

"Oh. Of course. I just thought that if the book is in the public domain we could publish it without the expense of paying the author."

"Or the illustrator," Junior chimed in.

Mother turned a pleased smile upon son.

"But how did you like the electro-optical reader?" Carl blurted, unable to stand the suspense any further.

Mrs. Bunker smiled again, but differently. "It's *wonderful*. It's everything you said it would be. The pages are crisp and clear, and the illustrations come out *beautifully*. I've never seen such brilliant colors in print. Well—let's say seldom, instead of never."

Reaching into his jacket pocket, Carl pulled out a half dozen more wafers and spread them out on the Boss's desk.

"Here we have *War and Peace, Asimov's Guide to Everything,* this year's *World Almanac*"—he pointed each one out with his index finger—"and these three contain the complete novels of James Michener."

"Really? All in those little disks?" Mrs. Bunker asked.

"All in these six wafers," Carl agreed. "I could provide you with the complete *Encyclopedia Britannica* in a pocketful more. Or two of Victor Hugo's novels in a single wafer."

"Hugo? Who publishes him?" asked Mrs. Bunker.

"Hey, Mom," Junior replied, "he does plays. He was big on Broadway the year I was born. Don't you remember, Dad almost named me John Val John." He pronounced the name like a New Yorker, and favored his mother with a condescending smile that pitied her lack of literary lore.

Carl glanced at Lori, who kept a perfectly straight face.

"It's a wonderful invention," Mrs. Bunker said again, "and I think you're right—this can transform the publishing industry. I believe that Bunker Books can become the nation's number-one publisher if we move ahead swiftly with this."

Carl felt a surge of—what? Satisfaction. Relief. Joy. Justification for all the months he had spent half starving and working twenty hours a day to create the electro-optical marvel that rested modestly on the desk of this woman in white. He felt gratitude, too. For deep within him, buried in the innermost convolutions of his mind, there lurked a stubborn fear that his invention was worthless, that any half-trained TV repair man could have figured it out, that it was nothing but a toy without any real value whatsoever.

But she thinks it's great, Carl told himself. She thinks it's going to transform the publishing industry, he rejoiced triumphantly to that inner voice of fear.

And the voice answered, Maybe so. She also thinks Victor Hugo is a Broadway playwright.

Carl found that he had to swallow a lump in his throat before he could say, "I'm very pleased, Mrs. Bunker. How do you want to proceed from here?"

"Proceed?" Her face suddenly looked blank.

"Do we sign a consulting agreement, or do you want me to become a contractor to Bunker Books? What kind of payments will Bunker Books make for the invention? What rights do you want to purchase? That sort of thing."

With a glance toward her son, Mrs. Bunker answered, "I'm not empowered to make any commitments of that sort. Only Mr. Bunker himself can do that."

"Then I suppose I'll have to demonstrate the device to him," Carl said, reaching for the reader.

Mrs. Bunker put on a smile that showed some teeth. "Couldn't you let me borrow it overnight? I'll show it to my husband this evening."

With alarm bells tingling in every nerve, Carl slowly slid the reader to the edge of the desk and gripped it in both his hands. "This is the only prototype in existence. I'm afraid I can't let it out of my sight. I'd be glad to show it to Mr. Bunker myself. . . ."

Mrs. Bee bit her lower lip. "That may be difficult. He's such a busy man. . . ."

Holding the reader firmly in his lap, Carl gestured with his other hand to the six wafers still resting on the desk top. "I can let you show the wafers to him. To give him an idea of how small and cheap books can be made."

"But he won't be able to read them without your device, will he?"

"I'm afraid not."

"What's the matter, don't you trust us?" Junior asked. His tone was light enough, almost bantering. But there was no levity in his face.

Carl replied, "This isn't personal. I decided before I left Boston that I would not let the prototype out of my sight."

A cloud of silence dimmed the all-white office.

"I'd be glad to show it to Mr. Bunker personally," Carl repeated.

"I suppose that's what we'll have to do, then," said Mrs. Bunker. "I'll see what I can arrange."

Feeling vastly relieved, Carl shot to his feet. "Thank you! You won't regret it."

He put out his hand to her, still staunchly grasping the prototype in his left hand. She made a sweet smile without getting up from her chair and touched his hand briefly, like a queen dispensing a blessing. Junior's eyes never left the device until Carl tucked it back into his black courier case.

Lori and Carl got as far as the door. Mrs. Bunker called, "Oh, Lori, dear. Could you stay a moment longer? There's something I want to discuss with you."

Carl stepped outside into the busy corridor where editors and other unidentified frenzied objects were dashing about. Mrs. Bunker had no secretary, no outer office. Bunker Books was a tightly run ship where computers and communications were used in place of salaried employees, Carl realized. It's criminal to use human beings in lackey jobs like secretarial work, he told himself. Nothing but ostentatious show for the people who hire them and degrading drudgery for the people who take such jobs. Electrons work more efficiently. And cheaper. Any job that can be done twice the same way *ought* to be done by a machine.

Then why do they have editors? he asked himself. Computers can check a manuscript's spelling and grammar much more thoroughly than any human being can. What do editors do that computers can't?

His ruminations were interrupted by Lori's stepping through

the Boss's office door and out into the corridor. A grim-faced gray-haired man clutching a long trailing sweep of narrow white sheets of paper fluttering behind him like the tail of a kite bolted past them like an underweight halfback being pursued by the first-string defense. He brushed so close to Lori that she jumped into Carl's arms.

"Who was that?" he asked, releasing her as the gray flash disappeared down the hall.

"Grenouille, the assistant managing editor," Lori said without moving from his side. "He's always in a rush."

Carl shook his head. "This is an odd place."

"Isn't it, though?" Lori laughed.

As they headed back toward her office, Lori said, "How's your hotel room?"

He shrugged. "It's a hotel room. Okay, I guess. It's walking distance to the office."

"My apartment's down in the Village. How about letting me cook you dinner tonight?"

"Fine!"

"And then you can come and watch me dance."

Carl tried to stop his face from reddening, but he could feel his cheeks turning hot. "Uh, okay, sure."

Lori grinned up at him.

Alba Blanca Bunker sat on the edge of the enormous round waterbed waiting for her husband. She was tired. It had been a hectic, exhausting day. The new line of historic novels was not selling well. It had seemed so _right_: a line of novels based on true history, the actual deeds and romantic exploits of some of history's greatest figures—Cary Grant, Lynn Redgrave, Willie Nelson, Barbara Walters. But despite a six-million-dollar publicity campaign, the books were moldering in the warehouses. Nobody seemed to want them.

She sighed deeply and lay back on the waterbed, allowing her filmy white peignoir to drape itself dramatically across the tiger-striped sheets. She studied the effect in the overhead mirror. This bedroom had been their fantasy place when they had first built this home out of a converted warehouse next to the Disneydome, years earlier. With voice command either she or her husband could convert the hologrammic decor from jungle to desert, from underwater to outer space. With a sad little smile she remembered how the circuitry had blown itself out in a shower of sparks during one particularly vocal bout of lovemaking.

Nothing like that had happened for many years now. The room was a cool forest green, the scent of pine in the whispering breeze, the hint of a full moon silvering the drawn draperies of the window.

She knew where her husband was. In his office talking to Beijing, trying desperately to nail down the deal that would open up the Chinese market. A billion potential customers! It could mean the salvation of Bunker Books.

Or could this MIT whiz kid be their salvation? His invention worked, there was no denying it. How much would he want for it? How much would it cost to start a whole new line of operations, electronic books instead of paper ones? *That's* why we need the China deal, she told herself, to provide the capital for developing the electronic book. Otherwise . . .

There was still the tender offer from Tarantula Enterprises. Pandro would never sell his company. Never. He had built it practically from scratch, with nothing but the ten million his father had loaned him. Bunker Books was *his* creation, and he would go to hell and burn eternally before he would sell the company or any part of it.

Still—if she could get him to pretend to consider the Tarantula offer, they might be able to raise some capital from a few insiders down on Wall Street. No, that wouldn't work. Pandro wouldn't stoop to such chicanery. He would plug ahead stubbornly trying to close the China deal with those elusive, wily Orientals. She did not trust men who spoke so politely, yet never quite seemed to do what they said they would.

The electronic book. We've *got* to have it. And somehow find the money to develop it. Nothing else matters. It's either that or bankruptcy.

She lay perfectly still on the beautiful bed in the beautiful room, waiting for her husband to come to her while her mind searched out a way to avoid the yawning black abyss that was ready to swallow Bunker Books. No path appeared safe; there was no way out of the financial chasm awaiting them. Except perhaps the electronic book. Perhaps.

She fell asleep waiting for her husband to leave his work and come to bed. She dreamed of electronic books and showers of golden coins pattering gently over the two of them as they lay coiled in a passionate embrace.

MURDER THREE ▬▬▬

JOHN Watson was a professor of sociology at the New New School, at Central Park North. The neat rows of condominiums marched northward through Harlem, each lovingly renovated building flanked on both sides by blockwide vegetable gardens, also lovingly tended by the neighborhood residents. Watson could have taken considerable pride in the role he had played in turning Harlem into a model of peace and prosperity.

All his younger years he had battled the city, the state government, the feds, and the people of Harlem themselves. His enemies had been hopelessness and resistance to change: the indifference of the masses and the brutal opposition of the dope peddlers and slumlords and crooked city officials who made their millions out of the sweat and suffering of Harlem's people.

His allies had been the mothers who had seen their children killed by narcotics, or guns, or knives. And the brighter youngsters who sought a way out of the endless cycle of misery and poverty. They had little power. But they had guts and brains. Then John Watson hit upon a stroke of genius. He made allies of the building contractors and their associated trade unions.

Rebuilding Harlem made jobs for nearly a generation of carpenters, plumbers, electricians, masons, truck drivers. It made hundreds of millions for the companies that employed them. The money came from taxes, of course: local, state, and federal. But the payoff, as John Watson spent twenty years explaining to appropriations committees, would be a Harlem that was productive, a Harlem that housed taxpayers, not welfare cases. Not criminals and diseased addicts.

Now, as he strolled along Martin Luther King Boulevard toward Rev. Jesse Jackson Park, Watson took no small measure of satisfaction in the happiness that he saw all around him. Harlem was not heaven; it was not even the Garden of Eden. But it was no longer the rotting, drug-infested ghetto that it had been when he was a child growing up in it.

It was a considerable shock, therefore, when a strange white man stepped out of a car parked in a clearly marked bus stop zone and sank a switchblade knife into John Watson's heart. He died almost instantly, while the white man got back into his car and calmly drove away. None of the stunned witnesses could provide the police with the car's license number, probably because the license plate had been carefully smeared with dirt beforehand.

It was a monument to John Watson's life work that this foul murder was treated as any other would be, both by the police and the media. Everyone was shocked. No one suggested that such an event was only to be expected in Harlem.

EIGHT

CARL sat sweating in the smoky Greek nightclub
on Ninth Avenue, watching a fleshy half-naked young woman
performing the artfully erotic Oriental ritual known in the West
as the belly dance.

The place was only half-full, but almost all of the customers
were men. Most of them sat up at the bar itself, squinting through
the haze of cigarette smoke and muttering an occasional "Ya-
soo!" at a particularly stimulating movement by the dancer up
on the tiny platform that passed for a stage. A three-piece band
—reedy clarinet, big-bellied stringed bouzouki, and the inevitable
drums—played weaving snake charmer's music. Now and then
the drummer would sing in a wavering, almost yodelling high-
pitched tenor.

Carl sat alone at a table near the stage, close enough to smell
the dancers' heavy perfumes and feel the breeze from their veils
as they twirled about. Men staggered up to the edge of the stage
now and then to press dollar bills into the dancer's bra or
g-string. Carl had never seen that before. In Cambridge, where

he had met Lori, the belly-dancing was more of an Armenian clan gathering. Everybody danced before the night was over, linking hands in a long human chain that wended around the restaurant and, sometimes, right out into the street.

But that had been in Cambridge. Now he was in New York. They played by different rules here. It had been a dizzying, stupefying couple of days. Now, as he sipped alternately at a water tumbler filled with milky iced ouzo and a tiny cup of powerful, muddy Greek coffee, Carl wondered how long it would take before P. T. Bunker, the founder and president of Bunker Books, would condescend to meet with him.

"Mrs. Bee wants me to entice you into turning the prototype over to her, so she can show it to Mr. Bee," Lori had told him in the cab as they rode to the club.

"She *what*?" Carl had snapped.

Patting his knee, Lori said soothingly, "Relax. I'm going to do no such thing. If P. T. Bunker wants to see your prototype, he'll have to see you along with it."

Carl felt his misgivings ease away. Slightly.

"It's just that it's almost impossible to get to see Mr. Bunker. He's so busy all the time."

"What about when he comes to the office?"

"He *never* comes to the office," Lori had said. "We never see him. Mrs. Bunker runs the office and he stays in their home down in the Lower East Side."

"That's a pretty posh neighborhood, isn't it?" Carl had asked. "Near the Disneydome and all."

Lori smiled bitterly. "Listen: I know plenty of starving writers, hungry artists, editors who have to take moonlighting jobs just to pay the rent on their studio apartments. But publishers live in posh neighborhoods and drink champagne every night."

No champagne for me, Carl told himself as he took another sip of the ouzo. It was powerful stuff, even iced. Strong flavor like licorice. The waiter had taken one look at Carl and decided he did not look Greek. When he brought the first ouzo, he also brought a stainless-steel bowl filled with ice cubes. "You don't drink it straight," he insisted. "You put ice in it. No friend of Yasmin's is going to throw up on this floor!"

The waiter was watching him now, from the shadows in the corner of the room, a dark scowl of suspicion on his swarthy mustachioed face. There was a table full of young, broad-shouldered men on that side of the stage, laughing and drinking and hollering to the dancer in Greek. They looked like stevedores from the nearby docks. Muscular types, shirts opened to their belt buckles to show off their hairy chests.

A crash from up near the bar made Carl swivel his head. The men up there, older, balder, paunchier, were laughing uproariously. One of them raised his emptied glass over his head and smashed it to the floor. Everybody laughed and applauded.

The ouzo should be relaxing me, Carl told himself. I ought to be loosening up, like everyone else. Instead he felt tense, wary, as if he had been trapped alone in a strange and dangerous land.

The dancer finished with a flourish and a hearty round of "Yasoos" and applause, then scurried offstage with dollar bills flapping from her costume.

The music died. Muttered conversations and occasional bursts of laughter were the only sounds in the club. Carl finished his glass of ouzo, then sipped carefully at the coffee. When he began to taste the mud at the bottom of the little cup, he put it down and signalled to the waiter.

The swarthy man was at his side like a shot. "Another coffee?"

"When does Yasmin come on?"

"She is next."

Carl pulled in a deep breath. His nose wrinkled at the acrid smell of cigarette smoke. "Another ouzo," he ordered.

"And coffee?"

"No. Just the ouzo."

"You don't like our coffee? Too strong for you?"

Carl looked up at him. "I love your coffee."

"Then I bring you another cup."

The man was being protective, Carl realized. "Okay. Another cup of coffee. And another glass of ouzo."

"Hokay."

The waiter also brought a glass full of ice cubes, with a fierce scowl that told Carl he would not tolerate his drinking the ouzo straight.

The band started tuning up again as Carl was pouring the clear liquor over the ice and watching it turn pale milky white, wondering what chemical reaction caused the change in color. Then the club's bass-heavy loudspeaker announced: "And now, our next Oriental dancer—Yasmin! The Armenian Dervish!"

It was Lori all right. She was beautiful. Bare flesh as smooth and flawless as the most perfect fantasy. She moved sensuously, sinuously, hips weaving a spell that soon had Carl breathing hard.

The first part of her dance was all right. The dancers all started with see-through veils that really hid nothing, but at least discouraged admirers from trying to stuff money into their costumes.

Carl gulped at his watered ouzo as slowly, tantalizingly, Yasmin removed her veils. She smiled at Carl as if to say she were dancing especially for him. But although his eyes were riveted on her, he could hear the raucous remarks coming from the table across the way.

Carl felt every nerve in him tightening. It's just their way, he told himself. They're not being crude or obscene. Still, as Lori danced, he found himself glaring at the table full of young stevedores.

She moved toward their side of the stage and, sure enough, one of the hairy grinning apes stood up and tucked a dollar bill in the g-string circling Lori's hips. She danced away from them, back toward Carl, bending over him slightly so that her breasts swayed with the music.

Carl was panting now. Then another one of the stevedores jumped up on the stage with a fistful of bills and started pushing them into Lori's bra. She looked slightly alarmed.

Before he could think, Carl was on the stage and pushing the young Greek away from her. The music stopped. All the other stevedores got to their feet, fists clenched. The mustachioed waiter dashed up onto the stage and stood between Carl and the others. The rest of the waiters gathered around.

Carl found himself being politely but firmly led by both arms out of the club and out into the street. His waiter shook his head sadly at him and said, "Not enough ice."

It was drizzling. Carl felt like a perfect idiot. And he also felt furious that there were men in there pawing Lori's body. And she was letting them do it! He started walking in the general direction of his hotel, letting the drizzling rain cool him off. He imagined it sizzling to steam as it struck his body, he felt so heated.

After what seemed like an hour's walking he found himself back at the same club. I must've walked around the block, he realized. Like a man lost in the desert, he had made a circle and returned to his starting point.

Briefly he wondered what would happen if the half dozen or so stevedores came out the door right at this instant. But instead, when the club's front door swung open, Lori stepped out, looking worried and slightly dishevelled, bundled in a beige raincoat.

"Carl!"

He started to say hello as casually as he knew how, but his throat was raw and it came out as a croaking "Hi."

"Whatever possessed you . . . ?"

"I got mad."

She did not seem angry. In fact, she was smiling. "You decided to protect my honor?"

"Something like that."

Almost, she laughed. But she caught herself. "Come on, you can walk me home." She pulled a miniature umbrella from her capacious shoulder bag and opened it. Carl had to snuggle very close to her just to keep his head under its tiny red canopy.

Quite seriously, Lori asked, "Don't you know that the waiters protect all the dancers? This is a respectable club; they don't allow any nasty stuff."

"Just feeling you up onstage, in front of everybody."

"That's nothing. It's like leaving a tip for the waiter."

"Do you enjoy having strange guys paw you?"

For a moment she said nothing. Then, in a small voice, Lori told him, "I'd enjoy it more if someone I knew very well pawed me."

Carl gulped and asked, "How far is it to your apartment?"

It was a studio apartment on the second floor of an old red-brick high rise in the Gramercy Park area. Once the neighborhood had been prime real estate, but it had been going steadily downhill for a generation. Still, Lori assured Carl, the building was safe. The automated security system kept strangers from entering the lobby, and the bars on the windows discouraged burglars.

Carl did not notice the automated security system or the bars on the windows or anything other than Lori, the nearness of her, the warmth of her, the scent of her. In his mind he heard swirling reedy music and saw her dancing for him alone. They danced together, the oldest dance of all, entwined in each other on a foldout bed until he fell into an exhausted sleep.

Lori lay next to Carl's peacefully slumbering body. It smoldered like hot lava, and she pressed herself against him. He was out like a light, poor baby. Too much ouzo, she diagnosed. She smiled at the cracked ceiling in the shadows of her little apartment. The noise from the traffic of Third Avenue and the wailing sirens of the ambulances from the hospital across the way did not bother her now.

But something else did. The novel. *The* novel. The greatest piece of literature she had ever read, in manuscript. Not as good as Tolstoy or Proust or even Dickens, but as good as anything ever written in America. As good as Hemingway or Twain or Fitzgerald, even when he was sober. Better.

They'll never let me publish it. They'll say it's not commercial. It's not a *Thorn Birds* or a *Shogun*. It's merely the finest piece of literature written by any American since Christopher goddamn Columbus stumbled ashore. And there's no market for fine literature. That's what they'll say.

But, Lori told herself, if I bring them Carl's electronic book, if the company gets rich on the idea that I brought to them, then I'll have the power to publish what I want to. I'll be able to bring this great work of literature to print.

Carl groaned softly and shifted in the bed. Lori gazed at his naked body, still sheened with perspiration. I'm using you, she said silently to him. She felt a pang of remorse at the realization. But it's all in the service of great art, she rationalized, great literature.

And besides, she almost giggled, I think I really do love you, you big silly knight in shining armor.

Capt. Ron Clanker, U.S.N. (Ret.)
c/o Army/Navy Home
Chelsea MA 02150

Dear Capt. Clanker:

It is my great pleasure to tell you that Bunker Books will be happy to publish your novel, *Midway Diary*. As you will see in the enclosed contract forms, we offer you an advance of $5,000 against all rights to the work.

Let me offer my personal congratulations. I think you have written a fine, sensitive novel that still contains stirring action. It is the best such work I've read since Richard McKenna's *The Sand Pebbles*. I only hope it sells as well!

Sincerely yours,
Lori Tashkajian
Fiction Editor

NINE

TWO men spent the rest of the week in an agony of suspense.

Carl Lewis felt like an astronaut lost in the dark vacuum of space, hanging weightless and alone, waiting for rescue. P. T. Bunker had agreed to see him, but not today. He was busy. Tomorrow. When the next day came, it was the same story. Sorry, Mr. Bunker is engaged in some very delicate negotiations and cannot be disturbed.

Mrs. Bunker was pleasant, even sweet, to Carl as he came by the office every day. Junior kept casting a shifty eye on Carl whenever they bumped into one another in the corridor. Each afternoon Carl went back to his hotel room, wondering if he should ask Lori to dinner, wondering if their night together was the result of ouzo or true love or just animal passion.

For her part, Lori did not mention their night of lovemaking, although she smiled at Carl warmly and cast him long-lashed glances as if she expected him to make the next move. And he was not certain what his next move should be.

So he waited for his moment with P. T. Bunker. And waited.

Twenty floors higher in the Synthoil Tower, P. Curtis Hawks

anticipated the weekend with barely concealed frenzy. He was not waiting for someone else to make himself available. Hawks yearned for the day, Saturday, when he did not have to be in the office. When he could sneak out to New Jersey without the Old Man knowing it. When he could start the machinery that would eventually remove Weldon W. Weldon and install himself as CEO of Tarantula Enterprises—the head spider.

Saturday dawned like a scene out of Edgar Allan Poe: dark and dreary. Rain slanted down from black clouds. The perfect day for sleeping late. But Hawks was up and out of his Westchester County house by seven, leaving his lumpy overweight wife snoring soundly in her bed, her usual tray full of tranquilizers on her night table in easy reach.

It never occurred to Hawks that the same technology that could turn his office into a veritable Hollywood sound studio could also keep track of his private automobile. An electronic chip the size of a fingernail paring could send a signal to a satellite orbiting more than 22,000 miles high, which in turn could pinpoint the car's position anywhere in the Western Hemisphere. If Hawks had realized that, it probably would have affected his driving.

As it was, he sped his heavy Citroën-Mercedes down practically empty throughways in the dreary pelting rain, crossed the Hudson on the Tappan Zee Bridge, and plunged into New Jersey. Within an hour he was at the warehouse.

His warehouse. The primary storage area and distribution center for Webb Press's books and magazines. Hawks's personal, concrete monument to himself. His albatross.

It was a long, low, gray concrete structure, more reminiscent of the bunkers and gun emplacements of the Siegfried Line than a publisher's warehouse. Rows of big trucks, each emblazoned with the stylized spiderweb of Webb Press on their flanks (and a small representation of a tarantula at the edge of the web), lined the parking area. The loading docks were shut tight. The place looked empty and deserted.

Hawks pulled his big sedan up to the front entrance, beneath the marquee that he had personally designed. It was rusting already, even though he had specified that it be made of stainless steel throughout.

Ignoring the streaks of ignominy defacing his creation, Hawks trudged the few feet from his car to the warehouse's front door, huddled inside his trenchcoat against the gusting wet wind.

He pushed at the door. Locked.

He tapped at the security buzzer.

"Name, please?" asked the security computer in the hard, no-nonsense voice of a retired cop.

"Hawks. P. Curtis Hawks."

"Just a moment for voiceprint identification, please."

Hawks fidgeted in the rain that slanted in under the canopy. A leak in the supposedly stainless steel dripped into a puddle that spanned the front doorway like a miniature moat. Hawks's immaculate Argentinean boots, with their clever inner soles and heels that raised him two inches taller than he deserved, were getting soaked and ruined.

"I'm sorry, sir. Voiceprint does not match."

"Whattaya mean it doesn't match!" Hawks shouted at the little speaker grille. "I'm P. Curtis Hawks. I'm the president of this goddamn company! Open this fucking door or I'll replace you with a Radio Shack robot, you goddamn stupid mother—"

The computer's flat voice cut through. "Voiceprint identification accepted, sir."

The door popped open.

Muttering to himself, Hawks stepped through and out of the rain. Goddamn idiot computer doesn't recognize my voice unless I scream at it. Who the hell set up the voiceprint IDs, anyway?

Fuming and steaming, Hawks stomped through the carpeted reception area and pushed through a steel fire door. The warehouse spread out before him, silent and still, a vast windowless conglomeration of row after row of twenty-foot-high shelving on which rested huge cartons filled with nothing but books. Even taller piles of magazines, neatly baled and wrapped in impervious protective plastic, lay in long rows on the floor. They were not on shelves because there was not enough shelf space for both Webb

Press's books *and* magazines. In his personal direction of the warehouse's design and construction, Hawks had badly underestimated the space needed to store all of Webb's many publications. The brand-new warehouse was far too small the day it opened.

And dangerous.

Hawks had insisted on a completely automated warehouse. "We have the technology," he had snapped. "Let's not be afraid to use it." So there were no human workers in the warehouse, in theory. All the lifting and carrying and sorting was done by clever robots. In theory. Overhead conveyor belts whisked heavy cartons of books from one end of the warehouse to the other with swift, silent efficiency. The only people working there were up in the control center, where they pushed buttons from the comfort of padded chairs. In theory.

In practice the robots were not quite clever enough. They could not reach the shelves higher than ten feet off the concrete floor, and not even the most patient Japanese technicians could teach them to climb like monkeys. The warehouse operators had to hire teenagers and unemployed laborers for that. To keep the facts secret from higher management, these employees were listed in the personnel files as assistant truck drivers. Once the Teamsters got wind of that, of course, they had to be *paid* as assistant truck drivers.

Hawks's footsteps echoed off the concrete floor as he made his way across the warehouse toward the control center. Should have placed it on the same side of the building as the front entrance and reception area, he told himself. I'll know better next time.

He looked warily above him as he crossed the shadow of one of the overhead conveyor belts. It was not in operation, but still, caution was the watchword. At top speed the conveyors developed a slight wobble, just enough to send a heavy carton of books toppling down to the floor below now and then. The concrete was chipped where the cartons had landed. And there were several chalked outlines of human figures, workers who had been conked by falling cartons. Some wiseass Puerto Rican had started putting up little crosses at the spots where people had been killed, but Hawks had put a stop to *that*.

The warehouse was costing Webb a fortune. The accident insurance claims alone were enough to keep the company in the red. If the Old Man ever started wondering why so many assistant truck drivers were receiving accident benefits, Hawks might end up working in the warehouse himself.

All the more reason to get the Old Man out of the picture. For good.

With grim resolve, Hawks climbed the clanging metal stairs that led up to the control room. He pushed open the heavy, acoustically insulated door, and saw that the Beast from the East was already there, smiling at him.

Vinnie DeAngelo had won his nickname many years earlier, when he had been in charge of Webb's magazine circulation for the western region of the country. Headquartered in Denver, responsible for getting Webb's magazines prominently displayed on every newsstand between the Mississippi and the Pacific coast, Vinnie had instituted a reign of terror among wholesalers, distributors, truck drivers, and newsstand operators.

He looked fearsome. Six feet even, in every direction. Built like a block of concrete. Absolutely no neck at all; his shoulders grew out of his ears, which were strangely petite and a shell-like pink. A nose that had been broken so many times it looked like a hiker's trail twisting up a steep mountain. Ice-blue eyes. Reddish-brown hair. The control center, built to accommodate three operators at their consoles and at least two more supervisors behind them, seemed crowded with Vinnie in it.

"Hello, Mr. Hawks," said Vinnie. It sounded almost like an old Mickey Mouse cartoon.

The Beast had a high-pitched little-girl's voice that made people want to laugh when they first met him. Those who did laugh never repeated the error.

"Hello, Vinnie."

"What can I do for you?" asked the Beast.

"I need a favor."

"Such as?"

Hawks glanced around the control center. It was small: merely three electronic consoles and the padded chairs for them, plus two more empty chairs behind them. The wide windows looked out on the warehouse floor. The only door was at Hawks's back. The walls were softly padded to keep out the noise of the machines that clattered during the working day.

"It's time for the Old Man to retire."

For the first time in the years that Hawks had known the Beast, Vinnie's glacial blue eyes widened with surprise.

"The Old Man? Mr. Weldon?" He whispered the name.

Hawks nodded.

Vinnie shifted his ponderous bulk from one foot to the other. "Gee, I don't know. The Old Man . . ."

"It's got to be done. For the good of the company."

"He's already had a stroke, ain't he?"

"A heart attack."

"Maybe he'll pop off by himself soon."

"This can't wait for nature to take its course, Vinnie." Besides, Hawks thought, the old bastard will probably live long enough to bury us all. Especially me.

"Gee, I don't know," Vinnie repeated.

"I can make it worth the risks you'd be taking."

Hunching his massive shoulders, the Beast replied, "I'm already special assistant to the national manager of magazine circulation. I get more money than I can spend as it is."

"Name your price."

"The Old Man? Gee, I don't know. . . ."

"Name your price," Hawks repeated.

Glancing furtively around, as if afraid that someone was eavesdropping, Vinnie hesitated for agonizingly long moments. At last he said, "See, I met this guy a couple months ago. In the airport in Dallas. He was autographin' books. He's a writer. An author."

Hawks felt his brows knitting. What was the Beast after?

"An' we got to talking on the plane back to New York, an' he told me I ought to write my life story. You know, I'd tell it to him and he'd write it and we'd split the money."

"You want me to publish your autobiography?"

Sheepishly, the Beast nodded his massive head. "Yeah. That's it."

"Aren't you afraid that the police would read it?"

"I ain't done nothin' illegal. Nothin' they got witnesses for."

Hawks started to smile, but quickly suppressed it. Not wise to smile at the Beast; he might get the wrong idea.

"All right, Vinnie," said Hawks slowly, carefully. "I'm sure that Webb Press will be happy to publish your autobiography."

"And make it a best-seller."

"We'll do our best."

"It's gotta be a best-seller," said the Beast ominously.

"Well, your people in distribution would have more to say about that than I would," Hawks replied smoothly. "We'll start with a print run of fifteen thou—"

"A hunnert thousand. Hardcover."

"That's not necessary, Vinnie. Fifteen to start, and we can go back to press as soon as we see they're selling well enough to warrant another press run."

"A hunnert thousand," rumbled the Beast. "This writer guy said it can't be a best-seller unless you print a hunnert thousand hardcover."

"Oh, come on now," Hawks countered—cautiously. "What do writers know about the publishing business?"

Vinnie scowled, a look that many a man had taken to the grave with him.

"I'll tell you what," said Hawks, trying to keep his voice from trembling. "We'll do a first print run of fifty thousand. That'll be enough to get the book on *The New York Times* best-seller list all by itself. Okay?"

Vinnie thought it over for a while. Hawks could almost hear the laborious grinding of gears inside the Beast's thick skull. Finally, he stuck out his right hand and Hawks let the enormous paw engulf his own hand. Weldon W. Weldon is about to enter that big publishing house in the sky, Hawks congratulated himself as Vinnie pumped his arm nearly out of its socket.

Then he added, And I'm going to publish the autobiography of a goon.

THE WRITER ▬▬▬▬▬▬

THE Writer drove his battered GMota across the George Washington Bridge and into Manhattan that same rainy, dreary Saturday morning. But to him, the fabulous skyline of the city sparkled like Arthur's Camelot.

For hours he drove through the midtown streets, seeing with own eyes for the first time the legendary Saks Fifth Avenue windows, the Cathedral of St. Paul, the United Nations complex, the Empire State Building. It was breathtaking.

By midafternoon he was running out of gas, with no idea of where a gas station might be, practically no money in his pockets, and not a clue about where he might find a motel room. But he did see a police precinct station halfway down the block, with half a dozen blue-and-white police cars double-parked in the narrow street, blocking traffic almost completely.

He double-parked behind a police car, got out, and started into the station. Then he remembered he was now in New York City, the Big Apple, and sprinted back to lock the doors of his old hatchback.

Contrary to what he had been led to expect by watching

hundreds of TV police shows, the precinct station house was drowsily quiet this Saturday morning. A few uniformed officers were standing off in the far corner of the room he entered, quietly talking together. Along the side wall stood four squat blue robots, silent and inert. The Writer paid careful attention to the equipment on the human police officers: pistols, stun wands, gas and concussion grenades, bulletproof vests, protective helmets with built-in radios and shatterproof sliding visors. Yes, he was in New York, all right.

The sergeant behind the desk was neither friendly nor gruff, just totally impersonal. He seemed to be looking *through* the writer instead of at him.

"Excuse me," said the Writer.

The desk sergeant sat up on a raised platform, like a judge. He seemed to take in the Writer's presence at a glance, his faded jeans and checkered polyester sports jacket. He made the barest perceptible motion of his head. Otherwise he remained as stolid as a robot.

"I just got into town, and I'm looking for a place to stay. Can you recommend—"

"Traveler's Aid," snapped the desk sergeant.

" 'Scuse me?"

"Grand Central Concourse. Traveler's Aid."

The Writer scratched his head.

Leaning forward slightly and peering down at the writer, the desk sergeant said slowly and carefully, as if speaking to a retarded child, "Go to Grand Central Station. That's at Forty-second Street and Park Avenue. Ask any officer there and he, she, or it will direct you to the Traveler's Aid desk. The people there will help you to find a hotel. Understand?"

The Writer nodded vaguely.

The desk sergeant started to repeat his instructions, this time in Spanish: *"Vaya a Grand Central Estación . . ."*

The Writer backed away, muttering his thanks and wondering if the desk sergeant actually was a robot.

Outside, it was drizzling again. But that was nothing compared with what had happened to the Writer's faithful old hatchback. Vandals had taken all four wheels, popped the hood and stolen the battery, the distributor, and all four sparkplugs, jimmied the hatch and taken his only suitcase, ripped out the seats, the radio, and the hand-stitched snakeskin steering wheel cover that his mother had made for him many Christmases ago, and broken each and every one of the windows. In front of the police station.

The Writer gasped and gaped at the pillaged remains of his car. Then he noticed a piece of paper stuck in the one remaining windshield wiper. A ticket for double parking.

He sank down onto the curbstone and cried.

TEN

FOR the fiftieth time that cheerless Saturday Carl picked up the telephone, then slammed it back down again. He paced to the window of his sparse hotel room again and looked out at the rain. It spattered the puddles growing on the rooftops across the street, it slanted down onto the cars and pedestrians in the avenue far below. The city allowed private cars into Manhattan on weekends. They and the umbrellas along the sidewalks made a shifting patchwork of colors against the gray stones, gray streets, and gray skies of this somber Saturday.

So you slept with her, Carl said to himself. That doesn't mean anything. Not in this day and age. You're both consenting adults.

But what did you consent to? the other half of his brain asked. A one-night stand? Or do you love her? Would you want to marry her?

Not so fast! This is no time to talk about marriage. Don't even *think* about it. You're in no position to take on responsibilities like that.

But you've got a tricky situation here. You're here in New York because she got her company to invite you. If you go ahead with them on the electronic book project, you're going to have to work with her. How are you going to handle that?

You can't mix business and romance, Carl insisted stubbornly. That's the one thing I learned out of all the management courses I took. Office romances lead to disaster.

So it was just a one-night stand, eh?

It has to be.

Carl nodded, satisfied that he had thought the problem through and come to the correct conclusion. But his hand reached for the telephone, and he asked the information computer for Lori's number.

Lori was in the middle of her morning calisthenics. Saturday she could sleep late, then do the week's wash and her exercises at the same time. Instead of riding down to the basement laundry room on the elevator, she jogged the three flights down and back up again. Not only was it better for her cardiovascular system and muscle tone, it avoided the jerk who lived on the ninth floor and seemed to lurk in the elevator, waiting for anything female to leer and lunge at.

She finished the deep bending routine and, wiping a sheen of perspiration from her face, was about to head downstairs again when the phone chimed.

Drat! she said to herself. If that's Momma she'll talk me blue in the face while the clothes wrinkle before I can get them into the dryer.

She touched the phone console's automatic answer button and heard the telephone's flat, emotionless voice say, "You have reached 999-5628. When you hear the tone, please leave your name, your number, and a brief message. Thank you. Please remember to wait for the tone."

Lori had one hand on the front door's knob when she recognized Carl's voice. "Uh, oh, Lori? This is Carl Lewis. I . . . I, uh, I'll call you back later."

She was at the phone before he could hang up.

"Carl? I'm here. It's me."

"Oh! I thought maybe I got a wrong number."

"No, that's just the answering program. It's not a good idea for a woman to use her own voice."

A long pause. Then, "I was wondering if you'd be free for dinner tonight."

Lori's first impulse was to say yes, and then explain that it would have to be early and brief, because she had to work and a belly dancer with a full belly was a belly dancer in trouble.

But she heard her voice replying, "Gee, I'm sorry, Carl. Not tonight. I have to work."

"Oh." Did he sound disappointed? Or relieved? Or some of each?

"How about brunch tomorrow?" she suggested. Brunch would be safer than dinner, she thought. Not so many complications afterward.

His voice brightened. "Sure. That'll be fine."

She gave him the name and address of a neighborhood restaurant. "Is one o'clock okay?" she asked.

"Sure. I've got nothing else to do."

"All right. I'll make the reservation. See you then."

And she sang to herself all the way down to the laundry room and back upstairs again.

Sunday morning was warm and bright, a perfect spring day in the city, like a scene from a Woody Allen film. The previous day's rain had washed the streets and the sky; everything seemed to sparkle as Lori walked from her apartment to the restaurant. People were actually smiling on the street and almost being polite to one another. A fantastic spring day in Manhattan.

Just what is it you expect of Carl? she asked herself. And she answered, grinning, Nothing. Not a damned thing. All I want is for him to be himself. And to stay near me.

That's *all* you want?

For now, she admitted. Carl is attractive, intelligent, a little shy, very gentle, very steady. Kind of old-fashioned. Not one of those macho beer-swilling clowns that this town is so full of. Or one of those phony name-dropping intellectuals who try to impress you with how much they know, and then take out a calculator to tote up the dinner check. I'm sick to death of them; the publishing business is filled with them.

And you think Carl's not like that?

Not at all like that. He got angry when those longshoremen were tucking money into my costume. He was ready to fight the whole crowd of them.

Foolish.

Gallant.

He was drunk.

But very lovable.

What was that word? Did you say "love"? Be careful girl, that's the way careers turn into pregnancies.

I know what I'm doing.

Do you?

Then she saw Carl sitting at one of the rickety tables on the sidewalk in front of the restaurant, and ended her dialogue with herself. He was staring off into some private vision, somber and serious, just gazing at nowhere as he sat there in the early afternoon sunlight. The Macy's Thanksgiving Day parade could have passed by and he wouldn't have noticed it. Still in that rumpled tweed jacket. But suddenly he did recognize Lori and his face brightened into a million-kilowatt smile. He stood up as she approached.

Carl saw Lori approaching and automatically got to his feet. She smiled brilliantly at him and he felt himself grinning back. In the warm spring sunlight she wore a sleeveless tan blouse and a knee-length skirt of darker brown. She seemed to glow, she looked so beautiful.

He held her chair for her as she sat down. The sunlight felt warm and good. Not even the foul-smelling diesel buses lumbering past on the avenue or the filthy bag lady rummaging through the dumpster on the corner could spoil the beauty of the moment.

They spoke about inconsequential matters at first: Would you

rather sit out here or go indoors? Do you think the eggs Benedict
would be better than the bagels and lox?

"What is lox, anyway?" Carl asked.

"A kind of smoked salmon."

"Oh. In the lab it's an abbreviation for liquid oxygen."
Lori laughed.

Carl ordered the eggs Benedict. After a tussle with her con-
science, Lori skipped the bagels and rich cream sauces and settled
for a salad. After the waiter had brought their trays, Carl started
to say, "Lori—about what happened a couple of nights ago . . ."

She stopped him by placing her hand gently on his. "What
happened, happened. It was lovely, and there's nothing we can
do to change it. So let's just forget about it."

He looked into her dark eyes and saw that there was no regret,
no anger, in them. "I don't think I can forget about it," he said.
"I don't think I want to forget about it."

With a smile, Lori replied, "Okay. Neither do I. But let's just
leave it as a nice memory. Let's not make it more important than
it is."

Now he felt puzzled. Does that mean she doesn't care? Or is
she trying to make me feel better about it?

"You're supposed to see Mr. Bunker tomorrow," she changed
the subject.

"If he doesn't cancel out again."

"He'll see you," she said firmly, then added, "Sooner or
later."

"What's he like?" Carl asked.

Lori shrugged her shoulders, a move that churned Carl's entire
glandular system.

"I've never met him," she said.

"But you've seen him around the office, haven't you?"

"I told you, he never comes to the office. Honest. Mrs. Bee
holds the title of publisher; she's in the office every day. Mr.
Bee is the president and owner of the company. We never see
him."

With an exasperated sigh, Carl asked, "What kind of a business is this, anyway? Nobody can do anything without Bunker's okay, and nobody gets to see him!''

"Publishing is unique," Lori admitted.

"It sure isn't anything like the business management courses I've taken."

She took a leaf of her salad and agreed. "What other business puts out a product that you can return for a full refund even after you've used it?"

"Huh?"

"No book sale is ever final. All the books we send out to the regional distributors and wholesalers, they're all taken on consignment. If they don't sell, they come back to us. If you buy a book in a store, you can return it a day or two later and they'll refund your money. The store management might argue, but they'll give your money back if you insist on it—and if the book is still in decent shape."

"But that's crazy! How can you tell what your sales are?"

"You can't. Not for a couple of years."

In the back of his mind Carl realized that his electronic book would change all that. He would bring the publishing business into the twenty-first century. By now, though, Lori had lapsed into tales of the editorial department.

". . . every year she would send us a manuscript, a totally unpublishable piece of junk," Lori was saying, "and every year we would send it back with a standard rejection form. You know, 'Dear Sir or Madam: Thank you for submitting the enclosed manuscript, but we find that it does not suit our needs at the present time.' ''

Without waiting for Carl to ask what happened next, Lori went on, "So one year Arleigh Berkowitz—he's not with us anymore—he gets fed up with Mrs. Kranston and her terrible prose, so he writes her a really nasty letter: 'Stop bothering us with this rotten material! It's a waste of your time and ours!' ''

"That must have hurt her feelings," Carl said.

"Are you kidding? We're talking about a would-be _writer_," Lori retorted. "She sent us a letter back in the return mail that said Arleigh's letter was the first personal response she's ever gotten from an editor, and she's so inspired she's going to work twice as hard. Now we get *two* unpublishable manuscripts a year from her, every spring and every fall."

Lori laughed, but Carl failed to see the humor. "And her stuff never gets better? She doesn't improve at all from one year to the next?"

"She doesn't learn a thing. I think it gets worse."

"You've read them?"

"We've all read them, at one time or another. They're *awful*!"

"It's a strange business, all right," Carl said. But in the back of his head he kept thinking, I'll change all this. Electronic books are going to totally change the publishing industry.

He mentally squared his shoulders in preparation for his meeting with P. T. Bunker, his rendezvous with destiny.

Telephone Transcript

"You have reached the Murray Swift Literary Agency. There are no humans at work over the weekend. Please leave your name and number and someone will get back to you first thing Monday morning."

"This is the Bunker Books automated message transmitter. Please have Mr. Swift call Ms. Scarlet Dean no later than three P.M. on Monday to discuss contract terms for Sheldon Stoker's new novel, *The Terror from Beyond Hell*."

"I am programmed to accept contract offers electronically. Please transmit the contract and state orally the amount of the advance being offered."

(Delay of four seconds.)

"Contract transmitted. Advance offered is one million dollars."

"Thank you. I am programmed to respond that the advance is too low. Mr. Swift will call you on Monday."

ELEVEN

MONDAY morning. The city stirred to life much as it did in O. Henry's time, bleary-eyed, reluctant. Gleaming silver subway trains streaked through their tunnels, their anodized surfaces immune to the spray paints and felt pens of even the most rabid graffitists. Inside the swaying, *swoosh*ing cars working men and women sat crammed in plastic seats, numbly inanimate, ignoring their fellow workers who stood jammed together shoulder to shoulder hanging by one arm from the overhead hand rails. Darwin smiled from the grave.

Most of the men read the sports sections of their newspapers. Most of the women read the fashion pages. After all, it was Monday, time for the latest new styles to appear. The columns were illustrated by color photographs showing the fashion of the week: the smoldering, sensuous, slutty look—tangled kinky hair, sloppy sweatshirts that exposed at least one shoulder, very tight knee-length skirts slitted to the hip, patterned stockings, and spike heels. Accessories included voluminous handbags that carried mace and tranquilizer dart guns.

The sports pages carried ads that showed subtle changes in last week's biker image: tear the sleeves off the leather jackets, add a new broad-brimmed hat, buy a pair of glitter gloves and elevator boots, and the new pimp image was yours, just in time to match your girlfriend's slutty look.

On the city's streets buses lumbered over potholes and detoured around repair crews, depositing streams of workers at every corner. The clothing stores were open early, of course, for those enterprising men and women who wanted to show off the new fashion first thing upon starting work.

Carl Lewis wore his usual corduroy slacks and tweed jacket as he walked through the sunny morning to the Synthoil Tower. Lori had taken him shopping after their brunch on Sunday, and he had bought some shirts and underwear and socks. But he had not yet worked up the nerve to try the flamingo-pink pimp slacks that the salesman had shown him as a special preview of the coming week's new style.

"You can be ahead of all your friends by buying now," the salesman had prompted.

While Lori could barely conceal her giggles, Carl had decided to remain behind.

A phone message inviting him to demonstrate his invention at the Monday morning editorial board meeting had been waiting for him when he returned to his hotel room after walking Lori back to her apartment. He had spent the night checking and double-checking the electro-optical reader, and then had slept with it under his pillow.

Now, with a small but discernible dent in his temple left by one of the reader's hard corners, he strode past fake bikers staring at the newest fashions in store windows, determined to make the editors realize that they were witnessing the dawn of an entirely new era in the history of publishing.

It's more than publishing, Carl reminded himself. Publishing is only the first step. Electro-optical communications is going to allow the human race to live in harmony with the whole Earth's ecology. No more chopping down forests to make paper. No more ignorance and poverty. The price for information will go down to the point where everyone on Earth can obtain all the knowledge they need. They won't even have to know how to read; the next improvement on my invention will be the talking book. The singing book. The device that speaks to you just like the village story teller or your own mother.

P. Curtis Hawks started the work week in the most unpleasant way imaginable. He found that Gunther Axhelm was waiting for him in his office when he arrived there, shortly after nine o'clock.

Since Hawks rode his private elevator from the underground parking garage directly to his office, neither his secretary nor his communications computer was able to warn him of the Axe's presence. Hawks stepped out of the elevator and saw a strange man leaning over the billiard table in the far corner of the spacious office.

"Who the hell are you?" Hawks grumbled, even while his brain (which was often slower than his tongue) told him that it could be no one other than the Old Man's newly hired hatchet man.

The tall, slim, blond stranger stood ramrod straight, the pool cue gripped in one hand like a rifle. He clicked his heels and made a curt bow.

"Sir. Permit me to introduce myself. I am Gunther Axhelm. Mr. Weldon ordered me to meet with you first thing this morning. I assumed that he meant nine A.M. precisely."

Hawks groaned inwardly. It was going to be a difficult relationship.

Hawks crossed to his desk and Axhelm carefully replaced the cue in its rack, then went to the padded leather chair in front of the desk and sat himself on it. Neither man offered to shake hands. Hawks took a long look at his new "assistant." Axhelm was long-limbed, athletic. Not an ounce of fat on him. His face was sculptured planes, sharp nose, slightly pointed chin, gray killer's eyes. Blond hair cut ruthlessly short. Instead of a business suit he wore a long-sleeved turtleneck shirt and form-fitting slacks. All in black. The uniform of a burglar.

"My assignment here," he began without preamble, "is to reduce the workforce by fifty percent before—"

"Fifty percent! That's impossible!"

Axhelm allowed a wintry smile to bend his lips slightly. "Sir. My assignment was given me directly by Mr. Weldon. He *is* the chief executive officer of Tarantula Enterprises, is he not? And therefore your superior."

"We can't cut fifty percent of the workforce," Hawks insisted. "We wouldn't be able to handle the work load with only half the people we have now."

Again the smile. "It is my intention to go further. I have examined the personnel files, and I believe it will be possible to cut perhaps seventy or even seventy-five percent."

Hawks gave a strangled little cry.

"Do not be alarmed, sir. Your position is quite secure."

That's what Macbeth told Banquo just before he hired the assassins, Hawks thought.

Leaning back in the leather chair, stretching his long legs casually, Axhelm explained, "You see, you have not taken complete advantage of the benefits of modern technology. You have computers, but you do not use them as fully as you could. For example—how many editors do you have on staff?"

"Um . . . thirty or so," Hawks guesstimated.

"Thirty-two, full time," corrected Axhelm, "and six part time. They can all be eliminated by a computer programmed to read incoming manuscripts and make selections based on criteria such as word length, subject matter, and writing quality."

"How can a computer judge writing quality?" snapped Hawks.

Axhelm's smile turned pitying. "Come now, sir. Programs capable of judging writing quality have been used in university examinations for nearly twenty years. Even high school teachers use such programs, rather than relying on their own faulty judgments."

"You can't use a program developed to grade freshman English compositions to judge the value of incoming manuscripts!"

"And why not?"

"Because the *quality* of the writing isn't really important! Take a look at the best-seller lists: none of those books would pass freshman English!"

Axhelm fell silent, stroking his chin absently with his long, slim fingers.

"It's *salability* that counts," Hawks insisted. "And to determine salability you need human judgment."

"Is that why ninety-five percent of the books that Webb Press publishes lose money?"

Hawks grimaced, but countered, "It's the five percent that *make* money for us that count."

With a nod and a sigh, Axhelm said, "Then we must develop a computer program that can determine salability."

"Impossible!"

"Of course not. If your editors can do it, a computer program can be written to do it better. More efficiently. I will make that my first priority."

Hawks said nothing.

"In the meantime, we will begin reducing the workforce. Today."

At precisely eleven A.M. the eight editors of Bunker Books filed into their shabby conference room, with Carl Lewis and Ralph Malzone added to their number. The two men took seats on either side of Lori, down at the end of the table.

Mrs. Bunker's chair remained vacant, as did the chair for the editor-in-chief. But all the others were there: the mountainous Maryann Quigly, the cadaverous Ashley Elton, ferret-faced Jack Drain, Concetta Las Vagas (who needed hardly any change of clothes at all to look slutty), and the rest. Before anyone could say a word, P. T. Junior entered the conference room, dragging his own chair from his own office.

"My mother will be here in a minute or two," he announced, sitting at the head of the table. "She's chatting with the new editor-in-chief." He eyed them all with his sly, smirking look.

A murmur went around the table. Before it died away, Junior spoke up again.

"You know, I've been looking over the publishing business for some time now . . ."

"Yeah, the whole weekend," Ralph Malzone whispered.

Unperturbed, Junior was going on, ". . . and I see that there are some books that get onto the best-seller lists, and they make a lot of money."

None of the editors said a word. All eyes were focused on Junior.

"What we ought to do," he said with the fervor of true revelation, "is stick to those books! Just publish the best-sellers and forget all the other stuff!"

There was a long, *long* moment of utter silence. Then someone coughed. Another editor scraped his chair against the uncovered floor. Maryann Quigly emitted a loud, labored sigh.

Ted Gunn rose to the occasion. "Uh—Junior . . . that's exactly what we try to do. We don't *deliberately* publish books that lose money. You just don't know which books are going to become best-sellers beforehand."

Junior stared at him disbelievingly. "You don't?"

Gunn slowly shook his head.

"Oh," said Junior, with vast disappointment.

"Wait a minute, though," said Ralph Malzone. "In his own way, I think Junior's got a point there."

All eyes turned to the wiry sales manager questioningly. Malzone, trying to curry favor with the Boss's son? Carl saw the expression on Lori's face: somewhere between surprise and disgust.

"What I mean is this," Ralph explained. "Most of the books we publish are doomed to lose money before they even get into print."

"How can you—"

"We publish them on the theory of minimum success," Malzone said.

"The theory of minimum success?"

"Yeah. Take this new novel Lori's just bought, this Midway book. We're giving the author the minimum advance, and we're putting out the minimum investment in the book all the way down the line. When we print it, it's going to be the minimum number of copies."

"That's to minimize our risk," snapped Ted Gunn.

"Yeah. Sure. But it also minimizes our chances of making the book profitable."

Lori started to ask something, but Malzone went on before she could frame the words.

"We print a small number of copies, we don't spend money on advertising or promotion. The book flops and we lose money on it—or break even, at best."

"But it's up to your sales people to *sell* the book," Jack Drain pointed out.

Malzone made a sour grin. "Sure. They've got a hundred-some books per season to push, and you expect them to spend any effort on an also-ran? A book the editorial department thinks so little of that they only print a couple thousand copies? Come on! My people ain't stupid, for chrissakes. They're not going to waste their time on a book after you've convinced 'em it's going nowhere."

"But it's a good novel," Lori insisted.

"Doesn't matter," replied Malzone. "What's inside the covers doesn't really matter at all. Not when my sales people are out there trying to get the wholesalers and bookstore managers to order the title. None of those people read! They take a look at the cover and ask how many copies we've printed. If *we* don't show any faith in the book, they sure as hell don't buy it in any quantity."

"But . . ."

"And how in hell can you sell books that haven't been printed?" Malzone went on with some heat of passion coloring his lean cheeks. "Suppose your author gets on all the TV talk shows and a zillion people go rushing to the bookstores for his novel. And the stores only have a couple thousand copies of the book because that's all we've printed. You think those customers are going to wait six weeks—or six months—while we make up our minds to go back to press? The hell they will!''

"So the book bombs," said Lori, "and the writer gets blamed for writing an unsuccessful book."

"Hey, it's not _our_ fault if a book doesn't sell! Why don't you . . ."

At that moment the door opened again and Mrs. Bunker entered, accompanied by Scarlet Dean. The argument ended like a light being switched off. Everyone snapped to their feet.

Mrs. Bunker was all in white, as always: she had bowed to the new slutty look only to the extent that her hair had been frizzed and her silk suit jacket had no blouse beneath it. Pearls adorned her throat, wrists, and earlobes.

Smiling, she said in her tiny voice, "I'm sure I really don't need to introduce Scarlet Dean. Even those few of you who haven't met her before know of her fine work at Webb and elsewhere. We're truly fortunate to have her join our team."

Still standing, the assembled editors gave their new chief a smattering of applause. Carl, noticing that Ralph Malzone smacked his hands together along with the rest of them, clapped a few times also.

Scarlet Dean was a vision in red. Tall and leggy, like a fashion model, her hair was flame, her eyes the green of a deep forest. She wore a sheath of fire-engine red adorned with spangles; Carl immediately thought of a circus trapeze artist. A rope of carnelians lay over her slim bosom. Her face had a slightly evil cast to it, the eyes darting from one person to another, the thin red lips twitching slightly in what might have been an attempt at a smile.

"Thank you," said Scarlet Dean. "Please—let's sit down and get to work." Her voice was low, sultry, suggestive. Despite himself, Carl felt a thrill of excitement stir him. He felt strangely stimulated and guilty, at the same time.

"I think the first order of business," the new editor-in-chief was saying, "is to let Mr. Lewis show us his wonderful new invention."

Suddenly all heads swivelled toward Carl. Feeling a flush of unexpected stage fright, Carl grasped the electro-optical reader in both his hands and got to his feet.

This time it was different. The device worked perfectly. Carl showed them pages from half a dozen different books. They oohed and aahed. Carl passed it around the table so that each editor could see for him- or herself how easy it was to use the device. Mrs. Bunker was smiling happily at him. All the editors beamed approvingly, now that they knew how the Boss felt about the subject. Lori, of course, was radiating delight and satisfaction. Even Ralph seemed to be pleased with the demonstration.

But Carl found himself ignoring all of them. He found that he was not looking at Mrs. Bunker, or any of the editors, not even Lori. His eyes were locked on Scarlet Dean, as if he were powerless to look elsewhere. She was smiling at him, a beguiling, bewitching little smile that perked the corners of her mouth and opened her lips just enough for the tip of her pink tongue to peek out at Carl. And her eyes were telling him that she would love to meet with him, alone, just the two of them with no one else.

He barely heard Mrs. Bunker when she announced that P. T. would definitely see him at five o'clock this afternoon, at the Bunker house.

MURDER FOUR

HOMICIDE Lieutenant Jack Moriarty knelt over the expired body of Nora Charleston, a grim look on his lean, weatherbeaten face.

"That's how they found her, Lieutenant," said the uniformed sergeant. "Musta been dead a couple days, at least."

Moriarty was glad of the head cold that had stuffed his sinuses so completely that he could smell nothing. Straightening painfully, his arthritis reminding him of his age, he asked, "Forensics been through the apartment yet?"

"They've finished with the living room, here. They're doin' the bedroom and bath now."

Moriarty surveyed the apartment. Once it had been very posh, but time had withered it all. The furniture was tattered, the carpeting threadbare. The old lady lying facedown on the living room rug was wearing what had once been an elegant robe. Now it looked frayed and hopelessly old-fashioned, like a faded photo from a high school yearbook.

"What do you think, Sergeant?" he asked the younger cop. "Burglary? Drugs?"

The sergeant pulled a long frown. "Nothing taken that we can see. No sign of forced entry. No struggle."

"Who called it in?"

"The super. He let himself in when he realized he hadn't seen her in a couple of days. Called the apartment on the intercom and got no answer. So he let himself in and found her layin' there."

Moriarty looked back to the frail body of Mrs. Charleston.

"Thought it was natural causes, at first," the sergeant continued. "She was ninety-nine years old, after all."

"Sonofabitch couldn't let her live out the full hundred," Moriarty muttered.

"She musta let him in. Door was shut when the super came in, but the inner locks weren't locked. She let him in, he conked her on the head, and walked out. No noise. No struggle. No fuss."

"We had another old lady knocked off for no discernible reason," said Moriarty. "Last month, down in Gramercy Park."

The sergeant said nothing.

"Wonder if there's any connection?" Moriarty made a mental note to check the homicide computer for similar recent murders and see if there was any common thread to them. Might be a nut case knocking off old ladies.

He glanced down at the body again. "Couldn't let her live out the full one hundred. Damned shame."

TWELVE

SCARLET Dean managed to seat herself in the limousine exactly opposite the young inventor from MIT.

Her instructions from her former boss, P. Curtis Hawks, had been explicit: find out everything there is to know about the man and his invention. Although Hawks had not revealed his strategy to her, Scarlet had a good idea of what it was. If young Tom Edison's invention is actually as good as it appears to be, Webb Press will buy out Bunker Books, thereby acquiring the electronic book in the process. Failing that, they would buy out the inventor himself.

There were four of them in the limousine: herself and Mrs. Bunker side by side on the limo's ultraplush rear seat, and on the jumpseats facing them, the slightly exotic-looking young editor who had discovered the handsome inventor and the young man himself. He looked distinctly uncomfortable locked into the car with three attractive women gazing fondly at him.

Scarlet glanced at the editor and then at Mrs. Bunker. Mrs. Bee's eyes had dollar signs in them; she saw Carl Lewis as a way to make money for Bunker Books. The editor, Lori Something-or-other, was smiling admiringly at the man. Were they romantically involved? No matter, she would put an end to that quickly enough. If nothing else worked she could always fire the editor.

She probed Carl Lewis's eyes with her own. He blushed slightly and looked away. He's vulnerable, Scarlet told herself. He can be had.

She began to consider various possibilities. Of course, Bunker does not want to sell his company. Hawks may be planning an unfriendly takeover, but Bunker himself owns virtually all the stock. There are only a few shares outside the family, and the people who own them are not quick to sell. She knew; she had ordered her broker to quietly buy up as much Bunker stock as could be found. Result: none available. Not one share.

"The few percent that Bunker and his family don't personally own are held mostly by retirees," the broker had told her. "Old friends of Bunker's father and mother. They just won't sell."

The thing to do, then, is to get Lewis and his invention away from Bunker. Which means getting him away from this dark-haired editor. That shouldn't be too difficult. In less than a week I'll have him eating out of the palm of my hand—so to speak.

Then Scarlet Dean had her inspiration. If Carl Lewis is personally attached to *me*, I can write my own ticket with Hawks and Webb Press. Or any other publishing house in New York! In the world!

She turned up the wattage on her smile and was pleased to see Lewis squirm a little on the jumpseat.

The limousine crawled through Manhattan's late afternoon traffic and finally pulled up in front of what had once been a five-story tenement in the Lower East Side. Now it was one of long rows of posh town houses, each with its own marquee and private parking space at curbside. The law banning private autos in Manhattan did not apply to residents of the borough, naturally. Eighty percent of the private cars registered in Manhattan were limousines, which also seemed natural enough.

A live doorman helped Mrs. Bunker out of the limo and escorted her to the front door of the house. Carl got out next and helped Lori and Scarlet Dean, while the chauffeur slowly strolled around the monstrously long vehicle just in time to close the rear door.

Mrs. Bunker ushered her three guests up the sweeping marble stairs and into the second-floor parlor, where still another live servant met them with a rolling cart laden with drinks.

"Please make yourselves comfortable," she said. "I'll go and tell P. T. that you're here."

Carl had never seen such splendor. The room was huge, richly carpeted, pillared with marble, panelled with rare Mayan tile. On the walls were hologram reproductions of the wonders of the world. Simply by turning around, Carl could look out upon the Sphinx guarding the great pyramids, or snow-capped Mt. Everest, or the original Disneyland romantically shrouded in sunset-pink smog.

Lori seemed equally impressed. "What a beautiful room," she murmured as the butler—she guessed he was the butler—poured her a diet cola.

Only Scarlet seemed to take it all in stride. "They found a good decorator," she said, and ordered a martini. Heading for the deep, fur-covered easy chair set before the fireplace hologram, she advised:

"Better relax and make yourselves comfortable. From what I know of P. T. Bunker, we have a considerable wait in store for us."

Mrs. Bunker, meanwhile, had gone to the splendid bedroom of their home. The master bedroom and the second-floor parlor were the only two rooms in the huge house that were decently furnished and decorated. The parlor, of course, was to impress visitors. The bedroom was for the two of them. The other rooms of the house were either bare and unused, or furnished with Spartan spareness. P. T.'s office, adjoining the bedroom, contained the same old pine desk that he had started with. Behind it was a magnificent hologram of the New York harbor. When P. T. talked with people by Picturephone, they saw the harbor and little else. And no visitor saw any part of the house other than the second-floor parlor.

They had intended to furnish the entire house just as sumptuously as the parlor and master bedroom. But running a business twenty-four hours a day saps one's energy and will. After a long, long day of frantic decisions and boring conferences, there just is no time or strength left to deal with decorators and painters.

Moreover, there was no money. Every cent the Bunkers had was tied up in the business. Being a middling-sized publishing house was a perilous existence. The big houses kept trying to buy out Bunker Books, or squeeze the company into bankruptcy. The smaller houses constantly undersold them.

Alba checked out her appearance in the full-length mirror next to the big circular waterbed. She frowned slightly. The slutty look was not for her. She had heard a rumor that next week's fashion would emphasize elegance: the Fred and Ginger look, from what she had been able to glean. She looked forward to it.

With a glance at her gold wristwatch she called through the open door to the office, "Pandro, dear, the guests are here."

No reply.

Alba went to the doorway. P. T. Bunker sat alone at the ancient desk of his childhood, an old-fashioned pair of bifocals perched on his nose, one finger running down a long column of computer printout figures, a semidesperate expression on his face. It was still a ruggedly handsome face, despite the years of worry and responsibilities that had carved deep lines into it. Worse, those years of sitting behind a desk and directing the firm had brought about a certain sagging around the jawline. Even his broad shoulders and brawny arms seemed to be withering. And his bulging stomach was stretching the buttons on his sport shirt, she noticed.

"Pandro, darling, we have guests downstairs."

He looked up at her, peering over the bifocal rims. "Do you know," he said, "that we've been losing money steadily on every category we publish, except for the self-help books." His voice was a sweet clear tenor, the voice of a born singer, a voice that should have led to the opera rather than conference calls with bankers in Beijing.

"Self-help books always sell, dear," Alba replied patiently. "The same awful people keep buying them, year after year."

"Don't the books actually help them?"

"Heavens, no! If they did, the entire category would have gone down the tubes ages ago."

Bunker wiped a bead of perspiration from the end of his nose. The office was uncomfortably warm. Windowless, totally undecorated except for the hologram view of the harbor, the stuffy little room held nothing but the desk and rows of aged filing cabinets. Despite the computer printouts that he was perusing, and despite the impressive array of electronic hardware on his desk, P. T. Bunker neither used nor trusted computers. Alba understood and sympathized; the poor dear had never learned to type, and it just would not be fair to expect him to embarrass himself trying to learn, since he was such an important and busy man.

"We shouldn't keep them waiting too long," she urged gently.

Bunker glanced at the calendar pad on his desk and the notes that his wife had written on it.

"Do I *have* to see these people?"

He had become a borderline agoraphobe, she knew. Over the years of his sweating and struggling to make Bunker Books profitable, he had slowly but steadily withdrawn into his own private, inner fortress. He trusted no one except his wife, and Alba wondered if the day would ever come when even she was shut out of his increasingly desperate broodings. He would much rather remain cooped up in this unhealthy little cell than come out and meet the people who had come to pay homage to him. He hardly ever left the house, and it was getting more and more difficult to get him to see anyone, even in the comfortable security of the downstairs parlor.

"You know I wouldn't bother you if it weren't important, dear."

"Why can't I talk to them over the Picturephone?" he asked unhappily.

"I think they might find that a little strange."

"We could tell them I'm . . . I'm . . ." His voice trailed off and faded away into silence.

"It's all right, darling," Alba said soothingly. "I'll be right beside you."

With an unhappy frown, P. T. Bunker got up from his desk. He wore only a pair of boxer trunks beneath his stylish open-neck sport shirt. Like a TV newscaster, Bunker had no need to clothe himself below his navel. Not as long as he remained behind his desk.

Now, however, he walked into the bedroom and began the ritual of showering, shaving, and dressing for company. He had been an impressive figure when Alba had first met him, nearly twenty years earlier. She had been an advertising copywriter for a small agency that still had its office on Madison Avenue. He had just started Bunker Books on the shoestring ten million his father had loaned him. It was love at first sight, a whirlwind courtship and marriage within a week. Never had either one of them regretted an instant of their life together. There had been hard times, businesswise, of course; in fact, the publishing business was *always* on hard times, it seemed. But Alba and Pandro loved each other with a steadfastness that defied all the strains and pressures of the lunatic world of publishing.

While he dressed she explained once again about Carl Lewis and the electronic book. Pandro cast her a skeptical look, but said nothing. Alba also reminded him that he would meet Scarlet Dean, their new editor-in-chief. He nodded and grunted as he tugged on his muscle suit.

It had been years since P. T. had taken the time to play tennis or swim in the four-lane pool they had built in the basement of their home. His once proud physique, with its flat stomach and powerful shoulders and arms, had slumped into middle-aged flabbiness. He avoided revealing this to the people with whom he did business over the Picturephone by wearing shirts that had impressive shoulder pads built into them.

But when he had to meet people in person, sterner measures were required. The muscle suit gave him the same athletic physique he had possessed decades ago. Once covered with a tight-fitting sport shirt and even tighter jeans, no one could tell that P. T.'s muscular build was made of plastic foam. He looked better than a matador, in Alba's eyes.

He complained about putting in his contact lenses, and worried that his toupee might have been askew. His cowboy boots returned the inch or so that had been taken away by years of bending over a desk. All in all, he looked handsome, trim, tanned, and ready to face the world—thanks to a touch of makeup and a constant stream of encouraging chatter from his wife.

Grasping her arm tightly, P. T. Bunker reluctantly entered the tiny elevator that took them down to the second floor. Alba reviewed the names of the people waiting to see him, and why they were there.

"This electronic book invention is very important, dear. It could mean the salvation of the company."

He nodded to show that he understood, but still he dreaded facing the people.

"Ralph Malzone has come up with a sexy name for the invention," Alba went on. "You know, we can't just call it the electronic book. We need a catchy name for it."

He nodded again. God, my stomach's turning itself inside out. I wish this was over and done with.

The elevator stopped and the door slid open automatically before Alba had a chance to tell him the name she had thought of. So she stood on tiptoes and whispered it into his ear.

To the three people waiting in the parlor, it looked as if Mrs. Bunker was whispering sweet nothings into the ear of the man she adored. He looked tight-lipped and slightly flustered. She smiled at their guests, as if somewhat embarrassed.

Carl's heart was thundering in his ribs. This is the big moment, he told himself. This is *it*. Go or no-go. This man holds the power of life and death over your invention.

Mrs. Bunker introduced her husband. As if in a dream, Carl took the prototype from his jacket pocket and showed P. T. Bunker how it worked. He watched in silence as Carl demonstrated with *The Illustrated Moby Dick*. Bunker said nothing. When Carl offered the device to him, Mrs. Bunker took it and played with it for a few minutes. They were all still standing, clustered around the great man a few steps in front of the elevator. No one had taken a chair.

"You see, darling?" said Mrs. Bunker. "It works beautifully."

Bunker finally made a single nod of his head as he handed the prototype back to Carl. "Okay. Looks good. We'll call it Cyberbooks."

And with that he turned abruptly and ducked back into the elevator, leaving Carl, Lori, Scarlet Dean, and his wife standing there gaping at his retreating back.

SUMMER,
Book II

THE WRITER ▬▬▬▬▬▬▬

IT was a blazing hot July day, the kind of molten heat and humidity that drives even the mildest man to thoughts of murder. An Ed McBain day in the city, where the detectives of the eighty-seventh precinct knew that each ring of the phone meant another body had met a meat cleaver.

The Writer had found a job. Not in the city. He could no more afford to live in Manhattan than he could fly to the moon by flapping his arms. His job, and his miserable one-room apartment, were in New Jersey. He could see Manhattan's skyline every day; see the myriad gleaming lights of the city each night. But he was separated from it by a river of poverty whose current was too strong for him to cross.

He worked in the warehouse of Webb Press, one of the dispensable men who were not supposed to be there, but who were needed because the automated machinery could not do what it had been designed to do, and ordinary expendable human beings were required to carry out the work of the imperfect machines.

Twice in the past month he had almost been killed by heavy cases of books falling from the wobbly overhead conveyor belts.

Six times he and his fellow nonentities had spent whole work shifts searching the entire warehouse for cartons of books that had been misplaced by the robots. On one frightening occasion the entire workforce had to battle a robot that resisted having a truckload of books taken out to the loading dock. Somehow the robot got it into its minuscule electronic brain that its job was to protect the huge crates from being moved. While the Japanese-American foreman screamed in two languages, the men risked injury and death to duck beneath the robot's menacing arms, pry off its access panel, and turn it off.

Now the Writer worked at the most thankless job of them all: the furnace. Another stroke of some architect's genius, the furnace burned the books that were returned from the stores unsold. In the brilliant design of the automated warehouse, the furnace supplied heat for the winter months and electricity all year long. During the summer the electricity not only powered the lights and computers, it ran the air-conditioning system.

But the heat of the burning books overburdened the air-conditioning system, so the computer program that ran the warehouse's environmental controls shut down the air-conditioning and there was no way to override its dogmatic decision. The supervisors up in their control booth sneaked in a few room-sized air conditioners for themselves. The men and machines on the warehouse floor worked in summer's heat—supplemented by the flames of the book-burning furnace.

The Writer knew that he was going mad. He spent his days shovelling paperback books into the furnace's hungry red fire. He worked stripped down to his shorts, sweat streaming along his scrawny ribs and lanky arms and legs, blurring his vision. The heat made him feel dizzy, crazy. Like O'Neill's Hairy Ape, he began to shout aloud, "Who makes the warehouse work? I do! Who makes the publishing industry work? I do!"

The other men on the warehouse floor started to avoid him.

But the Writer never noticed, never cared. He knew that he was right. If these books were not destroyed there would be no room for the new books coming off the presses. The whole industry would grind to a halt, strangled to death on a glut of books. So he shovelled the paperbacks into the flames: romance novels, westerns, mysteries, cookbooks, diet books, revealing biographies, lying autobiographies, books about God, about sin, about how to get rich in just ninety days. He scooped them all up in his heavy black shovel and threw them into the baleful blood-red fiery furnace.

These were the bad books, the books that did not sell, the books that had been returned to the warehouse by the stores and the distributors. Some of the books had been on store shelves for all of a week, some less. Some had never gotten to the shelves; their cartons came back to the warehouse unopened.

The Writer giggled as he worked. He cackled. These were *other writers'* books! If only he could burn enough of them, he told himself, there might one day be room in the world for his own book to be published. He scooped and threw, scooped and threw, making room for his own book and cackling madly all the while.

"Bad books! Bad books!"

Meanwhile, at the far end of the warehouse one of the robots trundled a newly opened carton of books to the inspection station next to the loading dock.

"Malfunction," it said in its limited vocabulary. "Malfunction."

The human inspector looked inside the box and turned pale.

THIRTEEN

C ARL Lewis's life was being dominated by three strong women, and he was not certain that he disliked it.

Since that brief, weird moment nearly three months earlier when he had met P. T. Bunker and the great man had okayed the project—and named it—Carl had become a full-time consultant to Bunker Books. That is, he worked for the company exclusively but was not entitled to any of the fringe benefits or government-ordained insurance that a regular employee received.

That did not matter to Carl one whit. He was being paid handsomely enough to afford a three-room apartment for himself, in the same Gramercy Park building that Lori lived in. He worked all day every day of the week and most of every night. His social life consisted of an occasional lunch with Lori, or a dinner with Scarlet Dean, who insisted on being kept up-to-date on the Cyberbooks project.

Cyberbooks.

Carl liked the name that Bunker had come up with; he did not realize that it was Ralph Malzone's original idea. Nor did it occur to him that the name was now formally registered as a trademark belonging to Bunker Books, Inc. Carl just plugged away at the task of turning his prototype into a device that could be manufactured as inexpensively as possible, while still maintaining quality and reliability. His goal was to have the device on sale nationwide for the Christmas buying season, priced at less than $200.

It was at one of the dinners Scarlet Dean insisted on that he first heard about the cruise.

"Cruise?" Carl almost sputtered out the salad he had been chewing. "Why do I have to go on a cruise?"

They were in the Argenteuil, one of the oldest and finest restaurants of Manhattan. Although it seemed to be Scarlet's favorite place, the restaurant always made Carl feel uneasy. An expense account restaurant, like so many in midtown Manhattan. Too formal and grand for his simple tastes. The maître d' always made Carl feel as if he were a shabby hobo who had drifted into the restaurant by mistake, even when he wore the new suit that Scarlet had sent him and his formal shirt with the blue MIT tie painted on it.

Daintily spearing an ear of asparagus, Scarlet replied, "It's the company sales meeting. We've rented out the ocean liner for the week."

"A week? I can't take a week off. . . ."

Scarlet smiled soothingly and touched his hand with her own. "Relax, Carl. Relax. You won't have to take the time off your work. I know how important it is. It's vital! We'll fix you up with a workshop and a satellite communications link to the office here in New York."

Somewhat relieved, he muttered, "I've also got to be able to work with the guys in the factory."

"That too," Scarlet assured him. "Interactive picture, voice and data links. Don't worry about it."

But he replied, "I still don't see why I have to go. Why can't I stay here?"

"Two reasons: First, Mrs. Bunker will be on the cruise, and she doesn't want you to be out of her sight."

"Really?"

"Really. Second, the whole sales force will be aboard. We'll need you to demonstrate the Cyberbooks hardware to them. And it will be good for you to meet them all informally, talk with them, get them pumped up about Cyberbooks."

"Hmm. I suppose so," he admitted grudgingly.

"And besides," said Scarlet, "think how much fun it will be to be out on the ocean for a whole week. It's very romantic, you know."

He nodded absently. "Will Lori be there, too?"

Her smile fading just a little, Scarlet said, "Yes, of course. The whole editorial staff will be aboard."

Sitting at the bottom of his swimming pool, P. Curtis Hawks made two telephone calls that night. Although he was certain that all the phones in his expansive Westchester home had been bugged by the Old Man's minions, he had obtained a surplus U.S. Navy underwater communications system from a Washington friend in the munitions business. In his fishbowl helmet and wet suit, breathing canned air that smelled faintly of machine oil and carcinogenic plastic, Hawks knew that the ultralow frequency of this communications equipment was beyond the range of the Old Man's tapping.

His first call was to Scarlet Dean, at a prearranged time and place: the ladies' room of the Waldorf Astoria Hotel lobby, at precisely ten minutes before midnight. A little square area of his glass helmet glowed with strangely shifting colors, then her face came into focus two inches in front of his nose.

"Good evening, Ms. Dean."

She frowned slightly. "Your voice sounds strange. Like you're in an echo chamber or something. Are those bubbles coming out of your ear?"

"Never mind that," Hawks snapped. "What's going on over there?"

"The entire sales and editorial staffs will be on the cruise. And

I've talked Mrs. Bunker into bringing young Tom Edison along, too.''

"Tom Edison? Who in hell is—"

"The Cyberbooks inventor, Carl Lewis.''

"Oh.''

"They'll all be on the ship together. There's talk that P. T. Bunker will be coming along, too, but so far that's just unconfirmed rumor.''

"Christ. If I had a submarine or a cruise missile I could wipe out the whole company.''

"Not before I get the complete data for the Cyberbooks machine,'' Scarlet said.

Hawks nodded inside his helmet. "Yes. Right.'' Then a brilliant thought occurred to him. "*You* could sink the ship and get away in a lifeboat with the device!''

She seemed startled for a moment, but she quickly composed herself. "Mr. Hawks, I'm an editor first, and a spy for you second. I am not an underwater demolitions expert.''

"Yes, of course, I understand,'' he mumbled, his mind filled with visions of the *Titanic* slipping beneath the ice-choked waves. He saw Bunker and his whole staff huddled on the slanting deck while the orchestra played "Nearer My God to Thee.'' Refuse to sell out to us, will you? Then down you go, Bunker, you and all your flunkies, down to a watery grave.

"Mr. Hawks?'' Scarlet Dean's insistent voice broke into his fantasy.

"Eh? What?''

"You were—cackling, sir.''

"Nonsense!'' he snapped. "Must be something wrong with this phone link.''

She said nothing.

"Get me the data on that Cyberbooks machine as quickly as you can. I don't care if you're in the middle of the ocean, as soon as you have the machine in your hands or a copy of its circuitry, send it to me over the special Tarantula communications satellite.''

"Yes, sir," she replied. "Of course."

"Don't call me otherwise. I'll call you each night at this time."

Scarlet nodded and cut their link. The tiny picture of her face winked out, leaving Hawks nothing to see but the blue-green haze of his swimming pool, lit by its underwater lights. He sat at the bottom of the pool for several minutes, the only sound coming from the frothy bubbles of his breathing apparatus.

As soon as she transmits the data on the Cyberbooks device, I could sink the damned ship and be rid of Bunker altogether. And all the evidence. Then I could present the Cyberbooks concept as my own to the board of directors. If the Old Man is still around, that by itself should be enough to remove him and put me at the top of the heap.

He resolved to find a reliable terrorist group that had access to speedboats and anti-shipping missiles. Maybe some of the Atlantic City boys, he mused. Didn't they sink a gambling ship that refused to pay them protection, a few years back?

At precisely ten minutes after midnight Hawks made his second phone call. The miniature image of Vinnie DeAngelo's beefy face screwed up in amazement.

"Gee, you look funny, Mr. Hawks. Like your nose is too close to th' camera, you know?"

"Never mind that. How are you coming along on the special project?"

The Beast's eyes evaded Hawks's. "Like I told you, this is a tough one. I been dopin' it out, but it don't look no easier than when I started. He's got snakes, for Chrissakes. Poison snakes."

"He doesn't stay in his office all the time. He goes home to his apartment."

"Yeah, but he takes th' snakes with him. His chauffeur got bit a couple days ago. Damn near killed him."

Exasperated, Hawks snapped, "Then find a mongoose!"

"Huh? A what?"

"Never mind. Keep working at it. There's got to be a weak link in the Old Man's defenses. He's a senile cripple, for god's sake. There's *got* to be a way to get to him."

"Not while all those snakes are sneakin' around." The Beast shuddered.

Hawks fumed silently. "Stay with it. And, by the way, Vinnie, who was that outfit that sank the gambling boat off Atlantic City a few years ago?"

"Oh, you mean my cousin Guido."

Alba Blanca Bunker allowed the chauffeur to help her out of the long white limousine and stepped onto the concrete surface of the massive dock. It was a gray, mean, John O'Hara kind of day in New York, threatening rain. But there alongside the shabby, deteriorating two-story passenger terminal rose the magnificently sweeping lines of the SS *New Amsterdam,* the cruise liner that would carry them off on a week-long jaunt on the sunny ocean. She took a deep breath of tangy salt air. Actually, the tang in the air was from a garbage barge being hauled down the Hudson River by a chuffing tugboat.

Alba felt thrilled anyway. For more than a year she had been working on the dozens of different strings that led to this moment. Now everything seemed to be in place. The Cyberbooks project had reached the point where they could brief the sales force. The medical specialists had agreed to come along on the cruise on a contingency fee basis. And P. T. himself would arrive soon.

In fact, there he was! Alba saw the blue-and-white helicopter loaned for the occasion by the American Express office droning purposefully against the gray sky up the river toward the pier. She knew that P. T. did not like to fly, did not like to leave the womblike safety of his office and bedroom, but she hoped that the panoramic view of lower Manhattan and the harbor would inspire him and be the first step toward reinvigorating her husband, the man she loved.

He needs this ocean voyage, she told herself for the millionth time. I'm doing this for him.

She watched as the helicopter settled briefly on the roof of the passenger terminal, its big rotors *whoosh*ing up a clatter of dust and grit. Even from this distance she recognized P. T., stuffed into his muscle suit and a double-breasted blazer topped by a jaunty white yachting cap. He scurried quickly up the special gangplank and into the ship without turning to see if his wife was watching. The chopper took off again, as though eager to hurry back to its ordained task of hunting down deadbeats with overdue bills.

Alba had suppressed her sudden urge to wave to him, knowing how silly it would look to the other people gathering on the pier. She turned to the chauffeur and ordered him to begin unloading her voluminous trunks and suitcases. P. T. was safely ensconced in their private suite; the medical specialists and the rest of the company could begin boarding the ship now.

Ms. Lori Tashkajian
Fiction Editor
Bunker Books
Synthoil Tower
New York NY 10012

Dear Ms. Tashkajian:

Thank you so much for accepting *Midway Diary*! I'm so delighted I almost got out of my wheelchair and danced a jig! The signed contracts are enclosed. How soon will the book be published? You know, I am the last surviving man to have been in the Battle of Midway, and I'd like to at least see the book before I report to the Big Admiral up yonder.

Thank you again. You've made an old man very happy. The advance money will come in handy when next month's bills arrive.

Thanks once again,
Capt. R. Clanker, U.S.N. (Ret.)

P.S. Do you think we could make a movie out of the book?

FOURTEEN

THE first night out of New York, the good ship *New Amsterdam* ran into a bit of foul weather. Nothing serious, merely a line of squalls that marked the leading edge of a weather front. Herman Melville would barely have noticed it. Yet the night resounded with the thump of landlubbers' bodies rolling out of their bunks.

Ralph Malzone leaned his scrawny forearms against the ship's rail and squinted out toward the bright, clean horizon. The morning was clear as crystal, the sun warm, the sea down to a light chop. Grinning dolphins rode along the ship's bow wave, gliding effortlessly up to the surface and disappearing beneath the sea, only to rise again glistening and sleek a few moments later.

Carl Lewis came up beside him and gripped the rail with white-knuckled hands.

"You okay?" Malzone asked.

"I think so. This is the first time I've been out of sight of land."

"You look a little green."

"I feel a little green," Carl admitted.

"Did you eat anything at dinner last night?"

"Not much."

"Keep it down?"

"Some of it."

Ralph chuckled. "Come on, kid. What you need is a decent breakfast."

Carl shook his head. "I'm not so sure. . . ."

"Trust me. I spent two years on destroyers. I've seen more upchucking than a men's room attendant at an ancient Roman banquet."

"Huh?"

"Don't worry about it. Every once in a while I forget that sales managers aren't supposed to know anything about literature. Neither are engineers."

"I read Classic Comics in my freshman English class," Carl said defensively.

Ralph sighed heavily and put an arm around the younger man's shoulders. "Come on, let's get some breakfast. You'll feel a lot better with something in your stomach."

Uncertainly, Carl let the sales manager lead him to the ship's dining room. It was a spacious, sumptuously appointed room, decorated in cool, soothing ocean greens and blues. Most of the tables were for four, a few for two, and only the captain's table big enough to hold eight or ten places.

Carl had to admit, half an hour later, that he did feel better. Some tomato juice, a couple of poached eggs, toast, and tea had revived him.

"You know a lot about a lot of things, don't you?" Carl asked.

Malzone shrugged his slim shoulders. "Mostly useless junk. How many times do you get the chance to help somebody get over a slight case of seasickness?"

Carl leaned back in his chair. The dining room was almost empty. Past Malzone's grinning face he could see the ocean through the ship's wide windows. The slight rise and fall of the horizon did not bother him at all now.

"Listen," Malzone said, his face growing serious. "I've been talking with my sales people, and I think you're in for some real problems.''

"Problems?"

"Yeah. Y'see, what you're doing with this Cyberbooks idea, basically, is asking the sales force to learn a whole new way of doing their job. It's kinda like asking a clerk in a shoe store to start selling airplanes to the Pentagon.''

Carl felt puzzled. "But selling Cyberbooks will be easy!''

Malzone made a lopsided grin that was almost a grimace. "No it won't. My sales people are used to dealing with book distributors, wholesalers, truck drivers, bookstore managers. If I understand the way Cyberbooks is going to work, we're going to be selling directly to the customer.''

"That's right. We eliminate all those middle men.''

"You eliminate most of my sales force.''

"No, no! We'll need them to—''

"They won't change,'' Malzone said quietly. But very firmly. Hunching forward in his chair, leaning on his forearms until his head almost touched Carl's, he said in a low voice, "They've spent their careers in this business doing their jobs a certain way. They work on the road. They live in their cars. They're not going to give up everything and sit in front of a phone all day.''

Carl felt a flare of anger at the pigheadedness Malzone was describing. But he saw that the sales manager was genuinely concerned, truly worried about the conflict that was about to break over his head.

"What should I do?'' he heard himself ask.

Malzone's lips twitched in a smile that was over before it started. "Nothing much you can do. Tomorrow morning you show them how Cyberbooks works. Half the sales staff will jump overboard before lunchtime. The other half will try to throw you overboard.''

"Terrific!''

"I'll handle them. That's my responsibility. I just wanted to warn you that they're not going to fall down and salaam at the end of your presentation.''

"But they all know the basic idea already, don't they?"

"Yep. And they're loading their guns to convince Mrs. Bee that Cyberbooks won't work."

Carl felt worse than seasick. "Jeez . . ."

Malzone straightened up and made an expansive gesture with both hands. "Like I said, that's not your worry. It's mine."

"But the whole purpose of this voyage is to familiarize the editorial and sales staffs with Cyberbooks," Carl insisted.

Laughing, Malzone countered, "Not exactly. That's the *excuse* for this sea voyage, but it's not the real reason for it."

"I don't understand."

"Didn't you notice the big contingent of medical people who came aboard with us?"

"Is that who they are?" Carl had noticed several dozen men and women, elegantly groomed and well dressed, who had arrived at the pier in limousines and shining luxury cars. Obviously neither editors nor sales people. Even their expensive matched luggage had stood out in pointed contrast to the worn, shabby bags of the Bunker Books employees.

"Plastic surgeons," Malzone explained. "It's time for Mrs. Bee's facelift again. And several other people are going in for lifts and tucks and some body remodelling."

"Here on the ship?"

"Sure. They get the job done and the bruises are all healed up by the time we get back to New York. Everybody home says how great they look, how much good the ocean voyage did them. Nobody knows they had plastic surgery aboard ship."

"My god," said Carl. "A facelift cruise."

Thus it was that the following morning, when Carl made his presentation of Cyberbooks to the assembled sales staff, he stood before an audience of bruised and bandaged men and women. They were dressed casually, in shorts and sports tops for the most part. Nearly all of them wore dark glasses. Maryann Quigly was in a whole-body cast, wrapped in white plastic from chin to ankles as a result of a fat-sucking procedure that had drained fifty pounds from her, and the follow-up procedure of tightening her skin so that her body would not be wrinkled like a dieting elephant.

Mrs. Bunker sat in the first row of the ship's auditorium, wearing an elegant hooded jacket and dark glasses that effectively hid the bandages around her eyes and jawline. Carl felt as if he were addressing the survivors of the first wave of an infantry assault team that had been caught in a deadly ambush. There was more bandaging showing than human flesh.

Unbeknownst to Carl or anyone else except Mrs. Bunker, at that very moment P. T. Bunker was on the surgical table, undergoing the multiple procedures that would replace his middle-aged flab with firm young muscle, a transplant procedure that was still very much in the experimental phase.

Just about the only two people in Carl's audience who were not bandaged were Ralph Malzone and Lori Tashkajian. Even Scarlet Dean, slimly beautiful and meticulously dressed as she was, sported a pair of Band-Aids just behind her ears. She had combed her hair into a smooth upsweep, obviously relishing the opportunity to show the bandages rather than hide them.

Feeling somewhat shaken by all this, Carl launched into his demonstration of Cyberbooks. Standing alone on the little stage at the front of the ship's auditorium, he used not his original prototype, but a new model fresh from the manufacturing center. It was exactly the size of a paperback book, small enough to fit in Carl's hand easily.

". . . and as you can see," he was saying, holding up one of the minuscule program wafers, "we can package an entire novel, complete with better graphics than any printing press can produce, in a wafer small enough to tuck into your shirt pocket."

"And how do you *sell* these chips?" asked someone in the audience.

"Two ways," replied Carl. "The customer can buy the wafers from retail outlets, or can get them over the phone, recording the book he or she asks for on a blank wafer, the same way you record a telephone message or a TV show."

"What about copyright protection?" asked Mrs. Bunker. Her

hood and oversized dark glasses reminded Carl of movie stars who pretended to avoid public recognition by a disguise so blatant you could not help but stare at it.

"The wafers cannot be copied," he answered. "Once a book is printed on a wafer, instructions for self-destruction are also printed into the text, so if someone tried to recopy the wafer it will erase itself completely."

"Until some ten-year-old hacker figures a way around the instructions," a voice grumbled.

Everybody laughed.

Carl shook his head. "I've had the nastiest kids in the Cambridge public school system try to outsmart the programming. They found a couple of loopholes that surprised me, but we've plugged them."

"You hope."

"I know," Carl shot back with some heat.

A man at the rear of the auditorium stood up, slowly. No bandages showed on him, but the careful way he moved convinced Carl that he must have had a tummy tuck done the day before, or worse.

"I'm just an old war-horse who's been workin' out in the field for damn near thirty years," he said in a rough voice deepened by a lifetime of cigarettes and alcohol. "I don't know anything about this electronics stuff. Hell, I got to get my nephew to straighten out my computer every time I glitch it up!"

The other sales people laughed.

"Now, what I wanna know is this: If this here invention of yours is gonna replace books printed on paper, what happens to the regional distributors, the warehouses, the truck drivers, and the bookstores?"

"The bookstores will still stay in business," Carl said. "They'll just carry electronic books instead of paper ones."

Maryann Quigly yelped from inside her body cast, "You mean there'll be no paper books at all?"

"Eventually electronic books will replace paper books entirely, yes," replied Carl.

"I ain't worried about eventually," the old salesman said. "I'm worried about this coming season. What do I tell the distributors in my area?"

"As far as Cyberbooks is concerned, you won't have to deal with them at all. You can show the line directly to the bookstores. We can supply them from the office in New York, over the telephone lines, with all the books they want."

A hostile muttering spread through the audience.

"In fact," Carl continued, raising his voice slightly, "the bookstores won't have to order any books in advance. They can phone New York when a customer asks for a Cyberbook and we can transmit it to them instantly, electronically."

The muttering grew louder.

"In other words," said the old war-horse, "first you're gonna replace the entire wholesale side of the business, and then you're gonna replace us!"

Carl's jaw dropped open.

Mrs. Bunker got to her feet and turned to face the salesman. "Woody—nobody could possibly replace you."

A ripple of laughter went through the group.

"Seriously," Mrs. Bunker continued, "we have got to learn how to adapt to this new innovation. That's why I've brought us all together on this ship, so we can hammer out the new ways of doing things that we're *all* going to have to learn."

"Mrs. Bee," retorted Woody hoarsely, "I been with you and P. T. for damn near thirty years. Through good times and lean. But it seems to me that this Cyber-thing is gonna mean you won't need us sales people. You won't need anything except a goddamned computer!"

"That's just not true," Mrs. Bunker snapped. "I don't care how the books are produced or distributed, they will not sell themselves. We will *always* need good, dedicated, experienced sales people. The techniques might change, the system may be altered, but your jobs will be just as important to this company with Cyberbooks as before. More important, in fact."

Ralph Malzone sprang to his feet. "Hey, listen, guys. How

many times have you come to me complaining about this knuckle-headed distributor or some dopey truck driver who brings the books back for returns without even opening the cartons? Huh?''

They chuckled. Somewhat grudgingly, Carl thought.

''Well, with Cyberbooks you eliminate all the middlemen. You deal directly with the point of sales. And you don't have to carry six hundred pounds of paper around with you!''

The discussion went on and on. Carl stepped down from the stage and let Ralph and Mrs. Bunker argue with the sales force. The editors shifted uncomfortably on their seats, whether from irritation, boredom, or low-grade postsurgical pain, Carl could not tell.

The men and women of the sales force were clearly hostile toward Cyberbooks. Even when Mrs. Bunker explained to them that since sales were bound to increase, the company would have to hire more sales people, which meant that most of the present sales personnel would get promoted, they expressed a cynical kind of skepticism that bordered on mutiny.

The most telling counterthrust came from one of the women. ''So we start selling Cyberbooks direct to the stores,'' she said in a nasal Bronx accent. ''So what about our other lines? They'll still be regular paper books. How do you think the wholesalers are gonna behave when they see us going around them with the Cyberbooks, huh? I'll tell you just what they'll do: they'll say, 'You stop going behind our backs with these electrical books or we'll stop carrying Bunker Books altogether.' That's what they'll say!''

Telephone Transcript

"I can hear you clear as a bell, Scarlet."

"You ought to, for what Bunker's paying to have its own satellite communications link from ship to shore."

"I'm glad you're with Bunker now. Webb seems to be going downhill."

"Stop fishing for dirt, Murray. We're discussing the Stoker contract and that's all."

(Laughing.) "Okay, okay. The terms are acceptable, all except the split on the foreign rights. Sheldon wants ninety percent instead of eighty."

"Eighty-five is the best I can do."

"Okay, I'll talk him into eighty-five. But just for you. I wouldn't do it for anybody else."

"You're a sweetheart."

"Oh, yeah. The advance. It's still no bigger than his last contract."

"That's because his last book still hasn't earned out, Murray. His stuff is getting stale. The readers aren't buying it the way they used to."

"Not earned out yet? Are you sure?"

"Sad but true."

"Hmm. Well, I guess Sheldon can live with a million until the next royalty checks come in. In his tax bracket, it isn't so bad."

"The self-discipline will be good for him."

"But how about making it a two-book deal?"

"On the same contract? Two books?"

"Right. You know he can pump out another one in six months or less."

"I think he pumps them out in six *weeks* or less, doesn't he?"

"Whatever. Two books, two million up front, and the same terms we've been discussing."

"You've got a deal, Murray."

"Nice doing business with you. Have a pleasant cruise."

FIFTEEN

WALKING through the vast offices of Webb Press is like walking through a mausoleum these days, thought P. Curtis Hawks. That damned Axhelm has depopulated the company. Where once there sat dozens of lovely red-haired lasses with dimpled knees and adoring eyes that followed his every gesture, now there was row upon row of empty desks.

Even worse, the Axe had brought in automated partitions for the editorial and sales offices. The amount of office space those people had now depended on how well their books were selling. "Psychological reinforcement," Axhelm had called it. What it meant was, if your sales figures for the week were good, your office got bigger; the goddamned walls spread out automatically, in response to the computer's commands.

But if your sales figures were down, the walls crept in on you. Your office shrank. It was like being in a dungeon designed by the insidious Dr. Fu Manchu: the walls pressed in closer and closer. Already one editor had cracked up completely and run screaming back home to her mother in the wilds of Ohio.

"The next step," Axhelm was saying as the two men surveyed

141

the emptiness that had once been filled with doting redheads, "is to sell all this useless furniture and other junk." Eyeing Hawks haughtily, he added, "The teak panelling in your spacious office should be worth a considerable sum."

Hawks chomped hard on his pacifier. Maybe I should put Vinnie onto this sonofabitch instead of the Old Man, he thought.

"And then we move to smaller quarters," Axhelm went on. "Where the rents are more reasonable. Perhaps across the river, in Brooklyn Heights."

"Never!" Hawks exploded. "No publishing house could survive outside of Manhattan. It's impossible."

Axhelm looked down at his supposed superior with that damned pitying smile of his. "If you don't mind my saying so, sir, your grasp on what is possible and what is impossible seems not to be very strong."

"Now see here . . ."

"You said it would be impossible to run Webb Press with only one-third of the staff that was present when I joined the company. Yet look!" The Axe gestured toward the empty desks. "Two thirds of the personnel are gone and the company functions just as well. Better, even. More efficiently."

"Our sales are down."

"A temporary dip. Probably seasonal."

"Seasonal nothing!" Hawks almost spat the pacifier out of his mouth. "How can we sell books when two-thirds of our sales force has been laid off?"

"The remaining one-third is sufficient," said the Axe smugly.

"You're going to run the company into the ground," moaned Hawks.

Axhelm eyed the shorter man as if through a monocle. "My dear sir, the task given me by corporate management was to make Webb Press more efficient. I have pruned excess personnel and now I shall reduce costs further by moving the offices out of this overly expensive location. *Operating* the company is your responsibility, not mine. If you cannot show a profit even after I have reduced your costs so drastically, then I suggest that you tender your resignation and turn over the reins of authority to someone who can run an efficient operation.''

Slowly, with the certainty of revealed truth dawning upon him, Hawks took the plastic cigar butt out of his mouth. So that's it, he said to himself. Axhelm wants to take over Webb Press. He wants my job. He wants my head as a trophy on his wall.

He said nothing aloud. But to himself, Hawks promised, I'm going to chop you down, you Prussian martinet. And I'm going to use your own methods to do it.

Sunset at sea. Scarlet Dean lay back on a deck chair, splendidly alone up on the topmost deck of the *New Amsterdam*, and watched the sun dip toward the horizon, blazing a path of purest gold across the sparkling waters directly toward her. It was if the huge glowing red sphere were trying to show her a path to wealth and happiness, she thought.

She knew she was in some danger. Not from anyone with Bunker Books. As far as she could tell they were all pleasantly incompetent nincompoops. Even Alba Bunker, who had a reputation for being the real brains behind the company, seemed totally unaware of what a tiger she had by the tail in Cyberbooks. Just about the only person who seemed to understand what was going on, really, was the sales manager. Ralph Malzone. A wiry, intense kind of guy. And a lot smarter than he pretended to be.

The danger came from Hawks and his temper. The man had no patience. God knows what demons are after his hide, Scarlet told herself. But it wouldn't be beyond him to order someone to sink this ship and drown everyone on it.

Including me.

But he won't do that unless and until he has the Cyberbooks machine in his grubby little paws. Or will he? Does he see Cyberbooks as a threat? Does he think he'd be better off putting the whole problem at the bottom of the Atlantic?

On the other hand, she thought, suppose I had control of Cyberbooks. Me. Myself. I could write my own ticket with Webb Press. Or with any publishing house in New York. I could probably get the top publishers together to buy me off, pay me millions to suppress the invention. I could retire for life.

Or start my own company. Take their money and then go to Japan and start a Cyberbooks company there. She smiled to herself. Or Singapore, even better. I could live like a queen in the Far East. The Dragon Lady. Empress of worldwide publishing. What a trip!

To do that, though, I'll have to get our young inventor to trust me. He's got to come along with me, at least at the beginning. The machine means nothing without the inventor to show others how to build it.

Scarlet realized, with a start, that she was sitting up tensely in the deck chair, every nerve taut with anticipation. She forced herself to lean back in the chair as she thought about Carl Lewis.

Lori Tashkajian is after him, she knew. Probably in love with him. Certainly the little twit understands that Carl is the key to her personal success. I'll have to pry Carl loose from her. More important, I'll have to pry him loose from his work. He's married to his damned invention, Scarlet realized. Oblivious to everything else. Lori is practically throwing herself at him and he just glides along without seeing it.

He's susceptible, though. I could see that the first time I met him. The tongue-tied engineer type. I'll have to be much more aggressive than Lori's been. His type calls for special measures.

Scarlet practiced smiling, alone up there on the top deck, while the sun slid slowly toward the gleaming red-gold sea and the sky turned to majestic flame.

Lori and Carl were standing side by side at the ship's rail, just one deck below Scarlet Dean's solitary perch.

"Isn't the sunset beautiful?" she murmured.

"So are you," Carl said. And she was, with the sea breeze caressing her shimmering ebony hair and the blazing red glory of the setting sun on her face. Lori wore a sleeveless white frock. In the last light of the sunset it glowed like cloth of gold.

She acknowledged his compliment with a smile, then looked back toward the sea.

"I think you and I are the only people on board," Carl went on, "who haven't had any plastic surgery done on them."

Lori giggled. "That's true enough! Have you seen Ted Gunn? Hair implants and artificial bone in his legs to make him two inches taller. Even Concetta has had her breasts and backside lifted."

Carl chuckled. "The one that gets me is Quigly. The pain she must have gone through!"

"And now she's eating five meals a day," Lori said, "even before the bandages come off! She'll be the same weight at the end of this cruise as she was at the beginning."

"But think of the great time she's having," Carl countered.

They both laughed. Then he said, "You don't need plastic surgery. You're gorgeous just as you are."

"I'm overweight. . . ."

"You're perfect."

"No I'm not."

"Yes you are."

"Carl, I'm far from perfect." Lori's face grew so serious that he did not reply. Then she went on, "In fact, I have a confession to make. I've been using you, Carl—for my own purposes."

"I don't understand."

She looked into his steady blue-gray eyes, a turmoil of conflicting emotions raging within her. As if beyond her conscious control, her voice said, "Carl, back in my office there's a manuscript. . . ."

"There's hundreds of 'em!"

"This is serious," Lori insisted. "One of those manuscripts is by a completely unknown writer. Nothing the author has written before has ever been published. And it's _good_, Carl! It's better than good. It's a masterpiece. It's raw, even crude in places. It's an unpolished gem. But it's a masterpiece. I want to publish it."

"So?" It was obvious from his puzzled expression that Carl did not understand the problem.

"It doesn't fit into any of the marketing categories. It's not a mystery, or a Gothic, or an historical novel. It's just the finest piece of American literature I've ever read. I get tears in my eyes whenever I think about it, that's how good it is. Pulitzer Prize, at least. Maybe the Nobel."

"Then why don't you publish it?"

"No New York publisher would touch it. It's a thousand manuscript pages long. It's not category. It's *literature*. That's the kiss of death for a commercial publishing house. They don't publish literature because literature doesn't make money."

"But if it's so good . . ."

"That's got nothing to do with it," Lori said, almost crying. "Quality doesn't sell books. Can you imagine the sales people on this ship going out and selling *Crime and Punishment* or *Bleak House*?"

Carl's expression turned thoughtful. "Didn't I read someplace that every publisher in New York turned down *Gone With the Wind* at one time or another?"

Nodding, Lori said, "Yes. And for twelve years none of them would touch *Lost Horizon*. There's a long list of great novels that nobody wanted to publish."

"But they all got into print eventually."

"But how many others didn't?" Lori almost shouted with a vehemence that surprised her. "How many truly fine novels have never been published because the people in this business are too blind or stupid to see how great they are? How many really great authors have gone to their graves totally unknown, their work turned to dust along with them?"

"My god, you're trembling."

Lori rested her head against Carl's shoulder. "It's a fine novel, a great work of art. And it's going to die without seeing the light of day—unless . . ."

"Unless what?" he asked, folding his arms around her.

"Unless we can make a success of Cyberbooks. Then they'll let me take a chance on an unknown, on a work of literature. I need to be able to tell Mrs. Bunker that the price of my bringing you to her is letting me publish this novel.''

"That makes sense, I guess.''

She pushed slightly away from him, enough to be able to look up into his eyes. "But don't you understand? I'm using you! I'm not interested in your invention just for its own sake. I want it to be a success so that I can have the power to publish this book!''

Carl smiled at her. "Okay. So what? I'm using you too, aren't I? Using you to get me inside a big New York publishing house so I can get my invention developed. Otherwise I'd still be sitting in some publisher's waiting room, wouldn't I?''

"But that's not the same. . . .''

"Listen to me. Cyberbooks can help you in more ways than one. How big is this great novel of yours? A thousand pages? How much would it cost to print a book that long?''

"A fortune,'' Lori admitted.

"With Cyberbooks it won't cost any more than a regular-sized book. And the retail price of the novel will be less than five dollars.''

Lori brightened. "I hadn't even thought about that part of it. I was still thinking in terms of printing the novel on paper.''

"Come on.'' He crooked a finger under her chin. "Cheer up. You help me bring Cyberbooks to life and I'll help you get your novel published. That's what the biologists call a symbiotic relationship.''

Dabbing away the tears at the corner of her eyes, Lori allowed Carl to lead her along the deck toward the hatch that opened into the dining salon. Neither of them noticed Scarlet Dean, leaning over the railing of the deck just above where they had been standing, a knowing little smile curving her narrow red lips.

MURDER FIVE

MILES Archer was an ex–police officer. A retired homicide detective, in fact. He had even been named after a detective. A small, unremarkable man who had gray hair by the time he was thirty, Archer had cracked many cases during his long distinguished career with the NYPD simply by the fact that hardly anyone could recognize the steel-trap mind behind his bland, utterly forgettable facade.

"He must have known he was being followed," said the uniformed cop.

Lt. Moriarty nodded. "Yeah. Miles would never have wandered up an alley like this for no reason."

Moriarty's steely gaze swept up and down the narrow alley. It was littered with paper, but otherwise clean enough. They were down in the financial district, near Wall Street. No winos huddled in the alleys here. Brokers might sneak martinis into their Thermos jugs, but they went home to posh suburbia after the day's frenzied work.

Archer's slight body lay facedown, where it had fallen, rumpled gray trenchcoat twisted around him, in front of a rusted metal door that led into the rear of a high-rise office building. The alley dead-ended at the brick rear wall of another high rise. A third skyscraper formed the other side of the narrow alley. Moriarty sniffed disdainfully; there was no garbage or urine smell to the alley. It seemed unnatural to him.

The forensics team was taking holographic pictures and lifting samples of litter from the area around the body. One of the team members was scanning the alleyway with an infrared detector for latent footprints. The binocularlike black detector steamed slightly as the summer evening's heat boiled away some of its liquid nitrogen coolant.

"He figured somebody was following him," Moriarty reconstructed the event aloud, "and ducked up here to see if whoever it was would come in too."

"And the perpetrator did follow him," said the cop in blue.

Moriarty nodded. "Must've been one person, and not a rough-looking type at all. Miles wasn't the kind for personal heroics. He must've thought whoever he was being followed by was lightweight enough for him to face down by himself."

"He made a mistake."

"The last one he'll ever make."

"Uh, Lieutenant . . ." The uniformed cop hesitated. "You don't think maybe he was deliberately meeting somebody here, do you?"

"In an alley?"

"They do a lot of designer drugs around here. Those brokers got a lot of money to throw around."

Moriarty dismissed the idea with a shake of his head. "Not Miles. He didn't even drink."

"Then what was he doing down in the financial district? He lived in Queens, didn't he?"

"He set up his own business after retiring from the force," said Moriarty. "Might have been down here on a case."

The cop went silent. Moriarty continued, thinking aloud, "I'll get the records from his office and see what he was working on. Must be a connection there." He watched as the medical team gently lifted the inert body onto a stretcher and carried it to the ambulance waiting at the head of the alley, lights flashing.

"You think there's a connection with the other Retiree Murders?" the uniformed policeman asked.

Moriarty looked sharply at him. "Is that what they're calling 'em? Retiree Murders?"

"In the newspapers, yeah. And on TV. This makes the fifth one, doesn't it?"

"That's right. But I don't think their murders have anything to do with their being retired. Hell, the Social Security clerks aren't going around bumping off their clients."

The cop shrugged and started up the alley. Their work here was finished. Moriarty followed behind him, thinking, I ran the other four through the computer to look for correlations. The only thing the victims had in common was that they were elderly, retired, and living off pensions, Social Security, and the income from a few odd shares of stocks.

SIXTEEN

WELDON W. Weldon frowned balefully at the computer's holographic display. It showed a graphic presentation of the owners of Tarantula's stock, twisted threads of colored lines that weaved and interlinked in a three-dimensional agony of confusion. Like a tangled mess of spaghetti. Like a pit of snakes slithering over and around one another. Or the snarled, twining stems of jungle vines struggling to find the sun.

He snorted in self-derision as he glanced from the display to the rotting jungle that infested his once immaculate office. Leaning forward in his powered wheelchair, he squinted at the display and tapped commands on the remote controller he held in one hand.

Who the hell really owns Tarantula? Ever since the Sicilians had started their takeover effort, that one question had burned through Weldon's brain like a laser beam cutting through naked flesh.

I don't have enough of the stock to stop them by myself, although I've climbed over the twenty-five percent mark. Synthoil is the largest single shareholder, that much is clear. The sky-blue line threading through the heart of the display was General Conglomerates, which owned eight percent of Tarantula. Are they in with the Sicilians? Not likely, Weldon thought, although you could never be entirely certain. The Benevolent International Brotherhood of Bureaucrats, a kinked muddy-brown line, owned twelve percent. Twelve percent! And the BIBB is a *known* Mafia subsidiary. Damnation.

And then there was the blood-red line pulsing through the others like an aorta: Rising Sun Electronics. They already had seventeen percent and were busily buying more. Weldon had encouraged the Japanese to buy Tarantula stock. Better in their hands than the Sicilians'. Play the Nips against the Wops, he had cackled to himself. But now the Japanese share of the company was becoming large enough to be a threat of its own.

The rest of the ownership was in the hands of individuals, thank god. Ordinary men and women who each owned a few shares apiece. Thousands of them. How would they vote at November's stockholders' meeting? Most of 'em never vote at all, never even send in their proxies, bless them. Then *I* vote their stock for them.

But what would they do if some smarmy jerkoff with olive oil in his hair offers to buy their stock at ten percent above the current market value? I'd have to make them a better offer, and the only way to do that is to liquidate half the company's assets to generate the cash for such a buy-back. Once Axhelm's finished with Webb Press I'll have to turn him loose on other divisions of the corporation. The old man sighed heavily. It can't be helped. We can't fight through an unfriendly takeover bid without spattering some blood on the floor, he thought grimly.

Maryann Quigly and Ashley Elton sat forlornly in the afterdeck lounge at the stern of the SS *New Amsterdam*. It was nearly midnight, and Quigly was working her way through her fifth meal of the day, a dainty snack of steak, french-fried potatoes, custard pie, and malted milk. Elton was nursing a tall concoction made of various rums and fruit juices.

The lounge was beautifully decorated in deep blue and silver, with glittering wall panels of faceted crystal that could be turned into giant display screens for video presentations. Beyond the curving windows that overlooked the ship's stern, the *New Amsterdam*'s churning wake glistened against the placid moonlit ocean. The muted strains of dance music from the main salon wafted through the afterdeck lounge.

"All these men on board," murmured the cadaverous Ms. Elton, "and not one of them has asked us even for a dance."

"I couldn't dance in this body cast," Quigly said through a mouthful of french fries. "It itches all over. I think they made it too tight for me."

Elton had availed herself of the plastic surgeons to transplant some of her gluteus maximus to her pectoral area. There was hardly enough meat on her to make any difference, but she felt better for it, although for the time being she had to sit on an inflated plastic ring, like a hemorrhoid victim.

"Well, I can dance, but nobody's asked me," she whined.

Maryann stuffed half the custard pie into her mouth. The afterdeck lounge was almost empty. The evening floor show had ended an hour ago, and now most of the ambulatory men and women aboard the ship were in the main salon, dancing to the syntho-rock music of a robot band.

"Don't feel bad about it," Maryann advised her colleague. "All the men on this cruise are either macho or gay."

"Yeah, I suppose so. Still, you'd think . . ." Ashley Elton's voice trailed off wistfully.

"That's not important," said Quigly, reaching for her malted milk. "What's important is this Cyberbooks deal."

"Yeah. What do you think of it?"

Quigly's eyes, small and deepset in folds of flesh that not even the cosmetic surgeons had been able to remove, shifted evasively. "It bothers me," she said.

"Me too."

"There's too many computers in this business already," muttered Quigly, glancing around to see if anyone was close enough to overhear. No one was. No one was sitting within thirty feet of them.

"Yeah. Did you see what they did at Webb Press? They've got computers doing just about *everything* now. Only three editors left in the whole house! They've got to do everything!"

"Who has time to do anything?" Quigly puffed out a weary sigh, then polished off the rest of her malted.

"I sure don't," admitted Elton. "What with meetings and meetings and more meetings, I'm lucky if I open the morning mail."

With a ponderous shake of her head, Quigly said slowly, "A book ought to have *pages*. It ought to be made out of paper."

"Yeah. Something you can curl up with in bed at night."

"Not some electronic box."

"It's so cold!"

"It isn't right," Quigly insisted. "Books should be made out of paper. That's the way they were meant to be made."

"Wrong, girls."

The two women jerked with guilty surprise. Standing over them was Woodrow Elihu Balogna, known to all as Woody Baloney, sales rep for the upper Midwest region.

"Books," Woody said genially, waving a cigarette in a grand gesture, "were meant to be made out of clay tablets—or maybe papyrus scrolls."

"Pass the bread," Elton announced ritualistically, "here comes the Baloney."

Woody pulled out the empty chair and sat himself carefully on it, sighing out a puff of smoke as he settled down.

"You know this is a no-smoking area," Elton said peevishly. "All indoor spaces on this ship are no-smoking."

"Yeah, but what the hell. You girls won't fink on me, will you?"

"They should have transplanted a human brain into your skull instead of just giving you a tummy tuck," Quigly chimed in.

"And you're adorable too," croaked Woody in his husky voice, a big grin on his weatherbeaten face. But he stubbed the cigarette out in the crumb-littered plate that had once held Quigly's custard cream pie.

He was a big man, and once had been handsome in a rawboned sort of way. But years of alcohol, cigarettes, sleeping in motels, and pounding his head against the ingrained obstinacy of wholesalers and jobbers had ravaged him. His face was seamed and scarred like the Grand Canyon, and scruffy with a day's growth of gray stubble. He wore a faded gray sweatshirt and patched jeans that hung loosely on his suddenly gangly frame.

"What you should have done," Ashley Elton said more seriously, "was let them give you a facelift. You're still handsome, underneath all those wrinkles."

Woody tilted his head back and guffawed. "Now, can you just picture me waltzing into Duluth Distributing's warehouse looking all prettied up! They'd throw me out on my ass!"

Maryann Quigly refused to smile. She waited for Woody's whoops to die down, then said, "Don't you go telling anybody what we were saying about the Cyberbooks idea. Just because—"

"Hey, I'm with you," Woody assured her. "I think this smart-aleck inventor is going to get us all thrown out of work. We gotta find a way to stop him."

Quigly's porcine little eyes widened. "You mean it?"

"It's him or us, that's the way I feel about it."

"But Mrs. Bunker . . ." whispered Elton.

"We gotta convince her that this Cyberbooks gadget is a mistake, a flop, a disaster. We gotta make her see that if she tries to market Cyberbooks it'll ruin the company."

"But her mind's already made up," Elton countered, "the other way."

"Then we've got to make her reverse her decision," said Quigly.

"But how?"

"That's the hard part," Woody admitted, his grin fading.

P. Curtis Hawks was standing at the sweeping windows of his spacious office, staring hard across the river toward Brooklyn.

The goddamned Junker bastard wants to move us to Brooklyn! He shook his head for the ten-thousandth time. Brooklyn. It's the end of the world.

He had to admit, however, that Gunther Axhelm's pruning was already showing results. The latest quarterly profit and loss statement on his desk was considerably better than it had been in years. The operation was actually in the black for the first time since the Reagan memoirs had swept the world with their candid charm and naively brutal insights.

Sales were slipping, but that was to be expected when the sales force had been reduced from two hundred men and women to a single voice-activated computer and a fleet of roboticized trucks. They would pick up again, Hawks fervently prayed, once the wholesalers got accustomed to seeing robots instead of human beings. The big chain stores, where the really massive orders came from, had not even noticed the difference. Book orders went from their computers to Webb's computer as smoothly as snakes slithering on banana oil.

Offsetting the downtrend in sales was the even larger downtrend in costs. The Old Man upstairs must be happy with the situation, Hawks told himself. He hasn't bothered me in weeks. Then he frowned. Or maybe he just doesn't want to see me anymore. Maybe Axhelm's axe is going to stab *me* in the back, too.

The warehouse. The goddamned, mother-humping, sonofabitching warehouse. So far I've been able to keep Axhelm's beady little eyes off it. But how long can I hold out? How long can I keep him from finding out what a fiasco the damned warehouse is?

His desk phone chimed.

"Answer answer," he called out, thinking that the goddamned phones were just like most goddamned people, you had to tell them everything twice.

"Sir," came the mechanical voice of his computer (where once there had been an achingly lovely red-haired lass), "Engineer Yakamoto is waiting to see you."

Oh Christ, thought Hawks. Just what I need. Yakamoto. Something else has gone wrong at the warehouse.

With a reluctant, shivering sigh, Hawks told the computer to let the Japanese warehouse manager enter his office.

Hideki Yakamoto was pure Japanese. He had come over from Osaka as a field engineer to oversee the installation of the robotic equipment at the warehouse. When it became apparent that he was the only man on the continent of North America who could make the robots function the way they should, Hawks had insisted to his parent company, Rising Sun Electronics, that they allow him to remain at the warehouse as supervisor. Rising Sun, happy to have a spy inside the Tarantula organization, allowed itself to be reluctantly persuaded.

Yakamoto, small, wiry, round-faced, clad in a Saville Row three-piece summerweight suit, bowed from the waist and inhaled through his teeth with a sharp hiss meant to express his unworthiness to breathe the same air as his illustrious superior. Hawks found himself bowing back. Not that he wanted to, his body just seemed to bow whenever the little Nip did it to him.

Annoyed at himself, he snapped, "What's wrong, Yakamoto?"

The Japanese engineer said blandly, "Nothing that cannot be put right by the wealth of knowredge that you possess. I am ashamed to bother you with what must be a small detail . . ."

"Come to the point, dammit!" Hawks went to his desk and stood behind it. It made him feel safer.

Yakamoto bowed again. "It is shameful for me to intrude on your extremery busy schedule . . ."

"What is it?" Hawks fairly screamed.

Yakamoto braced himself. Standing at rigid attention, he said, "The grue, sir."

"The grue? What grue?"

"The grue used to bind the pages of the books together, sir."

"You mean *glue!* Well, what about it?"

Yakamoto closed his eyes, as if standing before a firing squad. "It evaporates, sir."

"What?"

"The grue evaporates while the books are in their packing cases. When the cases are open, there is nothing in them but roose pages and covers."

Hawks sank heavily into his padded chair. "Oh, my sweet baby Jesus."

Yakamoto said nothing, he just stood there with his fists clenched by his sides, eyes squeezed shut. He did not even seem to be breathing.

"How many . . . cases . . ."

Without opening his eyes, "This month's entire print run, sir. We began receiving compraints from stores and warehouses rast week. Whenever a case is opened—nothing but roose pages, fruttering rike butterfries in the summer breezes."

"Spare me the goddamned poetry!" Hawks snapped.

"I have taken the riberty of firing a comprete report in your personal computer system," Yakamoto said, "so that you have all the details avairable at your industrious fingertips. However, I felt it necessary for me to tell you of this catastrophe in person."

Hawks grunted and reached out a reluctant hand to access the data. His screen soon showed the gory details. Millions of dollars' worth of books, reduced to millions of loose pages. Tens of millions of pages. Hundreds of millions . . .

He groaned. We're ruined. Absolutely ruined.

Yakamoto was making strange, gargling sounds. Hawks looked up. Is he trying to commit suicide, right here in my office?

No, the man was merely trying to get Hawks's attention by repeatedly clearing his throat.

"Don't tell me there's more," Hawks moaned.

Yakamoto stood rigidly silent.

"Well?"

"You told me not to tell you," the Japanese engineer said pleadingly.

"Tell me!" Hawks snapped. "Tell me all of it! Every god-damned ball-breaking detail. Give it to me, all of it. Then we can both jump out the frigging window!"

Yakamoto bowed as if to say, _You asked for it._ "Apparentry, exalted sir, the grue used to bind the books decomposes into a psychederic gas. When the crates are opened, whoever is within ten feet becomes intoxicated—they have immediate and invoruntary 'head trips' that approximate the effects of taking a sizable dose of harrucinogen."

Hawks felt his breakfast making its burning way up his digestive tract, toward his throat. Glue sniffing! With the effects of LSD!

"And . . ." Yakamoto said as quietly as a dove gliding through tranquil air.

"Still more?"

Barely nodding, Yakamoto said, "Those who have been affected by the narcotic nature of the residual gas from the faired grue are initiating rawsuits against Webb Press. Several such riabirity suits have already been fired against the company."

"Several? How many?"

With a pained expression, Yakamoto replied, "Seven hundred thirty-four, as of this morning."

Hawks slammed both palms down on his desk and hauled himself to his feet. "That's it! Hara-kiri! That's the only road left open to us, Yakamoto!" He strode toward the sliding glass partition that led to the terrace. "It's a fifty-story drop. That ought to do the job."

Yakamoto did not stir from where he stood. "Most respected and brave sir, it is not my place to kill myself over this matter. I had nothing to do with putting this unfaithful grue on the books. It is not my responsibirity."

Hawks stopped with one hand on the handle of the sliding glass partition.

"Wait a minute," he said. "You're right. I didn't order any new kind of glue for binding the books."

Yakamoto said softly, "Still, it is your responsibirity, sir."

"Is it? We've been binding books by the zillions for years without this kind of trouble. Who the hell ordered different glue? I'll nail his balls to the wall!"

Suddenly a happy thought penetrated Hawks's consciousness, and he broke into a slight grin. As eagerly as a teenaged boy reaching for a condom, he jumped back onto his desk chair and sent his fingers flying across the computer keyboard.

"Yes!" he shouted triumphantly after several frenzied minutes. "Yes! Yes! Yes!"

Yakamoto stood motionless, but his face showed unbearable curiosity.

"Axhelm ordered the new glue!" Hawks crowed. "The wise-ass ordered it because it's half a cent per thousand cheaper!"

While his faithful Japanese engineer watched incredulously, Hawks flung himself on the carpet and laughed hysterically.

THE WRITER

THE Writer cringed in terror in the farthest corner of the warehouse. They had all gone mad. Wildly, murderously mad.

His fellow employees—the bedraggled men and few equally unattractive women who worked the warehouse floor, those human dregs who daily risked life and sanity to do jobs that gleaming robots could not handle—they were capering and gibbering, ripping open the cartons that they were supposed to be neatly stacking, tearing out loose pages of books and flinging them high into the air until the entire warehouse looked like a blizzard was raging through it.

They sang. They screamed with laughter. They danced through the paper snowfall and howled with animal glee. Several heaps of paper the size of mating couples were twitching and shuddering here and there across the warehouse floor. Even the Japanese supervisors, who had raced down from the control booth shouting and gesticulating, were now capering through the littered warehouse, eyeglasses askew, reeling for all the world as if they were dead drunk.

"C'mon, pal! Don' be 'fraid!" One of the grimy-faced women was bending over the Writer, her faded blouse pulled open and her meager breasts hanging free.

With wordless terror, the Writer scrabbled away from her until his back was pressed against the concrete wall and he could retreat no farther.

. The woman laughed at him. "Don' be scared, pal. It's okay. It's our bonus. Lousy wages they been payin' us, we're entitled to a li'l bonus, huh?"

She advanced on him. The Writer tried to push his emaciated body *through* the concrete wall. Behind the woman's menacing form he could see the other warehouse employees gibbering and gamboling madly. Their insane shouts and laughter were a bedlam. All the robots stood immobile, inert, dead.

"Look, pal, I got a present for ya. . . ." The woman reached into the back pocket of her jeans and tugged out a brand-new paperback book. It had obviously just been taken from its packing crate. The cover glistened pristinely.

"Yer gonna love it," she said, shoving it under the writer's nose.

He tried to bat it away. The pages fell apart and spilled into his lap. A spicy, pungent odor filled the Writer's nostrils. His vision blurred for a moment. He rubbed his eyes, inhaling the wonderful perfume coming from the scattered pages of the book.

When he looked up at the woman again, he saw that she was beautiful. And the music was beautiful. The whole world was just as he had always dreamed it would be, someday.

Smiling, he began to sing the love duet from *Tristan und Isolde* in a better tenor voice than he had ever imagined possessing. She sang back in a breathtaking soprano.

SEVENTEEN ▬▬▬▬▬▬

SEVEN doctors and seven nurses, all in pale green smocks and masks, huddled over the surgical table beneath the shadowless light of powerful overhead lamps. In a corner of the tiny, intense room a row of electronic machines beeped and peeped, while miniature pumps and motors made a soft pocketa-pocketa sound. Otherwise the improvised surgical chamber was silent, except for the terse, whispered commands of the chief surgeon and the responses of the chief nurse:

"Clamp."

"Clamp."

"Retractors ."

"Retractors."

"Inserting left *flexor digitorum longus.*"

"Yes, doctor."

"Microviewer."

The nurse swung the elaborate electro-optical device toward the chief surgeon and deftly adjusted it to his eye level.

"Microstapler."

She put the tiny staple gun in his right hand.

For several moments the only sound from the group crowding around the surgical table was the clicking of the microstapler.

Then the chief surgeon straightened up and wiped his own brow with his own blood-smeared gloved hand.

"That's it," he said. They could all hear the smile behind his mask. "Close him up, Renshaw."

The thirteen men and women clapped their gloved hands in admiration. It sounded something like limp pillows clashing. The chief surgeon bowed, blew them all a kiss, and tottered off to wash up.

Hours later, consciousness returned to the newly rebuilt body of Pandro T. Bunker. He lay on the same table; it had been wheeled into the recovery room (actually a passenger's cabin four decks below the *New Amsterdam*'s waterline, a few yards down the passageway from the movie theater that the plastic surgeons had been using for their operations). A single nurse, young, blond, and nubile, was polishing her fingernails while a bevy of sensors kept tabs on Bunker's recuperation.

The nurse did not notice the first sign of her patient's return to consciousness, a slight trembling of Bunker's fingers. Then his eyelids fluttered.

P. T. Bunker took a deep breath. The sensors arrayed beside his table beeped along merrily. He growled at them. Then he saw the nurse, her back to him.

He felt—strangely powerful. Young. Virile. Horny as hell. Looking from the nurse to the white sheet that covered his body, he saw a large protuberance poking toward the ceiling.

With a malicious grin he slowly pulled himself up to a sitting position. The effort made him grunt slightly. After all, he had spent several hours in surgery.

The noise made the nurse turn toward him in her swivel chair. Her china-blue eyes went wide.

"Mr. Bunker, you're supposed to rest!"

He tried to reply that he did not feel like resting, that he felt strong and fine, but his throat was so dry that all he could utter was a sort of menacing strangled growl.

"No, no!" said the nurse, getting to her feet, never realizing that the sensors were reporting Bunker's condition to be completely healthy.

Bunker swung his legs off the table and stood up. The sheet dropped away. The surgeons had closed his incisions with quick-acting protein glue, so there was not a bandage on his rebuilt naked body.

The nurse's eyes went still wider, focusing on Bunker's aroused musculature. His eyes were focused on the strained front of her starched white blouse. She was panting. He began panting.

With a shriek, the nurse dropped her bottle of nail polish and bolted to the door. She ran down the passageway screaming, "He's alive! He's alive!"

Bunker lumbered after her, staggering slightly as he tried to make his newly muscled body obey the commands of his publisher's brain.

Three decks above the *New Amsterdam*'s waterline, Scarlet Dean was making up her mind—and her face. She stood before the mirror over the sink in her cabin's compact bathroom, wearing only a pink bra and panties, carefully applying as little mascara and lipstick as she dared. The tiny tucks of the plastic surgery had tightened up her face beautifully. And the biochemical toners made her skin glow like a young girl's.

The mirror seemed to be swaying slightly, and she felt a bit of a sinking sensation in the pit of her stomach. Frowning, she tried to concentrate on getting the lipstick on straight. Can't use too much of it, she told herself; can't have its scent masking the pheromone spray.

"Attention, all passengers," said a very male voice from the little speaker grille set into the ceiling. "We are approaching the edge of a small storm system. The sea will be slightly rougher than usual. Please take care walking, especially on the outside decks. Use the handrails, both inside and outside."

Scarlet shot an annoyed glance at the loudspeaker. They could at least wait until I've finished putting on my lipstick!

Satisfied with her work, she stepped through the hatch and opened the clothes closet next to her queen-sized bed. Her clothes swayed slightly on their hangers, like a chorus line in a speeding subway train. As she pondered over what to wear for dinner, she reviewed where her business matters stood.

The negotiation with Murray Swift over Sheldon Stoker's latest horror was successfully concluded. The other editors and most of the sales force were up in arms over the Cyberbooks project. Mrs. Bunker was fretting, and P. T. Bunker was getting his body rebuilt.

Now was the time to bring young Carl Lewis to heel. She had toyed with him for three months. Now she would reel him in and net him, and when she was finished with him she would mount his head on the wall of her trophy room.

She smiled at the thought.

She selected a slim sheath, bright red, of course, and dressed quickly, efficiently. The last thing she did before heading for the dining salon was to dig the tiny phial of pheromone spray out of her locked briefcase and slip it into her glittering red handbag.

Alba Blanca Bunker was also dressing for dinner. Her cabin was very spacious, of course, but it seemed terribly empty without P. T. to share it. She worried about him, alone without her, deep down in the lower decks that had been turned into a hospital. The doctors were using a new type of synthetic steroid mixture to speed his recuperation, but still it would take several days for him to recover from the body-rebuilding surgery.

She studied herself in the full-length mirrors that flanked both sides of the king-sized bed. Here on the ship she need not be a slave to the weekly fashions of New York. She wore a nineteen thirties ball gown of pure white silk that flowed gracefully to the floor and billowed behind her when she danced. She loved it and felt very beautiful and secure in it.

The plastic surgery had erased most of the worry lines in her face, but not in her heart. Ralph Malzone had warned her that the sales force would not like Cyberbooks. Now it looked as if they would openly revolt against the project. She sighed deeply at the prospect of having dinner with Ralph, Woody, and several other disgruntled sales people. But business is business, she told herself firmly. Squaring her bare slim shoulders, she picked up her handbag and went to the stateroom door.

The wind caught at her lovely gown and nearly twirled her around as she stepped out of the cabin. Up here on the topmost deck of the ship she could see in the last rays of the setting sun that the seas were heaving, whitecapped waves arching upward from the deep dark blue. Thick clouds were building up, gloriously crimson and violet in the dying sunset. Alba secretly thrilled to it. The deck slanted and rose beneath her feet, then dropped away. Even up here she could taste the tang of salt spray in the wind. It was exciting!

She made her way on delicate spike heels toward the ladderway that led down to the dining salon's deck. Gripping the handrails, she carefully went down the stairs and stepped through the hatch that opened onto the bar lounge. The ship had been designed so that it was impossible to enter the dining salon without passing through the lounge and bar first. Some of Malzone's salesmen never made it to dinner. Or lunch. The bar did not open before noon, or they might not have gotten any solid nourishment at all.

Ralph was standing in a little knot of people that included Woody, Lori Tashkajian, and Carl Lewis. Alba knew she would have to detach Carl and Lori from the sales people, but she expected that neither of them would mind. They would obviously rather have dinner by themselves than with the sales department.

As she started toward them, a worried-looking gray-haired man fairly dashed across the open space and intercepted her.

"Mrs. Bunker, I'm Dr. Karloff. . . ."

She recognized his immaculately groomed face, the carefully trimmed little gray mustache, the utterly expensive three-piece suit. He seemed unaccustomedly harried, not his usual smiling confident suave self.

"I'm afraid there's been something of a problem. . . ."

"Pandro!" she gasped. "What's happened to Pandro?"

"The surgery went fine, no problems at all, everything went very well." Karloff was visibly upset; perspiration dotted his brow, he was almost babbling.

"What happened?"

"The recuperative chemotherapy. You recall that I specifically explained to you both that the synthetic steroids were new and relatively untried. . . ."

"You assured us they were safe!" Alba felt cold terror clutching her.

"They are! They are! But the dosage . . . we may have given your husband a higher dose than he actually—"

Just then the double doors at the far side of the lounge were ripped off their hinges with a blood-chilling screech, and the naked lumbering figure of Pandro T. Bunker lurched into the area. Women screamed. Men ducked for cover. Dr. Karloff turned whiter than Alba's gown and fainted dead away.

"Alba!" came a strangled cry from deep within P. T. Bunker. Arms outstretched, he staggered across the thickly carpeted lounge toward her.

She stood frozen with shock, her eyes registering that Pandro seemed taller, stronger, more urgently virile than she had seen him in years. He was a naked Greek god, a young Tarzan, an Adonis with a hard-on.

"Alba!" He lurched toward her.

She ran to him. He scooped her up in his mighty arms and staggered off the way he had come, her virginal white gown trailing after them. Alba nestled her head against her husband's new bulging *pectoralis major* and let him carry her back to their private stateroom. He seemed rather clumsy, uncoordinated, but she was sure that he would learn to control his rebuilt body properly, given time. Tonight, self-control was the last thing she wanted from him.

Midnight once again.

Everyone aboard seemed to be still in a state of shock over

P. T.'s escapade at the start of the evening. In the main salon little foursomes and couples huddled over tiny cocktail tables, largely ignoring the dance music of the robot band, still talking about it.

"You can see why he's the top man." Woody was leering drunkenly at three of his cohorts, two of them women.

"It's a transplant," said the other man. "Must have been."

One of the women shot back, "And all you got was a tummy tuck, Woody."

Scarlet Dean had suffered through dinner with Maryann Quigly, Ted Gunn, and the boorish Jack Drain, just so she could keep Carl Lewis in her sight. Maryann had consumed food the way a horde of locusts does, then immediately waddled off to the afterdeck lounge to get ready for the late night snack. Ted had wisecracked that he could hear her body cast creaking from the pressure she was putting against it.

All through dinner, while Maryann stuffed herself and Drain sneered at everything, Scarlet watched for an opportunity to intrude on Carl and Lori. They gazed at one another adoringly and hardly noticed the meal being served to them. Scarlet knew they were not sleeping together, yet they were behaving like a pair of love-smitten teenagers.

Their romance has gone farther than I thought, she realized. The effects of too much salt air and moonlight. Well, I'll put an end to that tonight, she told herself, patting the handbag resting in her lap. One puff of the pheromone spray and he'll never look at another woman again.

The spray had come from the research laboratories of Tarantula Enterprise's biogenetic division in Stuttgart. It was actually an outgrowth of their genetic warfare work, an attempt to create a weapon that would selectively incapacitate only the enemy's troops and no one else. Based on an artificial virus that affected certain nerve pathways into the brain, it had been designed to make its victims fall asleep as long as they could smell the subliminal odor of their military uniforms. The Stuttgart scientists fondly hoped that once used on the battlefield, the spray would be so effective that the enemy troops would only wake up after their captors had stripped them down to their skivvies.

Alas, it never worked that well. The virus was *too* specific. In nature, it affected only one individual out of a hundred or more. And instead of putting a man to sleep, it imprinted unbearable sexual longing in the victim. Like a love potion of old, it made the victim fall hopelessly for whomever he or she first smelled after being hit by the spray. The scandal among the volunteer units of the Swabian Rifles led to a dozen resignations, three suicides, and five homosexual marriages.

Scarlet was going to spray Carl and make certain that the first person he smelled was herself. And after that, she knew, she would be the *only* person he would sniff after.

But she had to be very careful to get Carl away from Lori— and everyone else—before she spritzed him.

During dinner, Ralph Malzone had presided over a rowdy table of sales people. Afterward, looking thoroughly wrung out, he had stopped by Lori and Carl's table and the three of them had gone together into the main lounge.

It had been easy enough for Scarlet to insinuate herself into the threesome, and for the past several hours the four of them had been drinking, talking, and dancing. The robot dance band was built and costumed to look like a vague amalgamation of the Beatles, the Beach Boys, and other popular groups of the sixties and seventies. This cruise ship usually catered to retirees who were fixated on the music of their teen years.

Scarlet kept her drinks long and soft, and noticed that Lori did the same. Good old Ralph never drank anything but beer; he seemed to have an infinite capacity for it, although he excused himself every hour or so: "Time to recycle the beer," he would invariably say.

Carl, the innocent one, drank a steady stream of cuba libres. Rum and Coke. He downed them as if there was no rum in them at all, and Scarlet began to suspect that somebody—maybe Lori—had made a deal with the waiter to make his drinks innocuous. While he and Lori were dancing she had stolen a sip. No, the rum was there all right. Young Mr. Edison has a wooden leg, apparently.

Try as she might, though, she could not get Carl off by himself. The handsome young engineer danced with her several times, slipping and tripping as the dance floor sloshed back and forth in the storm-tossed sea. But Lori was either on the floor beside them, dancing with Ralph, or sitting at their ringside table watching Carl. And he was always looking around for her.

Maddening.

Scarlet danced with Ralph, too, from time to time. The wiry guy was athletically light on his feet, a good dancer despite the worried, preoccupied look on his lank face.

"The sales force giving you hell?" Scarlet asked him as they worked their way uphill on the tilting dance floor.

"Yeah," he said, making it a long flat exasperated syllable. "Worse than I thought it could be."

"Maybe they should drop the Cyberbook project."

Malzone shook his head. "P. T. *never* gives up on anything. You know that. And—dammit! It's a good idea. I think it could work if we'd give it half a chance."

The dance floor shuddered and then started slanting downhill. Ralph held Scarlet firmly in his surprisingly strong arms and guided her past the other dancing couples. The band was playing "Hey Jude" on its synthesized instruments. Carl and Lori were sitting at the table alongside the dance floor, gazing raptly at each other over a forest of tall glasses and empty bottles. Scarlet felt the anger of frustration heating her.

The song ended just as the dance floor gave another lurch. The couple next to Scarlet and Ralph staggered slightly into them. The woman's heel caught in the hem of her floor-length dress and she clutched at Scarlet for support. Scarlet's slim little handbag slid off her shoulder and hit the floor with a thunk as the woman—one of Ralph's sales people—straightened up and murmured an apology.

The couple scurried back to their table as Ralph bent down to pick up Scarlet's purse. She dropped to one knee beside him, anxious to scoop up the things that had spilled out of the bag and onto the polished wood of the dance floor.

Ralph helped her. "Hey, what's this?" he asked, picking up the pheromone spray.

"Ah . . . perfume," Scarlet improvised, making a grab for it. Her hand clutched for the phial just a touch too hard, and a microscopic mist sprayed from it with an almost inaudible hiss.

Malzone blinked as the spray hit his face. "Doesn't smell at all," he muttered, handing the phial back to Scarlet.

Scarlet felt the spray tingle on her face, too. She looked deeply into Ralph Malzone's eyes and knew beyond the trace of any doubt that this was the one man in the world that she absolutely had to have for her very own.

"Ralph," she said, her voice shuddering with the urgency of it all. "Would—would you please take me back to my cabin?"

Nodding absently, as though something had just happened that was beyond his understanding, Ralph straightened up, took Scarlet by the hand, and walked with her right past Lori and Carl without saying a word.

FISHING BOAT EXPLODES,
FOUR FEARED KILLED

Brigantine, N.J. A forty-five-foot fishing boat, *Calamara,* was blown to bits last night in a mysterious explosion a few miles off the south Jersey coast, according to a Coast Guard spokesman.

Four men aboard the vessel are missing and feared dead.

"It was like she was hit by a missile," said Lt. (j.g.) Donald Winslow.

Coast Guard radar, on a routine drug surveillance sweep, picked up the *Calamara* while it was heading out to sea. "One instant it was there, the next it was gone," said Lt. Winslow. A Coast Guard helicopter sent to investigate found only floating debris and an oil slick.

"The sea was getting rough, but not dangerously so. There were no other ships within fifty miles of *Calamara* except a cruise liner, the SS *New Amsterdam,*" Lt. Winslow stated.

The missing men are Marco DeAngelo, Guido DeAngelo, and Vincenzio DeAngelo, all of Brooklyn, N.Y., and Salvatore Baccala, of Brigantine, N.J., owner of the boat.

THEFT OF CRUISE MISSILE REPORTED

Staten Island, N.Y. An unnamed Navy official reluctantly admitted that a fully armed cruise missile was stolen from the Staten Island weapons depot three nights ago. She stressed, however, that the missile was armed with a conventional warhead, not a nuclear weapon.

Defense Department and F.B.I. antiterrorist teams are investigating the incident, which may be linked to the mysterious explosion of a New Jersey fishing boat last night.

The Navy spokesperson, who insisted on anonymity, claimed that all cruise missiles in storage are equipped with automatic self-destruct systems, as a protection against terrorist seizure. "If the people who stole the missile tried to launch it, it would blow up in their faces," she averred.

WHITE HOUSE BLAMED

FOR MISSILE THEFT

AND BOAT EXPLOSION

Washington, D.C. Sen. Mario Pazzo (D., N.J.) accused the White House today of "culpable guilt" in the explosion last night of a New Jersey fishing boat in which four men were apparently killed.

"The President should realize that all the Navy's cruise missiles are booby-trapped, and thus a danger to those who operate them," said Sen. Pazzo. "And if he doesn't know that, then he isn't doing the job he was elected to do."

Reminded that the only way the four men in question could have obtained a cruise missile was to steal it from the Navy weapons depot in Staten Island, Sen. Pazzo insisted, "The issue here is not crime. It's the safety of human lives."

A Pentagon spokesman, when confronted with the Senator's statement, expressed surprise. "Hell, there's red lettering eight inches high that says 'DO NOT ATTEMPT TO LAUNCH UNTIL SELF-DESTRUCT SYSTEM IS DEACTIVATED.' Maybe the guys who stole the missile couldn't read."

F.B.I. officials theorize that the missile was stolen as part of the gang wars over narcotics smuggling.

"If they're escalating to cruise missiles," said the F.B.I. agent in charge of the investigation, "then we're going to have ask Congress for antimissile weaponry to protect the lives of innocent citizens and the Bureau's agents."

EIGHTEEN

RALPH Malzone struggled up from sleep like a man clawing his way out of an immense, cloying, suffocating ball of cotton candy. He was still half dreaming of childhood guilts and terrors while the rational side of his brain was telling him to open his eyes and wake up.

It was not easy. He was physically exhausted and emotionally spent. But with a supreme effort of will he unglued his gummy eyes and focused blearily on the ceiling panels of off-white acoustical tile.

For long minutes he lay unmoving, almost afraid to look about him. Usually he sprang out of bed full of vigor, ready to start the new day. But he was not home in his bare little studio apartment now, he was aboard the cruise ship.

His heart skipped a beat. He was not in his own cabin, either.

With a mixture of dread and joy he slowly turned his head. Scarlet Dean lay sound asleep beside him, a sweet smile of bliss curving her red lips.

It's true! Ralph gasped to himself. It wasn't a dream. It really happened.

175

He stared at Scarlet, half-covered by a twisted bedsheet, her blazing red hair flowing across the pillow like molten lava.

It really happened, Ralph repeated to himself, so incredulous that he still could only half believe what he saw and remembered. He squeezed his eyes shut and tried to picture Lori's face. She was the one he truly loved. He had betrayed her. Even though she had no inkling of his unswerving love for her, he had betrayed her. Guilt. Sin. How many Hail Marys would he have to say for this?

But Lori's face would not come into focus for him. He saw her vaguely, but then her features melted and changed into the beautiful, willing, giving face of Scarlet Dean. Ralph popped his eyes open. Yes, it was her. She was really there. This was her cabin, and they had spent the night doing things that Ralph had only fantasized about.

He studied Scarlet's face. Until last night he had thought her to be unfeeling, calculating, a hard-hearted bitch whose only interest was her career. A flame-haired ice princess. Eyes as cold and shrewd as a snake's.

Now he wanted her to open those eyes, so that he could gaze into them while she gazed into his.

Then a horrifying thought caught him. She was drunk. It was all a mistake. Or—worse still—she's trying to use me.

For what? Why would she do that? Ralph sat up and tried to shake the cobwebs from his head. He turned back and stared at the sleeping woman. I love you, Red, he admitted silently. I love you.

As quietly as he could, Ralph got out of the bed and started searching for his clothes. They had been thrown all over the cabin, as if they had exploded off his body.

Scarlet Dean opened her eyes and saw the sinewy form of the man she loved. Without moving she watched him gathering up his clothes. She smiled inwardly at the bite marks on his naked chest and felt a glow deep inside her that she had never known before.

Far, far off in a remote region of her brain a voice—her

own—was warning her that this man was nothing more to her than a chemical dependency. Scarlet heard the voice and understood what it was saying. She remembered the pheromone spray and the accident on the dance floor.

So what? she asked herself. This is what I've wanted all my life: a man who loves me and whom I can love, completely, endlessly, forever. The rest of life is meaningless. This wiry redheaded guy is my life.

He had found almost all his clothes and was holding them in a rumpled, tangled mess in one hand as he tiptoed toward the bathroom. There was a puzzled, little-boy expression on his face. He had found only one of his shoes, she realized.

"It's under the bed, I think," Scarlet said in a lazy, happy, sultry voice.

"Oh!" He seemed startled. But then he grinned at her. "Good morning."

"Good evening," she countered.

"I . . . uh . . ."

But Scarlet merely stretched her bare arms out to him and he dropped his clothes in a heap and came back to bed with her.

Lori and Carl, who had spent a chaste and miserable night in their separate cabins, as usual, met for breakfast. As usual, he ordered bacon and eggs, she asked for yogurt and honey.

The dining salon was almost full and buzzing with three stories: P. T.'s dramatic entrance in the bar lounge last evening, Scarlet Dean and Ralph Malzone scurrying away arm in arm at the end of the evening, and the spectacular fireworks display off on the horizon around two in the morning.

"Woody says it looked like something exploding," Lori said to Carl as she dipped a spoon into the honey-covered yogurt.

He shrugged. "Somebody getting an early start on the Fourth of July, I guess."

Looking around the tables of the crowded salon, Lori said, "I don't see Ralph or Scarlet."

"Maybe they jumped ship."

With a smirk, Lori said, "They way they hurried off last night, I think they jumped each other."

Carl felt his face redden.

She smiled at him and patted his hand, which raised his temperature even more. "Ralph is supposed to be at the sales conference this morning . . . I wonder if he's going to make it on time."

"I don't see Mrs. Bee, either," said Carl.

"She usually has breakfast in her stateroom. She'll be at the conference. She never misses a sales meeting."

But when ten o'clock came, neither Mrs. Bunker, Ralph Malzone, nor Scarlet Dean was present. No one knew quite what to do, except that they all knew better than to ring their respective cabins. So the meeting was postponed until two in the afternoon.

Carl went off happily to his workshop, where he spent the morning in conference with the factory in Mexico where the Cyberbook units were being manufactured. Lori took a thick manuscript up to the top deck, ensconced herself on a lounge chair, and spent the morning doing what she was not allowed to do in the office: reading.

Woody Balogna also made use of the "free" morning. He called all the sales representatives together for an informal meeting in the forecastle lounge. Subject: mutiny.

The forecastle lounge was the smallest of the several lounges aboard the *New Amsterdam*. It was decorated in a "nautical" motif: ropes and nets looped around the portholes, fake buoys hanging from the ceiling low enough for the taller sales people to bump their heads. The lounge was furnished with a few small sofas and deep plush chairs, all in bilious shades of blue-green, plus a built-in bar and a spinet piano—both closed at this time of the morning.

Because it was up forward in the ship, the lounge rose and sank with each bite of the *New Amsterdam*'s bow into the sea's swelling waves. It felt to the assembled sales folk who crowded into the rather small compartment as if they were jammed in an elevator that could not make up its mind; it rose a few floors, then sank a few floors. The motion, the press of bodies in the overcrowded cabin, and the fact that somehow the air-conditioning was not working, quickly turned several of the sales people a sickly shade of green.

Including Woody Balogna. But despite the queasiness of his stomach, he called the meeting to order.

"Okay, quiet down," he said, trying to keep his eyes off the portholes that showed the horizon rising and falling, rising and falling.

"I don't feel so good," said one of the women sales reps.

"You're gonna feel a lot worse if we let the Bunkers put this Cyberbooks deal through," Woody snapped.

"So what do we do?"

"Yeah. What *can* we do—go on strike?"

"Something better than that," said Woody, struggling manfully to hold down his breakfast.

"Such as?"

"What does any red-blooded American do when somebody's tryin' to screw him?"

"Hire a hit man."

"Wait for them to fire you so you can collect your severance pay and pension."

"Relax and enjoy it."

His face growing greener by the millisecond, Woody waved down their asinine cracks. "Nah, you dummies. We sue the bastards."

"Sue?"

"Who?"

"Bunker Books, that's who."

"The Boss?"

"The company?"

"Mr. Bunker?"

"That's right," Woody snarled. "They wanna put in this Cyberbooks thing, right? Get rid of all the distributors, wholesalers, jobbers—all our customers, right? Next thing you know they'll get rid of the bookstores, too. And you know what they'll get rid of after that?''

''What?''

''Us, that's what!''

''But Mrs. Bee said—''

''I don't give a damn what she said! Once they got these friggin' automatic books coming out, they won't need us. Out we'll go, out into the cold on our bare asses.''

''She wouldn't do that!''

''The hell she wouldn't. And even if *she* wouldn't, P. T. would. So we sue the bastards.''

''About what?''

''About Cyberbooks, of course.''

''But how can . . .''

''It can't be done—can it?''

''What do we sue them for?''

Woody could feel the burning remains of breakfast searing up his throat. Still, he managed to say, ''Don't worry about that. We can always find some lawyer who'll find some reason for suing.''

The sales staff stared at one another, stunned.

''Well?'' Woody demanded. ''Anybody got a better idea?''

Total silence.

''Then we sue!''

For a moment nobody moved. Then suddenly, like a startled pack of lemmings, they broke for the double doors of the lounge and raced for the ship's railing. Woody stood alone in the empty lounge, satisfied that he had done the right thing. Then he threw up on the bilious blue-green carpeting.

P. Curtis Hawks sat alone in his grandiose office. It had been stripped bare. The electronics console, the conference table, the pool table, even his desk and beautiful leather swivel chair had been removed, sent on their way to (ugh!) Brooklyn. The teak panelling had been torn from the walls. The lighting fixtures had been taken from the ceiling. The carpeting from the floors. There was nothing in this room that he had once loved so dearly except a single cardboard carton, big enough to hold exactly two dozen Webb Press books.

Hawks stood at the window, breathing his final silent farewell to the grand view that once had been his. Now all he had to look forward to was a tiny slit of a window that looked out on a trash-to-energy powerplant. The plastic pacifier in his teeth tasted sour, bitter.

He heard the door behind him open, stealthily, as if a burglar or assassin was trying to slip in unnoticed.

"Come right in, Gunther," he called without turning from his magnificent view. He knew it was Axhelm, worse than any burglar or assassin.

"The movers have finished, except for this single packing case here on the floor," said the Axe in his usual precise, icy tones.

Hawks turned toward him, and made his lips smile. Axhelm was wearing his customary dark turtleneck and slacks, but this time he had a Luftwaffe-blue sports coat over them.

"That package isn't going to Brooklyn. It's a present, from me to you."

"A . . . present?" For the first time since Hawks had met the sonofabitch, Axhelm seemed surprised, unsure of himself.

"A going-away present, you might say." Hawks stepped toward the innocent-looking cardboard box, resting all alone on the vast empty expanse of the bare plywood flooring.

"This is unexpected."

It was laughable, watching the stiff-backed Axhelm trying to figure out how he should behave in the face of a personal gift. Hawks could see a shadow of suspicion in those cold gray Nordic eyes. *He's wondering if I'm trying to bribe him,* Hawks realized, *but he knows there's nothing left for me to bribe him about. He's ruined my life and wrecked my office. His work here is finished. The company will be out of business in another six months; he's seen to that.*

Just before they took away his computer (and the desk on which it rested), Hawks had run a check on Webb's sales projections. They were down. Shockingly down. Almost to zero. In his zeal to cut costs, Axhelm had decreed that the company stop buying new books and sell only the books it had already published. Like Scribley's and many another publishing house that depended too much on its backlist, Webb Press was on a steep, terminal dive into bankruptcy.

"Open it up," Hawks said as genially as he could manage.

Still somewhat suspicious, Axhelm muttered, "It looks like a carton of our books."

"Very perceptive of you," said Hawks smoothly. "That's exactly what it looks like."

For an awkward moment neither man moved. Then Axhelm slowly bent to one knee and pulled from his back pocket a Swiss army knife. I might have known he'd have one on him, thought Hawks. The model with *all* the attachments, even the AM/FM radio and earplug.

Deftly Axhelm sliced the tape holding down the carton's lid. He pulled it open and stared into his "present."

Frowning, he dug into the carton and came up with a handful of loose book pages.

"I don't understand. . . ."

Standing well away from the carton and quickly whipping a triply guaranteed Japanese filter over his face, Hawks replied with a vengeful chortle of glee.

Axhelm looked up at Hawks, his face a portrait of puzzlement. He started to say something, but suddenly his jaw went slack. His entire body sagged, as if every muscle in him had gone limp.

From behind his filter, Hawks crowed, "The goddamned glue you made us buy, you cheap asshole! It turns into a psychedelic gas! Take a *deep* breath, shithead! A *deep* breath!"

Axhelm was indeed breathing deeply, a blissful relaxed smile on his normally cold face. He plunged both hands into the carton and pulled a double handful of loose pages to his face, inhaling them as if they were the most fragrant flowers in the world.

Leaping to his feet, he flung the pages toward the ceiling.

"At last!" he shrieked. "At last I'm free! *Free!*"

Hawks watched with beady eyes as the Axe capered across the bare office, dancing like a Bavarian peasant at a maypole.

"I can sing! I can dance!" the erstwhile management consultant shouted. "All my life I have wanted to be like the immortal Gene Kelly! I'm si-i-ingin' in the rain . . ."

Axhelm was still gibbering and dancing (with a total lack of grace) when Weldon W. Weldon wheeled his power chair into what was left of Hawks's office. Hawks had, of course, arranged for the Old Man to come to his office at precisely this moment. The timing was perfect.

Crunching down viciously on his pacifier, Hawks took the filter from his face and let the astounded CEO of Tarantula watch his vaunted management consultant stumble and lurch up and down the bare office floor boards. The look on the Old Man's face was priceless.

Christ, said Hawks to himself, as happy as the first time he had shot a rabbit, if looks could kill the Axe would be stone cold dead.

AUTUMN,
Book III

THE BUYER ▬▬▬▬▬▬

THE first snow of November was gently sifting past
the window of Dee Dee Lowe's office as she held court. It was
a gray day in Des Moines, but the chief buyer for Cleaveland
Book Stores was dressed in bright oranges and flaming reds.
There were even brilliant yellow ribbons in her thick gray hair.
Her face was tanned and taut; she looked as if she had just returned
from a trip to the Bahamas. Actually, she seldom left her office
and had not been on vacation since the entire Cleaveland chain
was taken over by Tarantula Enterprises, many years earlier. Her
good looks were a combination of cosmetic surgery, makeup,
and the tanning parlor in the shopping mall across the road from
Cleaveland's offices.

Before her desk, four dozen sales people were seated in neat
rows of folding chairs. This was Dee Dee's monthly meeting,
where she deigned to allow the sales people into her office and
let them show her their companies' wares for the month.

Each sales person, male or female, had a laptop computer open
on his or her knees. Each computer was plugged into a complex
electronics console that squatted on the floor next to Dee Dee's

desk like a square fireplug. The tangle of wires among the folding chairs was so fierce that Dee Dee had put a printed sign on her desk:

CLEAVELAND BOOK STORES INC. IS NOT RESPONSIBLE FOR INJURIES TO VISITING SALES PERSONNEL DUE TO ACCIDENTS OR OTHER NATURAL OR MAN-MADE CAUSES.

Not a word was being spoken. Each sales person was busily tapping on his or her keyboard, relaying glowing information about his or her latest batch of books into the central Cleaveland Stores computer.

In the old days the salesmen—they had all been men when Dee Dee had started in this job—the salesmen would personally show her the information on each and every individual title they were trying to sell. They would show her a color proof of the cover, statistics about the author's previous books, monumental lies about how much money and effort the publisher was going to put into advertising and promotion for this individual title, tremendous whoppers about how wonderful this title was and how it was going to hit the top of the best-seller lists the instant it was released.

"But they can't *all* be best-sellers," Dee Dee would respond, smiling slyly.

The salesmen knew that only one out of a thousand of their titles would be successful. And they knew that if Dee Dee bought a hundred thousand copies or so for the vast chain of Cleaveland Stores, that particular title would be among the precious few. So they wined her and dined her and, when she felt like it, bedded her. Four times salesmen even wedded her. None of them took, although she now wore an impressive array of diamonds on her clawlike fingers.

But those were the good old days, Dee Dee thought with a sigh. Now it's all done by computers. We don't even need to have the sales people come to my office at all, she realized. They could pump their information into my computer system from their own offices, or even from New York.

But if they did it that way, she would not get to see any of the sales people, ever. And she clung to these monthly meetings because, after the computers had completed their intercourse, the sales folk—being sales people—hung around complimenting Dee Dee on her good looks, her great taste in clothes, her incredible business acumen, her deep love for literature.

Actually, Dee Dee had not read a book since she had graduated college, so many years ago that she dreaded even thinking about it.

Every month the sales people seemed to get younger, she said to herself sadly. None of them ever makes a pass at me anymore—except for old lechers like Woody Baloney, and even his leering suggestions were strictly routine these days. I wonder if he can still get it up? A couple of the saleswomen had hinted at availability, but Dee Dee felt she was too old to experiment.

She sighed as she looked out at the office full of bowed heads. All those eager young kids bent over their laptop computers instead of kissing my ass. No, the business isn't what it used to be.

Deep down in the basement of the Cleaveland Stores building, behind electronically locked steel fireproof doors, sat a single Nisei woman in front of a bank of four dozen display screens. The screens cast an eerie flickering light across the young woman's blankly impassive face. They curved around her single swivel chair like the compound eye of some giant insect examining her. But in truth, *she* was examining *them*. Each screen flickered for a bare three seconds with the cover proof and other data on each of the titles the sales people were pumping into the central Cleaveland computer. Then the next title came on. This one lonely woman's task was to select which titles Cleaveland would actually buy.

For the vaunted Cleaveland computer system could not actually decide which titles to buy, out of the thousands presented each month. No automated expert system or decision-tree program could handle the avalanche of incoming data that the sales people unloosed each month. So the entire international chain of bookstores depended on this one solitary young woman to make the selections. Each month she sat on that chair, watched the madly flickering screens, and made selections that determined the fate of most of the books published in North America.

Her right hand gripped a knobbed joystick while the fingers of her left flew madly across a small keyboard. With her left hand she indicated to the computer which screen she was glancing at; if she pushed the joystick *up* that meant the book would be bought by the chain, the amount of upward push indicated the number of copies bought—ten thousand, a hundred thousand, a million. If she pushed the stick *down* the book was bypassed, doomed to oblivion.

Her qualifications for this key position? She had been, as a teenager, the champion video game player of California.

NINETEEN

Even with the lawsuit looming over them, and the sales force virtually on strike as far as Cyberbooks was concerned, Bunker Books staggered along, trying to stay solvent.

Lori Tashkajian was in her cubbyhole office that same dreary November morning. The storm that was bringing snow to Iowa was already smothering the New York skyline with gray tendrils of fog and spatterings of drizzle. Mountains of manuscripts still littered Lori's tiny office. But she ignored them as she pondered over the data on her computer display screen.

According to the computer's program, it would be foolhardy to print more than five thousand copies of Capt. Clanker's novel about the Battle of Midway. The title for the book was still under discussion at the editorial meetings. Every one of the editors except Lori thought that *Midway Diary* would not sell, although Ralph Malzone (the only one with sales experience at the conferences) liked the title well enough. Currently its working title was *Forbidden Warrior's Love,* which Lori hated. But at least it was better than *Pacific Lust,* which she had narrowly averted, after several screaming matches.

The computer was saying that, no matter what the book's title, they could expect to sell no more than two or three thousand copies of the hardcover. That meant printing no more than five thousand.

Lori frowned at the glowing screen. Dammit, this novel deserves better than that! But it had been cursed with the strategy of minimal success. The editorial board had decided to take no chances with a first novel by an unknown writer. No money was to be risked on publicity or advertising. No effort made to sell the book to reluctant buyers in bookstore chains or major distribution centers. Minimum success. Spend as little as possible and "let the book find its own level of sales." The level would be on the bottom, Lori knew from bitter experience.

If only she could get to Mrs. Bunker and make a personal pitch for the novel. She *knew* it could sell much better, maybe even make a run at the best-seller lists, if they would give it some support.

But Mrs. Bee was hardly in the office these days. Ever since the cruise—and the lawsuit whipped on them by the sales force—Mrs. Bunker had spent more time out of the office than in it. Strange, though. Even though the company was in dire trouble, with sales down and morale even lower, with a lawsuit by its own sales force threatening to close down Bunker Books entirely, Mrs. Bee seemed smiling, radiant, even girlishly happy on those increasingly rare occasions when she did make an appearance in the office.

Then Lori's thoughts turned to Carl and his Cyberbooks project. The outlook for him was bleak. Very bleak.

But Carl Lewis was whistling while he worked. Hunched in front of his own computer display screen in the workshop/office he had made out of the apartment the Bunkers were paying for, Carl traced out the circuitry for an improved Cyberbook model that would reduce the costs of the hand-held reader by at least ten percent.

He leaned back in the little typing chair and let out a satisfied sigh. Yep, we can make it cheaper. The cheaper it is, the more poor people will be able to afford Cyberbooks. Carl had tried, during the last few months, to interest Mrs. Bunker in a program of giving away a few hundred thousand Cyberbook readers to the children of urban ghettos. Mrs. Bee had given him a puzzled look and a vague smile instead of a definite answer.

His phone buzzed. Carl rolled in his little chair to the desk and tapped the phone keyboard. Ralph Malzone's long-jawed face appeared on the screen.

"Hey, are we going to lunch or are you on a diet?"

"Lunch! I forgot all about it!"

"Okay. I'm down at Pete's. Meet me at the bar."

"I'll be there in ten minutes."

Carl was damp and chilled by the time he entered Pete's Tavern. The drizzle had not looked serious from his hotel window, but walking three blocks with no umbrella or raincoat had not done his tweed jacket much good.

"Where's the duck?" Ralph asked him, grinning from behind a schooner of beer.

"Duck?" Carl wondered.

"You look like a retriever that's just come out of the water."

Carl laughed, a little self-consciously, and ordered a double sherry to warm himself.

They took their drinks into the crowded dining room beyond the bar and ordered lunch.

"You're still working on the gadget?" Ralph asked, his face more serious now.

"Sure. Why not?"

"The trial starts next week."

"So?"

Ralph leaned forward, bringing his face close to Carl's. "So if Woody and his pals win this suit, the court will enjoin Bunker to stop all work on Cyberbooks."

Despite a slight pang of fear in his gut, Carl replied, "That can't happen."

"Oh no?"

"What judge in his right mind would stop a whole new industry just because some salesmen are afraid it will force them to learn a slightly different way of doing their work?"

Justice Hanson Hapgood Fish was a man of rare perceptions. So rarefied were his perceptions, in fact, that some whispered they actually were hallucinations.

He sat in his chambers, behind the massive mahogany desk that had belonged to Malcolm (Malevolent Mal) F. Fortunata until the unhappy day when the Feds had carted Mal away for seventeen counts of bribery, obstructing justice, and aiding and abetting organized crime. The room was large, panelled in dark wood where it was not lined with glass-enclosed bookcases. The leather chairs and solitary long couch were heavy, massive, uninviting. Thick curtains flanked the windows. A gloomy chamber, dreary even on the sunniest day.

Justice Fish's desk was neurotically bare, except for the inevitable computer display screen, blank and silent. In its empty screen, the judge saw his own face reflected: totally bald, tight-lipped and narrow-eyed, aging pale skin stretched over the skull so tightly that every blue vein could be seen throbbing sluggishly.

He was engaged in his morning ritual. First the mental exercises: reciting the logarithmic tables of his ancient school trigonometry text, then leaning his head back against the padding of his oversized chair and recalling from his memory the looks of every woman in his courtroom the previous day. There had been only two, both of them aging and lumpy. Nothing had happened in his courtroom except the sentencing of a miscreant embezzler. But he enjoyed replaying before his mind's eye the stunned look on the man's face when he sentenced him to ninety-nine years without probation.

The damned superior court will lighten his sentence, he thought grouchily. But still, that look on his face was worth it.

Now he rose slowly from his chair and went to the nearer of the two windows in his office. He moved carefully, with all due deliberation, as much from the desire to appear dramatically dignified as from the arthritis that plagued both his knees. The window was so filthy that he could barely make out the grimy gray City Hall across the way. Standing there, Justice Fish took three deep breaths. Never two, nor four. Never with the window open, either: he knew that fresh air, in Manhattan, could kill.

Now he returned, still with self-conscious dignity, to his desk and lowered himself onto his imposing chair. Reaching out a long lean finger that barely trembled, he touched the computer's keypad to see what his next case would be.

Bunker *vs*. Bunker. A publishing house's sales force was suing its employer over some new contraption that they felt would eliminate their jobs. Hm. Labor relations. Always a thorny issue.

Pressing keypads carefully, Justice Fish called up the secret, coded program that only he could summon from the computer because only he knew the special code word that accessed it: *Polaris*.

It was an astrology program, and the aging judge pecked at the keyboard, asking how he should decide the case he would soon be judging. The computer blinked and hummed, then gave him an answer.

Justice Fish nodded, satisfied. Now he knew what his decision would be. Now he did not have to listen to the evidence that the various lawyers would present over the next long, boring weeks. It was all decided. Sifting evidence and weighing the slick arguments lawyers dished up to him was just a waste of time, he felt. The stars told him what his decision would be, so he could relax and fantasize about the women in his courtroom without the fear of making a wrong decision. Pleased, he shut down the computer and leaned back in his chair for his morning nap.

MURDER SIX

DETECTIVE Lieutenant Jack Moriarty was not merely a good cop, he was a brave man. Brave in two ways: he had physical courage, the ability to stand up to a man with a gun or a gang of street toughs; he also had the courage of his convictions, the strength to play his hunches even when they seemed crazy.

Shortly after the murder of retired detective Miles Archer, several months earlier, Moriarty had come to certain conclusions about the Retiree Murders. The computer records of each victim hinted at the possibility of a motive that seemed so farfetched, so tenuous, that only a man as convinced of himself as Moriarty would dare to act on it. But act he did. He bought stock in a multinational conglomerate corporation called, of all things, Tarantula Enterprises.

It had not been an easy thing to do. Tarantula shares were expensive, more than $1,000 each. And the stockbroker he had contacted told him that not much Tarantula stock was available on the open market.

"Most of it is held by other corporations," the broker had

said, sniffling so much that Moriarty began to look for traces of white powder on his fingertips. "The big boys hold it and sell it in enormous blocks. It's not traded in onesy-twoseys very much."

Moriarty had assured him that he only wanted a few shares. He could not afford more; twenty shares cleaned out his savings account.

For months he waited patiently, even buying single shares now and then as they became available. Nothing had happened. His hunch had gone cold. The Retiree Murderer refused to strike at anyone, let alone an active police detective who held a grand total of twenty-four shares of Tarantula Enterprises, Ltd.

On that same foggy, drizzly day in November, Moriarty learned that his hunch was right. At the cost of his life.

He was on a routine call to question a witness to a liquor store holdup in the Village when it happened.

Moriarty stepped out of his vintage Pinto (the auto was his only discernible vice) in front of the liquor store in question. The street was slick from the chilly rain. Only a few people were passing by, and they all were hidden beneath umbrellas. Bunching his tired old trenchcoat around his middle, Moriarty got as far as the liquor store's front entrance.

He felt a sharp jab in his back, then a horrible burning sensation flamed through his whole body. He had stopped breathing before he hit the sidewalk.

The umbrella-toting pedestrians stepped over his prostrate body and continued on their way.

TWENTY

THAT evening, the cold November rain gave way
to the season's first snowfall. It was nothing much, as snowstorms
go, merely a half inch or less of wet mushy flakes that turned to
black slush almost as soon as it hit the streets. But the evening
newscasts were agog with the story of the storm: coiffed and
pancaked anchorpersons quivered with excitement while reporters
at various strategic locations around the city—the airports, the
train and bus terminals, the Department of Public Works head-
quarters, the major highway bottlenecks—stood out in the wet
snow and solemnly reported how the city *almost* had been hit by
a crisis.

"Although the traffic appears to be flowing smoothly through
the Lincoln Tunnel," said the bescarfed young lady on Channel 4, "it wouldn't take much more snow to turn this evening's
homeward rush into a commuter's nightmare." Behind her,
streams of buses proceeded without a hitch into the tunnel.

Channel 2's stalwart investigative reporter was at the airport
offices of the U.S. Weather Service, where he had collared a
wimpy-looking meteorologist.

"Why didn't the Weather Bureau provide warnings of this potential disaster?" he demanded.

The wimp's eyebrows rose almost to his receding hairline. "What disaster? You call a half-inch snow a disaster? The Blizzard of '88 this ain't!"

Still, all the channels buzzed with stories about the snow, the most inventive being a satellite report from a ski resort in Vermont, where the slopes were still green with grass.

The news of the storm smothered a human-interest story about a city police detective who had been the apparent victim of a senseless, purposeless murder. Thanks to the miracles of modern medicine, though, the detective had been revived from a state of clinical death and was recuperating in St. Vincent's Hospital, in the Village.

By morning the snow had been obliterated from the city by the ceaseless pounding of millions of buses, trucks, taxicabs, limousines, and pedestrians' feet. The Department of Public Works had not had to call out a single snow plow or digging crew. Still the trains ran two hours late, and the morning backup of traffic at the bridges and tunnels was ferocious.

Ferocious was the mood, also, of P. Curtis Hawks as he rode in his limousine through the crowded city streets to the annual board meeting of Tarantula Enterprises, Ltd. Vinnie DeAngelo, the Beast from the East, slept with the fishes ever since the fiasco of the cruise missile. Weldon W. Weldon, senile and crippled, still ran Tarantula from his infested jungle of an office. Webb Press—what was left of it—was now located in Brooklyn, in a building that had once been a fruit-and-vegetable warehouse. The place still smelled of onions.

This meeting is the shoot-out, Hawks told himself. High noon. There isn't room enough in this corporation for the Old Man and me. One of us has got to go, and it's not going to be me. He shifted the pacifier from one side of his mouth to the other and sucked in his gut. Got to make a good impression on the board of directors, he knew. Got to make them see that the Old Man has run Webb into the ground.

It would not be easy. But Hawks smiled a bitter, cold smile when he thought about his secret weapon. *I'll pin the Old Man's balls to the table, or what's left of them. And his own creature, Gunther God-Damned Axhelm, is going to do the job for me.*

"All rise."

From the front row of seats in the courtroom, Carl Lewis got to his feet together with everyone else as Justice Hanson H. Fish walked slowly, solemnly, in his black robes to his high chair behind the banc.

Lori stood beside Carl on one side, Ralph and Scarlet Dean were on his other side. Mrs. Bunker was at the table where the defense attorneys—all five of them—sat. Both Mrs. Bee and Scarlet were decked out in the latest fashion: the toothpaste-tube look. Their dresses were tight enough to asphyxiate, and shirred, ruched, pleated—wrinkled—so that they looked like the last moments of a toothpaste tube that had been squeezed to death. Skirts were midthigh and so tight that they could barely walk. Alba Bunker wore all white, of course, while Scarlet Dean was completely in red. Between them they wore enough jewelry to ransom a planeload of OPEC oil ministers.

Lori, as usual, ignored the weekly fashion and had dressed in a sensible plaid suit with a light green turtleneck beneath the jacket. Her skirt was knee-length, her jewelry confined to a small pair of earrings and matching copper bracelet and necklace.

Woody Balogna wore his best suit, which still looked ten years old and badly in need of a cleaning. He sat at the table for the plaintiff, with a single odd-looking attorney who represented the sales force.

Woody's lawyer was dressed in a deep blue velvet leisure suit, the kind that had gone out of style with Alan Alda, countless ages ago. A western-type string tie was pulled up against his prominent Adam's apple, cinched by a lump of turquoise big enough to be used in a shot-put contest. The man's wide-brimmed cowboy hat rested on the table before him, next to a battered slim leather case that looked like the saddle bag of an old Pony Express rider. Apparently it contained all the notes and papers he had brought to the courtroom. He had a rugged, seamed, weatherbeaten face and long flowing dark hair with a wild streak of silver in it. He looked as if he had not shaved that morning; his jaw was covered with grayish stubble.

Mrs. Bunker's five defense attorneys all wore traditional gray flannels and Ivy League ties painted on their starched white shirts. Their faces were shaved clean and scrubbed glowing pink. They looked young, confident, yet serious. Their briefcases were huge and thicker than parachute packs. Mrs. Bee looked nervous, though, and kept glancing over her shoulder toward the door that opened onto the corridor as if the one thought in her mind was to get up and flee from the courtroom.

Carl thought the courtroom was strangely empty, considering the importance of the case. No news reporters, no TV lights, hardly anybody in the visitors' pews at all except for the few Bunker employees and himself. And no jury. Both sides had waived their right to a jury trial; this case would be decided by Justice H. H. Fish alone, in his impartial wisdom. And then appealed, of course, by the loser. The lawyers saw the prospects of many years of high-priced work ahead of them.

While the bailiff read the title of the case and the charges, Carl studied the judge sitting up there above them all. His utterly bald head looked like a death's skull glaring down at them. Carl felt his easy confidence in the unassailable righteousness of the Cyberbooks project begin to melt away under the baleful glower of the judge's implacable eyes.

"Motions?" asked the judge.

One of the defense attorneys popped to his feet. They all looked so much alike that Carl thought they might be clones.

"Move to dismiss," said the attorney in a clear, crisp voice. "This suit is without grounds and totally irrelevant. . . ."

"Motion denied," snapped Justice Fish.

The young lawyer looked surprised. He sat down.

"Opening statements," the judge said. "Plaintiff?"

The westerner gangled to his feet. He was tall and lean as a fencepost.

"What we've got here," he drawled, "is a clear case of a deliberate, intentional—I might even say evil and pernicious— attempt to eliminate the jobs of a whole flock of hardworking, loyal, and faithful employees, and to substitute in their place a heartless, soulless, newfangled machine whose only purpose is to make money for the greedy employers of these poor and long-suffering working men and women."

The lawyer's words shocked Carl. How could he describe Cyberbooks that way? It wasn't true. None of what he was saying was true.

But then he saw the expression on the judge's face. A benign smile, such as saint might bestow on a nativity scene.

We're in deep trouble, Carl belatedly realized.

Detective Lieutenant Jack Moriarty opened his eyes and saw a smooth, featureless expanse of pastel blue. I must have made it to heaven, he said to himself.

Then he heard a faint humming sound, and a rhythmic beeping. He tried to turn his head and found that there was no difficulty with it. It's not heaven, he realized as he focused on a bank of electronic monitoring instruments, their screens showing a steady heartbeat and breathing rate. He felt slightly disappointed, immensely relieved. I'm in an intensive care ward. His detective's brain concluded it was St. Vincent's Hospital, in the heart of Greenwich Village.

For an immeasurable length of time he lay in the bed unmoving, reliving in his mind those last few minutes in front of the liquor store. Whoever had attacked him, it was no random act of violence. The perpetrator knew who he was, and had followed him to the liquor store. Of that Moriarty was certain. It was the Retiree Murderer; the method of operation fit, and so did the fact that the victim—himself—owned a few shares of Tarantula Enterprises, Ltd.

"Welcome back to the living!"

Moriarty turned his head toward the heartily cheerful voice and saw a grossly overweight black man in a white doctor's smock with a day's stubble on his fleshy, wattled face. He's got more chins than the Chinatown phone directory, Moriarty said to himself.

"I am Dr. Kildaire," said the medic in a lilting Jamaican accent. "And no jokes, if you please."

For all his unlikely appearance, Kildaire was a first-rate physician. Moriarty learned that he had been clinically dead when the ambulance had brought him in.

"A very rare poison, the kind you only see in the tropics. Distilled from the sap of a jungle flower known in Brazil as the Rita Hayworth orchid, for some obscure reason. Lucky for you I spent my military service in Central America; I bet I'm the only M.D. this side of the Panama Canal who'd recognize the symptoms of Rita Hayworth poisoning."

They had restarted Moriarty's heart and detoxed his bloodstream. Brought him back to life, quite literally. Moriarty mumbled his embarrassed thanks, then asked how the poison was administered.

"The murderer jabbed you with a sharp instrument, right between your shoulder blades. Might have been a needle coated with the toxin. Might even have been a thorn from the plant itself. Did you get a look at him?"

Moriarty closed his eyes briefly and relived the scene. Yes, the sharp pain in his back. He was falling to the sidewalk—no, the entryway of the liquor store. It was all going black. But he had turned his head to glance over his shoulder and he saw a man in a blue trenchcoat, shapeless brimmed hat pulled down low, umbrella in one hand. For the barest instant he had looked into the eyes of his murderer.

"I saw him," Moriarty said. "I'd know him if I see him again. I'd know those eyes of his anywhere."

* * *

In all honesty, Weldon W. Weldon had not expected to be stabbed in the back. He sat in his powered wheelchair at the head of the long gleaming conference table and listened with growing incredulity to Curtis Hawks's tirade.

". . . and with all due respect," Hawks was telling the board of directors, the blistering acid of scalding irony dripping from his words, "in this time of crisis we need a CEO who is physically and *mentally* sharp enough to repel the pirates who are trying to take over this corporation."

Hawks was pacing up and down the length of the long polished table, forcing the directors who sat on that side of it to turn in their chairs to follow him. The head of Webb Press was wearing a military-style suit vaguely reminiscent of a World War II general named Patton. Even down to his glossy calf-length cavalry boots and the fake ivory-handled revolvers buckled to his waddling hips.

"Snotty ungrateful sonofabitch," Weldon muttered to himself. I streamline his operation for him, get Webb Press ready to shift over to electronic publishing, and he rewards me with this stab in the back.

". . . and to show you just what kind of senility we're dealing with here"—Hawks had raised his voice to a near shout—"let me introduce you to the vaunted efficiency expert that was foisted on me, the superbrain who was given carte blanche by our beloved CEO to wipe out most of Webb Press's staff and move our base of operations out of Manhattan altogether!"

He snapped his fingers, and the flunky sitting next to the conference room's only entrance jumped to his feet and opened the leather-padded door. There was a slight commotion in the outer room, and then two burly men in white uniforms led in Gunther Axhelm, who was securely wrapped in a straitjacket.

Gasps went around the long conference table. Cigars fell out of hanging mouths. Pouchy eyes widened. They all knew Axhelm, by reputation if nothing else. They knew of his Prussian precision and the ruthless thoroughness of his operations. What they now saw was a wild man, red-rimmed eyes and drooling maniacal grin, straitjacket stained with spittle, baggy gray hospital drawers and bare feet. Even his crew-cut blond hair seemed askew.

"This is the result of breathing too much of the glue that he himself demanded we use in binding our books, instead of the glue we normally used. It has cost Webb Press roughly a hundred million dollars; it's cost Gunther Axhelm his sanity."

Of course, Hawks had made certain that Axhelm had all the glue he wanted to sniff in the private hospital where he had stashed the loopy Axe. That, and a steady diet of Gene Kelly videos.

Axhelm suddenly shouldered free of his two handlers and, with a deranged shriek, ran to the conference table and jumped atop it. Two directors tumbled backwards in their chairs and fell gracelessly to the floor. The others backed away in sudden fright.

But Gunther Axhelm meant them no harm. In his bare feet he capered along the table in a mad parody of tap dancing, the strap ends of his straitjacket flapping away, singing at the top of his lungs in a decidedly Teutonic accent, "Be a clown, be a clown, all the world loves a clown. . . ."

THE WRITER ━━━━━━━━━━

IN his miserable roach-infested room in the welfare hotel, the Writer pored over the current issue of *Publishers Weekly* that he had stolen from the local branch of the public library.

The State had stepped in and taken charge of his life. When the drugged-out staff of the warehouse had tried to burn the building down (with materials and helpful instructions from the management, incidentally), the apparatus of the State wheeled itself up in the form of (in order of appearance) Fire Department, Police Department, Bureau of Drug Enforcement, the Public Defender's Office, Department of Rehabilitation, Bureau of Unemployment, and the welfare offices of the state of New Jersey and the city of New York, borough of Queens.

Now he lived in a crumbling welfare hotel in Queens, detoxified, unemployed, and seething with an anger that seemed to grow hotter and deeper with every passing useless day.

But now it all focused down to a single point in space and time. For in his trembling hands he saw how and why it would all come together.

BUNKER SALES FORCE SUIT
OPENS IN FEDERAL COURT

The headline in *Publishers Weekly* caught his eye. Bunker Books. They were in a courtroom. All of them. The publisher, the editors. Out there in a public courtroom, where any member of the public could come in and see them, face to face.

With an immense effort of will, the Writer forced his hands to stop trembling so he could read the entire article and learn exactly where they would be and when.

As he finished reading, he looked up and saw a single ray of light shining through the filth that covered the room's only window. The shaft was blood red. Sunset.

The Writer smiled. Where can I get a gun? he asked himself.

TWENTY-ONE

IT was not easy being the son of Pandro T. Bunker. Junior sat in the last row of the half-empty courtroom, listening with only half his attention to the testimony being given up on the witness stand. No one sat near him; he had the entire pew of seats to himself. None of the sales people in the audience wanted to be seen sitting near the son of the publisher. And all of his dad's people, including his mom, were up in the front.

But Junior smiled to himself. They all think I'm just the owner's son, he told himself. They all think I'm a spoiled brat who doesn't know nothing and gets everything handed to him on a silver tray. I'll show them. I'll show them all. Even Mom and Dad.

Junior's work in the office, as a special assistant to the publisher, had not been terribly successful. Most of the editors either distrusted him as a snoop for his parents or belittled his intelligence. After weeks of being alternately ignored and avoided, he transferred to the sales department just in time for Woody's lawsuit to explode in everybody's face. Naturally, the sales people regarded him as a pariah.

But Junior leaned back on the hard wooden bench of the courtroom and grinned openly. I'm smarter than they think. I'm smarter than any of them.

Up on the witness stand, Woody Baloney was being questioned by the cowboy lawyer the sales department had brought in from Colorado.

"And what, in your professional estimation, will be the result of the Cyberbooks program?" asked the cowboy, his weathered, crinkle-eyed face looking serious and concerned.

"The result?" Woody said, glancing at the judge. "We'll all be tossed out on our butts, that's what the result will be!"

"Objection!" shouted three of the five defense clones in unison.

"Overruled," snapped the judge. "The witness will continue."

The lawyer prompted, "So this electronic book gadget, this . . . *thing* they call Cyberbooks, will result in the whole sales force being laid off?"

"That's right," said Woody.

"In your professional opinion," the lawyer amended.

"Uh-huh."

Junior slouched farther on the hard wooden pew. Mom and Dad have pinned everything they've got on this Cyberbooks idea, and the sales force is going to stop it cold. Then what happens? They can't fire Woody or anybody else; they'll be back in court before you could say "prejudice." They won't be able to work with Woody or the rest of the sales force; too much hard feeling.

No, Junior concluded, the company's doomed. Finished. Mom and Dad are going down the tubes.

Which only made him smile more. Because I've been smart enough to take the money I have and invest it wisely. In one of the biggest multinational, diversified corporations in the world. *My* fortune isn't going to depend on some crazy invention, or on a lawsuit by my own employees.

Two days earlier, P. T. Bunker, Jr., had taken every penny in his trust fund and sunk it into Tarantula Enterprises (Ltd.). He had not merely acted on his own, nor did he trust a stockbroker

with his money. Junior had first bought the latest computer investment program, and used his own office machine to examine
all the various possibilities of the stock market.

Tarantula Enterprises was a great investment, the computer
had told him. In order to fight off an unfriendly takeover bid,
Tarantula was buying its own stock back at inflated prices. Although this had removed most of the stock from the open market
and made the price for Tarantula shares artificially high, the
computer program predicted that the price would go even higher
as the takeover battle escalated. So Junior instructed his computer
to automatically buy whatever Tarantula stock was available, and
to keep on buying it until he told it to stop.

Glowing with self-satisfied pride, he told himself that he could
even retire right now and just live on the dividends.

Lt. Moriarty, meanwhile, was causing no end of anguish
among the staff tending the intensive care unit at St. Vincent's
Hospital.

The usual routine was to keep ICU patients calm and quiet,
sedated if necessary. Usually such patients were so sick or in-
capacitated by trauma that there was little trouble with them.
Generally the intensive care ward looked somewhat like a
morgue, except for the constant beepings and hums of monitoring
equipment. Except when there was an emergency, and then a
team of frantic doctors and nurses shouted and yelled at one
another, dragged in all sorts of heavy equipment, and even
pounded on the poor patient as if beating the wretch would force
him or her to get better.

No one knew how many times a screaming emergency at bed
A had resulted in heart failure at bed B. No one dared even to
think about it.

Moriarty was different, though. All the monitors showed that
he was in fine fettle, and since he had been in the hospital less
than twenty-four hours, the nurses could not even claim that he
was too weak to be allowed to get out of bed. But the hospital
rules were ironclad: no one got out of the intensive care ward

until their physician had okayed a transfer or release—and his insurance company had initiated payment for the bill.

Moriarty insisted that he was detoxed and feeling fine. They had removed the IV from his arm; the only wires connected to him were sensor probes pasted to various portions of his epidermis. He wanted *out*. But Dr. Kildaire was out for the day; he would not return until the midnight shift started. And the accounting department, its computer merrily tabulating hourly charges, absolutely refused to discharge a patient whose insurance was provided by the city.

Threatening bodily harm and a police investigation produced only partial results. The head ICU nurse, a slim Argentinean with a will of tempered steel, at last agreed to allow Moriarty to sit up and use a laptop computer.

"If you stay quiet and do not disturb the other patients," she added as her final part of the bargain.

Moriarty reluctantly agreed. He had to check out a thousand ideas that were buzzing through his head, and he needed access to the NYPD computer files to do it. The laptop was not as good as his own trusty office machine, but it was better than nothing.

For hours he tapped at its almost silent keys and examined the data flowing across the eerily blood-red plasma discharge screen. Yes, all of the victims had indeed been Tarantula stock owners; most of them had owned shares for years, decades. But he himself had only recently purchased a few shares. So new owners were just as vulnerable to the Retiree Murderer as old ones. The murders had nothing to do with being retired, the victims were owners of Tarantula stock who lived in New York.

Which meant that the murderer was connected in some way to Tarantula. And lived in New York. Or close enough to commute into town to commit the murders.

Pecking away at the keyboard, Moriarty used special police codes to gain access to the New York Stock Exchange files. What happened to the stock of the murder victims? Who was buying the shares?

It was impossible to trace the shares one for one, but there *was* a buyer for the shares of the murder victims. Within weeks after each murder, the victim's shares were sold—and bought immediately. But by whom? Tarantula shares were traded by the thousands every day of the week. Who was buying the shares of the murder victims?

For hours that question stumped Moriarty. Then he got an inspiration. He asked the NYSE computer if any one particular individual person was acquiring shares of Tarantula on a regular basis.

The stock exchange computer regarded corporations as individual persons, and gave Moriarty a long list of buyers that included corporations headquartered in New York, Tokyo, Messina, and elsewhere. It was almost entirely corporations, rather than human beings, who were regularly buying Tarantula stock.

Again Moriarty stared at a blank wall. But slowly it dawned on him that Tarantula Enterprises (Ltd.) was itself one of the largest regular buyers of its own stock. The corporation was buying back its stock wherever and whenever it could. Not an uncommon tactic when a company was trying to fend off an unfriendly takeover, and if Moriarty read the data correctly, Tarantula was fighting savagely to beat off a takeover attempt by a Sicilian outfit.

The Mob? Moriarty asked himself. Could be.

Then could it be the Mob that is knocking off these little stockholders and buying their shares?

Not likely, he concluded. The Mafia-owned corporations were buying Tarantula stock in big lots, tens of thousands of shares. Not the onesey-twoseys that the Retiree Murder victims had owned. Moreover, there hadn't been much selling to the Mobsters over the past several months. Tarantula was buying back its own stock pretty successfully and preventing the Mafia from gaining a controlling interest.

So who's buying the murder victims' stock? Moriarty asked himself for the hundredth time that afternoon. The computer could not tell him.

It takes two talents to be a good detective: the ability to glean information where others see nothing, and the ability to piece together bits of information in ways that no one else would think of. Perspiration and inspiration, Moriarty called the two.

He had sweated over the computer for practically the entire day. It had told him everything he asked of it; a most cooperative witness. But it had not been enough. Now he had an inspiration.

While the nurses were making their rounds, replacing the IV bottles that fed the comatose patients in the intensive care ward, Moriarty asked the computer for photographs of the members of Tarantula's board of directors. Maybe. Just maybe.

The pictures were slow in coming. The simple laptop computer, with its limited capability, built up each photo a line at a time, rastering back and forth across the screen like the pictures sent by an interplanetary probe from deep space.

The chief nurse herself brought Moriarty a skimpy dinner tray and laid it on the swinging table beside his bed with an expression on her face that said, "Eat everything or we'll stick it into you through an IV tube. Or worse."

Moriarty actually felt hungry enough to reach for the tray and munch on the bland hospital food while the computer screen slowly, slowly painted pictures of Tarantula's board members, one by one, for him to examine.

It wasn't until the very last picture that his blood pressure bounced sky high and his heart rate went into overdrive.

"It's him!" Moriarty shouted. "I'd recognize those eyes anywhere!"

He flung back the bedsheet and started to get to his feet, only to be surrounded instantaneously by a team of nurses and orderlies that included two hefty ex–football players. Despite Moriarty's struggles and protests, they pushed him back in the bed. The chief nurse herself stuck an imperial-sized hypodermic syringe into Moriarty's bare backside and squirted enough tranquilizer into him to calm the entire stock exchange.

"You don't unnerstand," Moriarty mumbled at the faces hovering over his suddenly gummy eyes. "There's a life at stake. Whoever bought Tarantula stock . . . his life's in danger. . . ."

Then he fell fast asleep and the team of nurses and orderlies left, with satisfied smiles on their faces.

Weldon W. Weldon was forced to call a recess to the board of directors meeting after the orderlies had finally cornered the all-singing, all-dancing Gunther Axhelm and carted him away. The conference table was a scuffed-up mess, and several of the older directors needed first aid.

He sat in his powered chair, Angora blanket across his lap, and watched the maintenance robots polish the table and rearrange everyone's papers neatly. The conference room's only door swung open, and a malevolently smiling P. Curtis Hawks stepped in. His red toupee was slightly askew, but Weldon said nothing about it.

"You wanted to see me?" Hawks snapped. He self-consciously planted his fists on his hips, just above the pearl handles of imitation Patton pistols.

"Yes I did," Weldon replied, adding silently, You stupid two-faced idiotic clown.

"Well?"

"Close the door and come down here," said Weldon. "What I have to tell you shouldn't be shouted across the room."

Hawks pushed the leather-padded door shut and slowly walked down the length of the long conference table, avoiding the robots that were industriously polishing its surface back to a mirror-quality sheen.

Pulling up a heavy chair and sitting directly in front of the Old Man, Hawks slowly took the pacifier from his mouth and said, "You forced me to do this."

"Did I?"

"Yes you did," the younger man said, his voice trembling just a little. Like a little boy, Weldon thought. A little boy who's mad at his daddy but knows in his heart that he's being naughty.

Weldon said carefully, "You thought that I sent Axhelm into your operation to destroy you."

"Didn't you?"

"No. I sent him to Webb Press because the operation had to be cleaned out before we could transfer to electronic publishing. And you wouldn't have the kind of cold-blooded ruthlessness it took to clean house."

"Clean house? He's driven us out of business!"

"Not quite," said Weldon. Then he added with a smirk, "Your losses are going to save Tarantula a walloping tax bite next fiscal year."

"Webb Press shouldn't be run as a tax loss. . . ."

"And it won't be," said Weldon softly, soothingly, "once you've converted to electronic publishing."

"You mean you . . ."

"Haven't you been paying attention to the industry news?" The old man was suddenly impatient. "Haven't you seen what's happening at Bunker Books? Their own sales force is suing Bunker over Cyberbooks."

Hawks gaped at him, uncomprehending.

"I had to clean out Webb Press," Weldon explained, "before you could even hope to start with electronic publishing. One thing I've learned over the years, never expect a staff to change the way it does business. If you're going to go into a new venture, get a new staff. That's an ironclad rule."

"So you were going to get rid of me, too," said Hawks grimly.

Weldon felt exasperation rising inside him like boiling water. "Dammit, Curtis, you can be absolutely obtuse! I *told* you your job was safe! I *told* you I wanted Webb to lead the world into electronic book publishing. What do I have to do, adopt you as my son and heir?"

Hawks thought it over for a long moment, chewing hard on his pacifier.

"It would help," he said at last.

Now it was Weldon's turn to go silent as he thought furiously. *This is no time for a split on the board. The Sicilians will take advantage of it and move in for good. Yet—Hawks has already risen to his level of incompetence. If I promote him one more step . . .*

The old man smiled at his erstwhile protégé, a smile that had neither kindness nor joy in it, the kind of smile a cobra might make just before it strikes, if cobras could smile.

He wheeled his powered chair up to Hawks's seat and reached out to pat the younger man on his epauletted shoulder.

"All right, Curtis," Weldon said softly, almost in a whisper, "I'll do just that. Make you my heir. How would you like to take over the responsibilities of chief executive officer of Tarantula Enterprises?"

The pacifier dropped out of Hawks's mouth. "CEO?"

Nodding, Weldon said, "I'll remain chairman of the board. You will still report to me. But instead of merely running Webb Press, you'll have the entire corporation under your command."

Hawks looked as if he were hyperventilating. It took several gasping tries before he could say, "Under . . . my . . . command!"

"I take it you accept the offer?"

"Yes!"

"Fine. Now let's get the rest of the board in here and finish our business."

Taking a deep breath to calm himself, Hawks agreed, "Right. Let's tell them the good news."

Weldon smiled again. Chief executive officer, he snorted to himself. I'll let you enjoy the office and the perks for a few months, and then out you go, my boy, on your golden parachute. Or maybe without it.

Hawks was grinning ear to ear. Chief executive officer! From that power base I'll be able to get rid of the Old Man in six months and take over the board. You're a gone goose, Weldon W. Weldon, only you don't know it yet.

Telephone Transcript

Harold D. Lapin: Hello, this is Lapin.

Mobile Phone: (Sounds of street traffic in background) Yes, I can hear you.

Lapin: The trial adjourned for the day, just five minutes ago.

Mobile: Justice only works a short day, eh?

Lapin: It will resume tomorrow at ten o'clock.

Mobile: Okay, okay. So how did it go today?

Lapin: The plaintiff scored all the points. Judge Fish seems to be leaning over backwards in their favor. I don't think Bunker has a chance.

Mobile: Good. Good.

Lapin: Bunker himself did not show up. His wife and several of his editorial employees were present. And the inventor, Carl Lewis.

Mobile: He didn't recognize you, did he?

Lapin: No, certainly not. I sat in the last row, while he was all the way up front. I'm wearing a false mustache and an entirely different style of clothing.

Mobile: Good. Good.

Lapin: Bunker Junior was there, too.

Mobile: What did you find out about him?

Lapin: It wasn't easy. I had to bribe three members of the family's personal law firm.

Mobile: But what did you find out? Has he made out a will or hasn't he?

Lapin: He has not.

Mobile: So if he should suddenly die, he dies intestate.

Lapin: That's right.

Mobile: His estate will be tied up in probate court for months, maybe years.

Lapin: Yes.

Mobile: And the Tarantula stock the little fool has been buying will be tied up along with everything else. No one will be able to vote the stock. Not even the Sicilians.

Lapin: I believe that means his proxies will automatically be voted by the corporation, isn't that right?

Mobile: I'm not sure. The lawyers will have to look into it. But at least the Sicilians won't be able to get their hands on it.

Lapin: If young Bunker should suddenly die.

Mobile: When he dies, yes. When he dies.

TWENTY-TWO

SCARLET Dean ran a lovingly manicured blood-red fingernail along Ralph Malzone's hairless chest and all the way down to his navel.

"Don't stop there," Ralph said, pulling her closer to him.

She giggled girlishly. They were in Scarlet's apartment, where Malzone spent almost every night. It was a spacious room in an old Manhattan building that had once been used as the setting for a horror movie. But although the outside of the building was dark and ornately Gothic, it had been completely modernized inside. The only way to tell it was an old building, from the inside, was to realize that no modern building would have such high ceilings. Nor such elegant moldings where the walls and ceiling met.

Scarlet's bedroom was completely mirrored. All of the walls, including the closet doors (where roughly half of Malzone's haberdashery was stored) and the high ceiling. On the rare occasions when sunshine made it through the polluted air and grime-covered window, the room dazzled and sparkled. It was like being inside a gigantic jewel.

But now the window blinds were drawn tight, and the only light was a dull red flicker from the artificial fireplace.

"Do you still love me?" Scarlet asked him.

Malzone turned his rusty-thatched head to gaze into her emerald eyes. "You bet I do."

"Even though our romance started with chemical warfare?"

It was by now a private joke between them. "I don't care how it started, Red. It started. And I never want it to end."

"Me neither," she said, snuggling closer.

Malzone sighed. "But we'll probably both be out of a job in another few days, the way the trial's going."

"This was just the first day," Scarlet said. "Our side didn't even get a chance to speak, yet."

"You mean management's side."

Propping herself on one elbow, Scarlet replied, "You're on management's side, aren't you?"

"Kinda." Malzone shifted uncomfortably on the bed.

"What do you mean?"

His lean, long face contorting into a miserable frown, Malzone admitted, "I know how Woody and the rest of the sales staff feel. Hell, I was one of them for a lot of years before I got kicked upstairs to sales manager. . . ."

Scarlet's expression softened. "You feel sorry for them."

"I feel sorry for all of us. I don't see this as one side versus the other side. I don't think of us as management versus labor. This is a family fight. It's damned unhappy when members of the same family have to fight. In public, yet."

She plopped back on the mattress and looked at their reflection in the ceiling mirror. Ralph was a coiled bundle of muscle and nervous energy; it excited her to look at his naked body. And she was glad that she kept herself ruthlessly to her diet and exercises; she wanted to keep on looking good to him.

"Maybe there's a way to get both sides together," Ralph was saying, "so we can stop this fighting and be all one happy family again."

Scarlet shook her head. "I don't see how."

"I do," he muttered, so low that she barely heard him.

Without taking her eyes off the ceiling mirror, she asked, "How?"

"We give up on Cyberbooks."

"What?"

"It's the only way. We tell Carl to pack up and leave."

"But you can't do that to him! And P. T. would never—"

"I know P. T. won't back down, so it's all a pipe dream. And I know Carl's a good guy, a friend, somebody I like a lot." Malzone hesitated a moment, then went on, "But the only way to save Bunker Books is to drop the Cyberbooks project. If we don't, the company's going to be torn apart and go down the tubes."

She turned toward him again, her heart suddenly beating faster. "Ralph, I have a confession to make to you."

"Another one? You sure you're not a closet Catholic?"

"Be serious!"

"Okay."

"I was planted at Bunker Books by my boss at Webb Press. I was supposed to be a spy. My assignment was to steal Cyberbooks away from Bunker."

Malzone's face brightened. "Great idea! Let's give it to them! Let *them* tear themselves apart!"

Scarlet stared at him. "Do you think . . . I mean . . ."

Ralph slid a wiry arm around Scarlet's trim bare waist. "Let's do it! And afterward, let's figure out how to get Cyberbooks to Webb Press."

Alba Blanca Bunker was in bed also, but for more than an hour she had nothing to say except moans and howls of passion. The voice-activated computer that ran the bedroom's holographic decor system had run its gamut from deep under the sea to the exhilarating peaks of the Himalayas, from a silent windswept desert in the moonlight to the steaming raucous orchid-drenched depths of the Amazonian jungle.

Ever since his body-restructuring operations, Pandro had been a half-wild animal: a passionate, powerful animal who would sweep Alba up in his strong arms the minute she arrived home from the office and carry her off to bed, like some youthful Tarzan overwhelming a startled but unresisting Jane.

Over the months since his operation, Alba had expected his ardor to cool. It did not. It was as if Pandro were trying to make up for all the years he had allowed business to get in the way of their lovemaking; as if he had stored all this passion inside himself and now, with his newly youthful and energetic body, was sharing his pent-up carnal fury with her.

Now they lay entwined together, tangled in a silk sheet that was thoroughly ripped, soaked with the sweaty musky aura of erotic sexual love. The room's decor had shifted to a warm moon-lit meadow. Alba could hear trees rustling in the soft wind, smell fresh-cut grass. Fireflies flickered across the ceiling.

As if struggling up from a deep, deep sleep, P. T. asked in the darkness, "How did things go today?"

"Oh—all right, I suppose. It's only the first day of the trial." She hadn't the heart to tell him her worst fears.

But he sensed them. "All right, you suppose? That doesn't sound too good."

"It wasn't so bad."

Bunker looked into his wife's face. Even in the flickering shadows he could see how troubled she was.

"Maybe I should go to the court with you tomorrow," he muttered.

Her heart fluttered. He's willing to leave the house, in spite of his fear of people and crowds, just for me. He's willing to face the world, for me!

Struggling to hold her emotions in check, Alba said, "That's not necessary, darling."

"Are you sure?"

"Yes, of course. It's all right."

"Are you sure?" he repeated.

All day long in that dreadful courtroom Alba had maintained her self-control. She had not cried or screamed when Woody's lawyer accused her of being a heartless money-mad despoiler of the poor. She had not taken after him with one of her spike-heeled shoes, as she had wanted to. She had remained cool and reserved, and had not said a word.

But now, after the evening's wild lovemaking, all her defenses were down. She broke into uncontrollable, inconsolable sobs.

"Oh, Pandro," she wept, "we're going to lose everything. Everything!"

The Writer was astonished at how easy it had been to acquire enough armaments to equal the firepower of a Vietnam War infantry platoon. He had been asweat with nervous fear when he walked into the gun shop. He had nothing bolstering him except the memory of an ancient video of an old Arnold Schwarzenegger flick.

The gun shop owner had been wary at first; a shabby-looking customer coming in just before closing time, dressed in a thread-bare gray topcoat and baggy old slacks. But the Writer smiled and explained that he was doing research for a new novel about terrorists, and needed to know the correct names and attributes of the kinds of guns terrorists would use. Within fifteen minutes the owner had locked his front door and pulled down the curtain that said CLOSED. He picked out an array of Uzi, Baretta, Colt, and laser-aimed Sterling guns. With the smile of a man who really cares about his merchandise, the shop owner proceeded to explain the virtues and faults of each weapon.

"And they all use the same ammunition?" the Writer asked naively.

"Oh no! The Baretta takes nine-millimeter . . ." Before long the owner was showing how each gun is loaded.

It was simple, then, for the Writer to pick up the massive Colt automatic and point it at the owner's head.

"Stick 'em up," he said with a slightly crazy grin.

The owner laughed.

The Writer cocked the automatic and repeated, minus the grin, "Stick 'em up."

He walked out of the gun shop burdened by nearly thirty pounds of hardware. He actually clanked as he hurried down the street. The owner lay behind his counter, bound and gagged with electrician's tape that the Writer had bought earlier from a nearby hardware store with his last five dollars.

"I can't believe it," Carl said with a shake of his head.

He and Lori were strolling slowly around Washington Square, still numb with the shock of the first day of the trial. They had gone to a tiny restaurant in the Village for dinner, but neither of them had much of an appetite. They left the food on the table, paid the distraught waiter, and now they walked aimlessly toward the big marble arch at the head of the square.

The November evening was nippy. Carl wore an old tennis sweater under his inevitable tweed jacket; Lori had a black imitation leather midcalf coat over her dress. A chilly breeze drove brittle leaves rattling across the grass and walkways. Only a few diehard musicians and panhandlers sat on the park benches in the gathering darkness, under the watchful optics of squat blue police robots.

"I just can't believe it," Carl repeated. "That lawyer made Cyberbooks sound like something Ebenezer Scrooge would invent just to throw people out of work and make them starve."

"And the judge let him get away with it," Lori said.

"This isn't a trial. It's an inquisition."

With a deep sigh, Lori asked, "What will you do if the Bunkers lose? If the judge actually issues an injunction against Cyberbooks?"

Carl shrugged. "Go find another publishing house, I guess, and sell the idea to them."

"But don't you understand? If the judge issues an injunction against Cyberbooks, it will be a precedent that covers the whole industry!"

Carl looked at her, puzzled.

"If Bunker is enjoined from developing Cyberbooks," Lori explained, "it sets a legal precedent for the entire publishing industry."

"That doesn't mean . . ."

"If any other publishing house decided to develop Cyberbooks with you, what's to stop their sales force—or their editorial department, or anybody else—from doing just what Woody's doing? And they'll have the legal precedent of the Bunker case."

Carl stopped in his tracks, his face awful.

Lori felt just as bad. "No other publishing house will go anywhere near Cyberbooks if we lose this case."

"Cyberbooks will be dead," he muttered.

"That's right. And I'll never get to publish *Mobile, USA.*"

"Huh? What's that?"

"The novel I told you about."

"Oh, that great work of literature." Carl's tone was not sarcastic, merely unbelieving, defeated.

"I'll have to spend the rest of my life working on idiot books and dancing nights to make ends meet."

"You could leave Bunker Books."

"It would be just the same at another publishing house."

"You could leave the publishing business altogether," Carl said.

"And go where? Do what?"

Before he realized what he was saying, Carl answered, "Come back to Boston. I'll take care of you."

And before she knew what *she* was saying, Lori snapped, "On an assistant professor's salary?"

"But I'll have Cyber—" His words choked off in midsentence.

Lori fought back tears. "No, Carl, you won't have Cyberbooks. You'll be back to teaching undergraduate software design and I'll be belly dancing on Ninth Avenue and we'll never see each other again."

His face became grim. He pulled himself to his full height and squared his shoulders. "Then we damned well had better win this trial," he said firmly.

"How?" Lori begged. "Even the judge is against us."

"I don't know how," said Carl. "But we've just got to, that's all."

PW Forecasts

The Terror from Beyond Hell

Sheldon Stoker.
Bunker Books
$37.50. ISBN 9-666-8822-5
Sheldon Stoker's readers are legion, and they will not be disappointed in this latest gory terror by the Master. Terror, devil worship, hideous murders and dismemberments, and—the Stoker trademark—an endangered little child, fill the pages of this pageturner. The plot makes no sense, and the characters are as wooden as usual (except for the child), but Stoker's faithful readers will pop this novel to the top of the best-seller charts the instant it hits the stores. (January 15. Author tour. Major advertising/promotion campaign. First printing of 250,000 copies.)

Passion in the Pacific

Capt. Ron Clanker, USN (Ret.)
Bunker Books.
$24.95. ISBN 6-646-1924-0
A better-than-average first novel by the last living survivor of the epic Battle of Midway (World War II). Tells the tale of a bittersweet romance in the midst of stirring naval action, with the convincing authenticity of a sensitive man capable of great wartime deeds. The characters are alive, and the human drama matches and even surpasses the derring-do of battle. (January 15. No author tour. No advertising/promotion campaign. First printing of 3,500 copies.)

TWENTY-THREE

As a bullet seeks its target, dozens of men and women from all parts of greater New York converged on the single oak-panelled courtroom in which the Bunker *vs.* Bunker drama was to be played out.

Lori Tashkajian, foreseeing a lifetime of dreary editorial offices and smoky Greek nightclubs ahead of her, rode the Third Avenue bus to the courthouse.

Carl Lewis, after a sleepless night trying to think of some way to turn the tide that was so obviously flowing against Cyberbooks, decided that he could use the exercise and so walked the forty blocks to the courthouse, through the crisp November sunshine.

Scarlet Dean and Ralph Malzone took a taxi together, each of them wrapped in their own gloomy thoughts.

The Writer rode the crowded subway downtown, his heavily laden topcoat clanking loudly every time the train swayed.

P. Curtis Hawks, glowing with his new title of CEO, directed his chauffeur to whisk down the FDR Drive for a firsthand look at the trial that was going to break Bunker Books. Even though his limousine was soon snarled in the usual morning traffic jam (which often lasted until the late afternoon traffic jam overtook it), Hawks smiled happily to himself at the thought of Bunker going down the drain.

P. T. Bunker, Jr., rode with his mother in her white limo the few blocks that separated their Lower East Side mansion from the courthouse. Junior hummed a pop tune to himself, grinning, as he contemplated how the computer in his room at home was busily buying up every spare share of Tarantula stock it could find.

Alba Bunker did not notice her son's self-satisfied delight. She dreaded another day in court and longed to be in the powerful arms of her oversexed husband.

Dozens of curious and idle people with nothing better to do headed for the courtroom, after learning from their TV and newspapers of the fireworks the cowboy attorney had lit off the day before.

Lt. Jack Moriarty had the most difficult course. Upon awakening from the sedatives administered to him the previous evening, he realized with the absolute certainty of the true hunch-player that the Retiree Murderer was going to be in that courtroom. Half an hour with his laptop computer convinced him that P. T. Bunker, Jr., was grabbing Tarantula stock like a drunken sailor reaching for booze, and the murderer was going to strike again that very morning.

Knowing it was hopeless to try to gain release from the hospital through normal channels (which meant waiting for Dr. Kildaire, who had just signed out at the end of his midnight-to-eight shift), Moriarty slowly, carefully detached the sensors monitoring his body functions and, clutching the array of them in his hands so that they would not set off their shrill alarms, he tiptoed to the bed next to his and attached them to the sleeping hemorrhoid case there. The spindly wires stretched almost to the breaking point, but the alarms did not go off.

With barely a satisfied nod, Moriarty raced to the closet and pulled on his clothes. Years of shadowing suspects had taught him how to seem invisible even in plain daylight, so he slithered his way out of the ward, along the corridor, down the elevator, and out the hospital's front entrance in a matter of minutes.

Using his pocket two-way he summoned a patrol car to take him to the courthouse. When the dispatcher asked what authority he had to request the transportation, Moriarty replied quite honestly, "It's a matter of life and death, fuckhead!"

Justice Hanson Hapgood Fish allowed his clerk to help him into his voluminous black robes, then dismissed the young man for his morning pretrial meditation. He sank onto his deep leather desk chair and closed his eyes. The vision of all the lovely women in his courtroom immediately sprang to his mind. Mrs. Bunker, looking so vulnerable and hurt in virginal white. The one in red: stunning. The dark-haired one with the great boobs. This was going to be an enjoyable trial. Justice Fish determined that he would drag it out as long as possible.

Let the goddamnable lawyers talk all they want to, he said to himself. Let them jabber away for weeks. I'll give them all the latitude they want. They'll love it! After all, they bill their clients by the minute. The longer the trial, the more money they squeeze out of their clients. And the longer I can sit up there and gaze at those three beauties. He smiled benignly: a blonde, a redhead, and a brunette. Too bad they're all on the losing side of this case.

One other person was thinking about the Bunker trial, even though he was not heading toward the courtroom.

P. T. Bunker sat alone in his half-unfinished mansion, at the old pine desk he had used since childhood, reviewing the videotape of the previous day's session in court. Thanks to freedom of information laws and instant electronic communications, it was possible for any informed citizen to witness any open trial.

He wore an old *Rambo XXV* T-shirt, from an ancient promotional drive to tie in the novelization with the movie. It was spattered with bloody bullet holes, and showed a crude cartoon of the elderly Rambo shooting up a horde of Haitian zombies from his wheelchair. Below the shirt Bunker was clad only in snug bikini briefs, his legs and feet bare. He no longer needed padding to look impressive.

His handsome face grimaced as he watched the plaintiff's attorney attacking Bunker Book's management—himself! his wife!—in his relentless western invective.

A low animal growl issued from P. T. Bunker's lips as he watched the videotape. After nearly an hour, he glanced once at the Mickey Mouse clock on his desk top, then rose and headed for his clothes closet.

Carl Lewis arrived in the courtroom precisely at one minute before ten. Half a dozen other people were filing in through the double doors and finding seats on the hard wooden pews. Carl saw Lori up in the front row, talking earnestly with Scarlet Dean and Ralph Malzone. As he started toward them, a scruffy man of indeterminate age, wearing a long shapeless gray topcoat and a day's growth of beard, accidentally bumped against him. Carl felt something hard and metallic beneath the man's coat, heard a muffled clank.

But his mind was on Lori and the others. He mumbled a "Pardon me," as he pushed past the man and headed for his friends. He did not even notice Harold D. Lapin sitting on the aisle in the next-to-last row. Lapin sported a dashing little mustache and wore a yachting outfit of white turtleneck, double-breasted navy-blue blazer, and gray flannel slacks. Hidden in plain sight.

P. T. Junior entered the courtroom right behind Carl. He was followed by P. Curtis Hawks, dressed in a fairly conservative business suit. Neither of them recognized the other.

"All rise."

Carl had not yet sat down. The courtroom buzz quieted as Justice Fish made his slow, dramatic, utterly dignified way to his high-backed padded swivel chair. His completely bald skull and malevolently glittering eyes made Carl think once again of a death's head.

There was more of a crowd this morning. The news of the

western lawyer's tirade had drawn dozens of onlookers and news reporters, the way a spoor of blood draws hyenas. Just as Judge Fish rapped his gavel to open the morning's proceedings, two more men slipped through the double doors and took seats on opposite sides of the central aisle, in the very last row. One of them was Detective Lieutenant Jack Moriarty, freshly escaped from St. Vincent's Hospital. Just behind him came a rather tall, slim figure in a blue trenchcoat. Neither man paid the slightest notice to the other; their attention was concentrated on the drama at the front of the courtroom.

Judge Fish leaned forward slightly in his chair and smiled a vicious smile at the western lawyer.

"Is the plaintiff ready to continue?"

The man was dressed in a tan suede suit cut to suggest an old frontiersman's buckskins. "We are, Your Honor."

"Are you ready to call your first witness?"

"Yes, sir."

"Then proceed."

"I call Mr. Ralph Malzone to the witness stand."

Carl felt a moment of stunned surprise. The courtroom fell absolutely silent for the span of a couple of heartbeats, then buzzed with whispered chatter. The judge banged his gavel and called for silence.

Ralph looked more surprised than anyone as he slowly got to his feet and made his way to the witness box. He ran a nervous hand through his wiry red hair, glanced at Woody Balogna sitting at the plaintiff's table, then at Mrs. Bunker, at the defense table with her five interchangeable lawyers.

The bailiff administered the oath and Ralph sat down. Uneasily.

The western lawyer strolled slowly over to the witness box, asking Ralph to state his name and occupation. Ralph complied.

"Sales manager," drawled the lawyer. "Would y'all mind explaining to us just exactly what that means?"

Slowly, reluctantly, Ralph explained what a sales manager does. The lawyer asked more questions, and over the next quarter of an hour Ralph laid out the basics of the book distribution system: how books go from printer to wholesalers and jobbers, then from those distributors to the retail stores.

"There's a lot of different steps involved in getting the books from the publisher's warehouse to the ultimate customer, the reader, wouldn't you say?" the lawyer prompted.

Nodding, Ralph replied, "Yes, that's right."

No one noticed P. Curtis Hawks, sitting in the audience, wincing at the word "warehouse."

"A lot of jobs involved in each of those steps?" asked the lawyer.

"Yes."

"Now, if Bunker Books went into this Cyberbooks scheme, how would your distribution system change?"

Ralph hesitated a moment, then replied, "We would market the books electronically. We could send the books by telephone directly from our office to the bookstores."

"Eliminating all those steps you just outlined?"

"All but the final one."

"Isn't it true that you could also sell your books *directly* to the ultimate customer, the reader? Transmit books *directly* to readers over the phone?"

"Yeah, I guess we could, sooner or later."

"Thereby eliminating even the bookstores?"

"I don't think we'd—"

"Thereby eliminating"—the lawyer's voice rose dramatically —"*all* the jobs of *all* the people you deal with today: the printers, the wholesalers, the jobbers, the truck drivers, the store clerks —*and even your own sales force!*"

"We have no plans to eliminate our sales force," Ralph snapped back with some heat.

"Not today."

"Not ever. Books don't sell themselves. You need sales people."

The lawyer strolled away from the witness box a few steps, then whirled back toward Ralph. "But you *admit,* don't you, that all the jobs in the middle—all the jobs involved with book distribution—will be wiped out by this devilish new invention.''

"The distribution system will be totally different, that's right.''

With a triumphant gleam in his eye, the lawyer strode to his table and pulled a batch of papers from his slim leather saddle bag.

"Your Honor,'' he said, approaching the bench, "I have here affidavits from each of the nation's major book distribution companies, and both of the national bookstore chains. They all ask that their interests be considered in this trial. Therefore, I ask you to consider enlarging the venue of this trial. I ask that this trial be considered a class action by the thousands—nay, tens of thousands—of warehouse personnel, truck drivers, bookstore clerks, wholesalers, jobbers, distributors, and their associated office personnel, against Bunker Books!''

The courtroom broke into excited babbling. Judge Fish whacked away with his gavel until everyone quieted down, then said, "I will consider the motion.''

The news reporters sitting at the media bench along the side wall of the courtroom tapped frantically at their computer keyboards.

With a satisfied grin, the western lawyer handed his papers to the bailiff, who passed them up to the judge. Then he smirked at the quintet of defense attorneys and made a little bow.

"Your witness,'' he said.

"No questions,'' squeaked five mousey voices in unison.

"Court will recess to examine these papers,'' said Justice Fish. Glancing at the clock on the rear wall of the courtroom, he added, "We might as well break for lunch while we're at it.''

THE ACCOUNTANT ▬▬▬

GREGORY Wo Fat squinted at the printout on his computer screen through old-fashioned eyeglass lenses thick enough to stop bullets.

As chief accountant for Webb Press (and one of the few employees still on Webb's payroll after the company's pruning by the Axe), Wo Fat's duties included supervising the royalty statements sent out to the authors of Webb's books.

The computer screen displayed the new layout for next year's royalty statements, a tangled skein of numbers designed to be as confusing as possible.

Wo Fat's grandfather, the esteemed accountant for the Honolulu branch of the Chinese Mafia, had drilled into his bright young grandson's mind since babyhood one all-important concept: "More money is stolen, my grandson, with a computer than with a gun."

Wo Fat had eschewed a life of crime. Almost. Instead of carrying on in the family tradition in Honolulu, he had come to New York and accepted a position as a lowly accountant with the publishing firm known as Webb Press.

"Your job is a simple one," said his first boss, an elderly gentleman named Kline. "No matter how many books an author sells, we should never have to pay royalties over and above the advance that the dumb editors gave the author in the first place. Got it?"

Wo Fat grasped the concept immediately. Of course, it did not apply to the firm's most prestigious authors. If they did not receive royalty checks every six months they would undoubtedly move to another publishing house. So they were paid—not as much as they actually earned, of course, but enough to keep them and their agents reasonably satisfied.

It was the other authors, the "midlist" authors who made up the great bulk of any publisher's titles and the new writers who had no experience, those were the ones whom Wo Fat slaved over. He regarded it as a personal failure if they received one penny in royalties over and above the advance they got before each book went on sale.

Wo Fat glowered at the computer screen. This new design was seriously lacking! What fool is responsible for this? This column here, if subtracted from the figures in the third column and multiplied by the square root of the figures in the first column, would actually tell the author how many books had been sold during the six months that the statement reported on!

Unacceptable! Someone's head would roll for this. Why, if he let this new design go through, Wo Fat would be besieged by authors demanding to know why they had not been paid for each and every book sold. That would never do.

TWENTY-FOUR ━━━━━━

CLAUDE Le Forêt had been born in a logging camp in Manitoba. He had grown up in logging camps, where his father was nothing more than an average cutter of trees and his mother a cook. But Claude had gone far beyond his humble beginnings.

Thanks to two lifetimes of hard work and sacrifice by his parents, Claude had gone to university. He had obtained a degree in management, and when he returned to the logging camp where his parents still slaved away over their tele-operated cutting machines and microwave cookers, he wore a business suit and carried a portable computer rather than a chain saw.

Yet he was still true to his upbringing. Beneath his gray flannel suit jacket he still wore a plaid lumberjack's shirt.

For many years Claude worked his way up the tree trunk of success. He had the brains and the inherited conservative instincts of his parents: he never went out on a limb, never barked at either a superior or an underling, never made a sap of himself. He stayed on the main trunk and rose quietly, unspectacularly, steadily to the very crown of Canada's largest lumber and paper-pulp combine.

Now he sat wedged into a tiny booth in the coffee shop on the ground floor of the courthouse, facing the suede-suited westerner who was representing what seemed to be the entire U.S. book distribution industry. The coffee shop was filled with lunchtime customers. It buzzed with gleaming-eyed lawyers and glumly downcast clients, all of them hunched head to head over tiny tables in cramped little booths, whispering secrets to one another over croissant sandwiches and Perrier.

"Your telegram said the affair was urgent," said Claude with a hint of Quebecois in his accent.

"Shore is urgent," smiled the lawyer.

Claude studied the weather-seamed face of this outlandish-looking lawyer. He himself was a handsome man, his face a bit fleshy from too much rich food, his eyes a bit baggy and bloodshot from the wine he drank with each meal, but otherwise he looked almost dashing with a touch of gray at his temples and a splendid mustache that curled up toward his slightly rouged cheeks. He wore a conservative two-button maroon suit, with his trademark lumberjack's plaid shirt and a tiny little bow tie of forest green. It took no great detective to deduce that he was totally color blind.

"You wish my corporation to join with you in this suit against the book *électronique*, is that it?"

"Yup," said the lawyer in his best Gary Cooper style.

"This would be a serious commitment by my corporation. Not only that, it would create an international incident. Canada would become heavily engaged in this lawsuit. The Canadian government would certainly take an interest. Ottawa and Washington would send observers to the trial, at the very least."

With a nod and a grin, the lawyer said, "Listen, Mr. Le Forêt." He pronounced the final "t," but failed to notice the shudder it sent along Le Forêt's spine. "If we let Bunker bring out Cyberbooks, what do you think it will do to the lumber business in Canada? To the paper and pulp industry?"

Le Forêt shrugged gallicly.

"I'll tell you what it'll do, friend. The more books they publish electronically, the less paper they'll need. Paper mills will shut down. Men will be thrown out of work. Whole cities will become ghost towns. The demand for lumber will be cut in half, then cut in half again. Thousands of lumberjacks will be unemployed. All those fancy tree-cutting machines of yours will be sitting out there in the forest, turning into rust. It'll be a disaster for you. And for Canada."

If there was one thing Le Forêt had learned in a long and successful career, it was to examine carefully the enemy's side of the matter. He sat pensively for a long moment, then steepled his fingers and played devil's advocate.

"If I do as you wish," he said slowly, "do you not think that the movement of environmentalists will come out on the side of Bunker and his Cyberbooks?"

"The environmentalists?"

"*Oui*. After all, they have been scheming for generations to close down the paper mills. They, with their silly nonsense about pollution. How can you make paper without sulfur and smoke? They even demand that we purify the water once we are finished using it!"

The lawyer smiled a thin, superior, knowing, nasty, lawyer's smile. "The environmentalists won't bother us," he said.

"Pah!"

"I have their word on it."

Le Forêt put on his pensive look again. "Their word? How so?"

"It's simple. I pointed out to them that if the paper and pulp industry goes under, the economy of Canada goes down with it."

"That has never bothered them in the past."

"Well, I also pointed out that if the paper mills close down, they lose one of their best targets for raising money. Everybody will think that they've won their battle against you, and stop contributing to the environmental movement. They'll go out of business, too!"

"Diable!" Le Forêt broke into a grin that pushed the tips of his mustache almost into his eyes. "And they believed you?"

"Sure they did. They know I'm right. They can't exist without you."

With a thoughtful rub of his chin, Le Forêt murmured, "I must remember this after the trial is finished. It is an interesting new light on a problem that has plagued me all my life."

The lawyer grinned back at him. "Then you'll join our suit?"

Sticking out a huge hand that was made to chop down trees, yet bore nary a callus, Le Forêt said, "I am with you. *Moi,* and the entire Canadian lumber and paper-pulp industries!"

When the trial resumed that afternoon, the lawyer grandly anno ced that the Canadian lumber and paper-pulp combine had joined in the class action suit against the rapacious forces of evil known as Bunker Books. Woody and the sales personnel attending the trial whooped loudly. Mrs. Bunker went pale, while Carl and the others on that side of the courtroom sagged visibly.

Judge Fish glowered at the cowboy lawyer as he accepted the papers filed by the Canadians.

"Will there be anyone else joining this suit?" he asked in a sharp, almost sneering tone. "Outer Mongolia, perhaps? Or maybe little green men from Mars?"

The lawyer bowed his head slightly, as if embarrassed. "Your Honor, I know this has been a somewhat unusual procedure, but in the interests of justice I beg you to overlook the slightly unorthodox course that this trial has taken so far."

The judge snorted at him.

"I assure you there will be no further enlargement of the plaintiff's co-complainants."

Turning to the clone group of defense attorneys, Justice Fish asked acidly, "Does the defense have any objection to this motion?"

The lawyer closest to Mrs. Bunker got to his feet, looking perplexed. "May we have five minutes to review our position on this, Your Honor? This motion has come as a complete surprise to the defense.''

"Yes, I imagine it has," the judge retorted. "Five minutes recess.'' He banged his gavel and stalked out of the courtroom.

Carl Lewis felt his temperature rising. "This trial is turning into a circus,'' he whispered to Lori.

"More like a Roman gladiatorial contest,'' she whispered back. "We're the Christians and they're the lions.''

Staring at the defense attorneys, all five of whom were frantically tapping at their briefcase computers, desperately searching for a precedent that would block the entry of the Canadians, Carl pleaded, "Isn't there some group that we could call in to back our side? I mean, how come we're all alone here and they've got so many people to back them up?''

Lori's eyes suddenly sparkled. "You're right! I've got an idea!''

She jumped up from her seat and pushed past Ralph and Scarlet to get to the aisle. Carl came right behind her.

"What is it?'' he asked as he followed her to the courtroom doors. "What?''

But Lori said nothing as she half ran to the row of public telephones down the marble corridor.

Picking up the nearest handset, she said to the voice-activated telephone computer, "The Author's League of America.''

Carl smiled with sudden understanding.

Raymond Mañana had never been a practical man. The fact that he had now served slightly more than seven years as president of the Author's League of America proved that fact.

Never very tall, Raymond had allowed years of poor eating habits and lack of exercise to round out what had once been a spare body into a globule about the size of a modest weather balloon. His glistening pate was bald, but his chin was covered with a dirty-gray beard of patriarchal length. His once keen vision had fallen victim to endless hours of peering at word processor screens, so he now sported heavy trifocal contact lenses that made his eyes seem slightly bugged out, like a frog's.

But despite these physical failings, Raymond had the heart of a lion. He had practically surrendered a mediocre career writing potboiler novels to accept the onerous and thankless responsibilities of the presidency of the Author's League. He was deeply immersed in reading the latest round of inflammatory letters sent in to the ALA *Bulletin* when the phone unit on his computer chimed out the first few bars of "Brush up Your Shakespeare," the ALA's official song.

Raymond welcomed the call. The letters were boring: two of the most widely read authors in the country reduced to boyish slanders and insults over the issue of whether or not the organization should have an official necktie. He poked the button that consigned the libelous words to the computer's memory bank.

Lori Tashkajian's lovely, worried face took form on the display screen.

"Lori! I thought you'd be in court this morning."

"I am," she answered. "We're on a short recess."

"Oh."

"Ray, we need your help. I need your help. The future of publishing depends on you!"

"On me?"

"On the Author's League."

"I don't understand."

Swiftly, Lori outlined what had been happening at the trial. Raymond nodded his understanding.

"So we need the Author's League to come in here and support us. Otherwise we're going to go down the drain and Cyberbooks will be strangled in its cradle."

"A mixed metaphor," said Raymond.

"We don't have time to argue syntax!" Lori almost shouted. "You've got to get the biggest number of authors you can contact to come into court on our side. Today! This afternoon!"

Raymond sadly shook his bald, bearded head. "What makes you think they'll come out to support Bunker Books? After all, authors and publishers aren't usually the best of friends."

"It's in your own best interest!" Lori insisted. "Cyberbooks will bring down the costs of publishing to the point where thousands of writers who can't get their works published now will have a viable marketplace for their books.''

"I know. I understand. And I applaud what you're trying to do. But . . ." His voice trailed off.

"But what?" Lori asked.

Feeling weak and helpless, Raymond explained, "Well, you know this bunch. They're *writers*, Lori. They can't agree on what to have for lunch, for Pete's sake. Half of them think Cyberbooks is the greatest idea since Gutenberg, the other half think it's an invention of Satan.''

"Oh, god.''

"And they don't like to go into courtrooms. Can't say I blame them. The idea gives me the chills.''

"But if the ALA won't support this innovation in publishing, you're dooming all the writers. . . .''

Raymond raised a pudgy finger. "I understand and I agree with you, Lori. I'll do what I can. I'll start calling people right now. But don't expect too much.''

"Maybe Sheldon Stoker!" Lori suggested.

"He's in Indonesia, directing the movie they're making from *The Balinese Devil*.''

"Oh.''

"I'll do what I can," said Raymond, knowing it sounded feeble.

"Please," Lori begged. "And quickly!''

"I'll do what I can.''

Lori nodded and broke the connection. Raymond Mañana sighed a great, heaving sigh and, like a general issuing orders for a hopeless charge against overwhelming odds, he began tapping out phone numbers on his keypad.

"She doesn't understand," he muttered to himself. "Editors just don't understand writers. We're not really organized. It's tough to get us to do *anything* except argue among ourselves. Christ, if we had any real organization, would the tax laws read they way they do?''

THE BOOK SIGNING ▬

CONRAD Velour sat in the middle of the bookstore, ballpoint pen poised, surrounded by stacks and stacks of his latest steamy novel, *Inside Milwaukee*. (After seventy-some "Inside" novels, he was running out of interesting cities.)

Not only was the table at which he sat heaped with copies of *Inside Milwaukee*. All the bookshelves in the front of the store were packed with the novel. Even more were stacked by the cash register, where a discreetly small sign suggested, HAVE YOUR COPY OF *INSIDE MILWAUKEE* SIGNED BY THE AUTHOR.

But the bookstore was strangely, maddeningly, eerily quiet. No customers had come to the table where MR. CONRAD VELOUR, AUTHOR!!! sat under the garish sign proclaiming his presence. Not a single book had been purchased. The ballpoint pen held in his white-knuckled fist had not scrawled out one autograph.

An icy anger was inching along Conrad Velour's blue veins. The store manager was definitely avoiding him. The clerks were tiptoeing across the store's plush carpeting and whispering behind his back.

Someone in the promotion department of S&M books was going to hang by the thumbs for this foul-up, Velour told himself. *Someone* was going to pay for this humiliation. More than an hour sitting on this hard bridge chair at this table heaped high with the best novel anyone's seen in years, and no customers. Not one.

They got the address wrong in the advertisements. Instead of 333 Fourth Avenue, the ads had all read 444 Third Avenue. Velour had discovered the mistake too late to do anything about it. He himself had gone to the address the S&M publicist had given him, only to find that it was not a bookstore at all. It was Ching's Pizza and Chinese Take-Out. He had found the bookstore after some frantic screaming into a street corner telephone's voice-activated computer directory.

Now he sat alone, flanked by piles of unbought books, while the store personnel avoided his furious stare. He had asked the youngsters behind the counter at Ching's to send the thousands of readers who would undoubtedly show up there to the proper address. But they barely understood English and—most crushing of all—not a one of them recognized him or his name.

You'd think that at least *some* of my faithful readers would recognize the mistake and find their way here, he groused to himself. But no, they're probably filling up on pizza and Chinese dumplings, making Ching rich while I sit here like a leper with bad breath and psoriasis.

Oh, they'll pay, he told himself for the millionth time. They'll pay!

A little old lady wandered into the hushed and nearly unpeopled store. Velour straightened up on his chair and gave her his most charming smile. He could be very charming when he wanted to be. He had the slim, elegant, slightly decayed looks of a bankrupt British lord. He wore the uniform of a successful author: white silk turtleneck shirt, informal Angora cardigan of royal blue, crisply creased gray slacks, and butter-soft moccasins of genuine artificial squirrel hide.

The little old lady doddered around the front of the store,

casting furtive glances toward the table where Velour and his oversupply of novels were stashed. She hesitated, took a few uncertain steps toward the author, stared up at the sign proclaiming who he was, then made a sour face, shook her head, and turned around and left the store.

Velour's hand clenched so tightly the ballpoint pen snapped in two.

The store manager, a young wisp of a man, approached him as if he were a live bomb.

"Uh, sir . . . there's a telephone call for you, sir."

Velour fixed him with an evil stare. Sweat broke out on the youngster's upper lip.

"Uh . . . I could bring the mobile phone here, I guess."

Velour raised his left eyebrow one centimeter.

"It . . . uh, it doesn't have a picture screen, though. Sir."

"Good," he snapped. "Then whoever is phoning will not see the humiliation I'm being put through."

The store manager scuttled away and returned half a minute later with the portable phone instrument in his trembling hand.

Velour took a deep breath, then made himself smile as he sang, "Velour here!"

"Conrad. Glad I located you. It's Raymond Mañana."

"What can I do for you, Ray?"

"I'm not interrupting important business, am I?"

"For you, Ray, I can set aside business for a few moments. What's so important that you tracked me down here in the middle of a signing session?"

"It's about the Cyberbooks trial, Conrad."

"Oh, yes. I read something about that in *PW* last week, I think."

For the next ten minutes Mañana explained what was happening in the courtroom. "So I thought, you're almost around the corner from the courthouse already, maybe when you've finished your signing you could pop over there and offer them some moral support."

Conrad Velour sighed a patient, long-suffering sigh. It was *so* difficult to deal with fools. "Raymond, it's impossible. I'm not a Bunker author, to begin with, and I don't see why authors should be called upon to pull Bunker's chestnuts out of the fire. If this Cyberbooks deal falls through, so what? It won't affect me or my sales."

"But—"

"No, Raymond. I will not lift a finger to help P. T. Bunker." And he clicked the phone's disconnect button.

It won't affect me or my sales, Velour repeated to himself as he stared out across the empty bookstore. It won't affect me or my sales.

TWENTY-FIVE

CARL was surprised to hear his own name called as the plaintiff's next witness. For a moment he felt the cold pain of fear surging through him. But then he looked the cowboy lawyer squarely in the eyes and rose to his feet. The fear burned away in the rising heat of righteousness. I'll show this hotdog what Cyberbooks is all about. I'll set them *all* straight. He patted his jacket pocket, where he always carried one of the Cyberbooks readers. I'll show them all.

Swearing to a deity he did not believe to exist, Carl took the witness chair and calmly watched the lawyer approach him the way a gunfighter in the Old West might saunter up a dusty town's main street.

"Your name?" the lawyer asked.

"Carl Lewis."

"Your profession?"

"I am an assistant professor at the Massachusetts Institute of Technology."

"That's your position," the lawyer corrected. "What is your profession?"

"Software composer."

"And what does that entail? What do you actually do?"

Glancing up at the judge, who hovered over him like an implacable death's head, Carl said, "I create the software programs that make computers run. Without such programs, a computer is nothing but a box full of electronic or optical switches."

"You make the computers actually perform, is that it?"

"Yes."

"You bring the machines to life."

"Right."

"Sort of like Dr. Frankenstein, huh?"

Carl felt his cheeks heat up. "It's not at all—"

But the lawyer cut him off with more questions. Soon Carl was explaining how Cyberbooks worked, and he even pulled his electro-optical reader from his jacket pocket to show the lawyer and the judge how to operate it. Justice Fish seemed fascinated with the device. The book it showed was Robert Louis Stevenson's *Kidnapped*, complete with dozens of beautiful full-color illustrations.

After nearly fifteen minutes of tinkering with the Cyberbooks reader, while the lawyer and the entire courtroom waited with growing impatience, the judge finally put the device down on his banc next to his silver-plated water pitcher.

"Exhibit A," he instructed the bailiff. Carl began to wonder if he would ever get it back.

"Now, Mr. Lewis," the lawyer said smoothly, running a hand through his long silver-streaked hair, "just what motivated you to invent this here Cyberbook machine?"

"What motivated me?" Carl felt puzzled.

"Why'd you do it? What was going through your mind while you were working to perfect it? The desire for money? Wealth? Fame? A way to get promoted to full professor?"

Shaking his head, Carl said, "None of those."

"Then what?"

Carl smiled slightly. The lawyer had talked himself into a trap.

Now I can tell them the real truth, make them understand why Cyberbooks is so important.

He took a deep breath, then began, "The main difference between human beings and other animals is our ability to communicate. Speech. Without true speech you can't have a truly intelligent species. The two most important inventions in the history of the human race were writing and printing. Writing allowed us—"

"Mr. Lewis," intoned the judge, "spare us the history lesson and answer the question."

Surprised, Carl said, "But I am, Your Honor."

"The question was about your motivation for creating this invention, not about the history of the human race. Be specific."

There was a slight commotion at the defense table. Carl saw Mrs. Bunker whispering furiously to the lawyer closest to her, who abruptly turned to the one next to him, and so on down the line until the last of the five clones got to his feet and said— rather weakly, Carl thought—"Objection, Your Honor."

"On what grounds?" Judge Fish demanded.

"Plaintiff's counsel asked the witness about his motivations for inventing Cyberbooks. The question permits the widest allowable interpretation. Restricting the witness to—"

"Denied," snapped the judge. Turning to Carl, he commanded, "Restrict yourself to the time period when you were inventing the device, young man."

Carl's guts churned with boiling hot anger. He glared at the judge, then turned back to the smirking cowboy lawyer.

"My motivations were simple. I wanted to make this world a better place to live in."

Carl had expected a gasp of awe from the audience. Perhaps some scattered applause. Nothing. Dead silence.

He plunged ahead. "Books are the life blood of our society. Our racial memory. Poor people can't afford books. Kids in ghetto schools hardly ever even see a book. Certainly they don't buy any. That's because they can't afford them. Books are too expensive for poor kids. Too expensive for the poor people in Latin America and Africa and Asia. Cyberbooks will bring the cost of buying books down to the point where even the poorest of the poor can afford it.''

''But as I understand it,'' the lawyer said, ''the reading device will cost several hundred dollars. How do you expect the poor to buy your fancy machines?''

''The government can buy them and distribute them free, or at nominal cost. The publishing industry could even donate a certain number of them, out of the profits they'll make from Cyberbooks.''

''And then all these poor people will have to buy Cyberbooks and nothing else, is that right? You'll have them hooked on your product. Very neat.''

''They will be reading books!'' Carl countered. ''They will be learning. They'll be able to *afford* to learn, to grow, to pick themselves up and make better lives for themselves. Even people who've never learned to read will be able to use Cyberbooks that talk to you. The books themselves will teach them how to read.''

''While Bunker Books makes a fortune and corners the entire publishing industry.''

Ignoring that, Carl went on. ''There's another factor here. Today the publishing industry consumes millions of acres of trees every year. Paper mills pollute the air and water around them. They contribute to the greenhouse effect and alter the world's climate. They contribute to acid rain. When the publishers turn to Cyberbooks we'll be able to stop that awful waste and make the world cleaner and greener.''

''Is that so?'' The lawyer smiled craftily as he turned back toward the plaintiff's table. He opened his saddle bag and took out a slim sheaf of papers bound in a set of green covers.

''I have here in my hand a report by the Wildlife Foundation, a respected international environmental organization.'' The lawyer waved the report over his head as he approached the witness box. ''It says here that if the existing Canadian logging industry were to cease its operations—which they find environmentally sound, by the way—then the beaver population of the forests would undergo a population explosion that could upset the ecological balance of the entire Canadian forest system!"

Now the audience gasped. One odd-looking fellow in a maroon suit and plaid shirt actually clapped his hands together once.

"Far from making the world cleaner and greener," the lawyer continued, "your invention could lead to an ecological catastrophe!"

Carl sat in stunned silence, unable to summon a word of rebuttal.

The cowboy turned dramatically to the defense table. "Your witness."

The middle one of the five identical mice peeped, "No questions."

"Witness may step down. Call your next witness."

Shakily, Carl walked away from the witness box and headed for his seat. Lori looked sad and sympathetic, waiting for him in the first row of benches. Just before he sat down, Carl heard the western lawyer boom out:

"I call Mrs. Alba Blanca Bunker."

"Mrs. Bunker to the stand."

It was a nightmare. The lawyer badgered and hounded Mrs. Bee, trying to twist every word she said into an admission that Bunker Books was attempting to drive thousands of innocent, hardworking men and women out of their jobs and into miserable lives of perpetual poverty.

Mrs. Bunker, all in white as usual, seemed to shrink on the witness chair like a little girl being scolded by an unforgiving parent. Her face was so pale that Carl thought she was about to faint.

"And isn't it true," the lawyer snarled at Mrs. Bee, "that the *only* reason you became interested in Cyberbooks was your vision of making huge fortunes in profits? That you didn't care if thousands of ordinary men and women were thrown out of work? That sheer, vicious greed was driving you to commit this horrible act of economic mass murder?"

Mrs. Bunker's eyes went wide and her mouth dropped open. She was staring not at the tormenting lawyer but beyond him, at the muscular figure who had barged through the courtroom's double doors, past the startled uniformed guard there, and now strode up the aisle toward the front of the courtroom.

Vaulting over the low rail that divided the audience from the front of the court, Pandro T. Bunker reached the cowboy before Judge Fish could even grasp his gavel. P. T. grabbed the westerner by a padded suede shoulder, whirled him around, and socked him squarely on the jaw. The lawyer sailed four feet off the ground and landed in a crumpled suede heap at the foot of the judge's banc.

Pandemonium broke out. Alba ran to the powerful arms of her protective husband. The judge banged his gavel so hard the head broke off and fell over the edge of the banc, bopping the semiconscious lawyer on the top of his head. The audience was on its feet, pointing, laughing, roaring. The five defense attorneys were running around in circles. The news reporters stared in frozen amazement.

And then a shot rang out.

The Writer, standing on the wooden bench of the rearmost pew, his long topcoat flapping open to reveal a veritable arsenal of small arms, held a smoking automatic pistol over his head.

"Nobody move!" he screamed, his scrawny face red, his eyes wild. "You're all my hostages! First one to make a move gets a bullet!"

THE FIVE O'CLOCK NEWS

BOBBI Burnheart elbowed her way through a phalanx of carefully coiffed and jacketed news reporters to a spot where she could be seen dramatically posed against the besieged courthouse. Behind her trailed the highly trained team of dedicated specialists who made Ms. Burnheart the most popular TV anchorperson in New York: her hairdresser, her makeup man, her wardrobe manager, and her speech coach.

Behind *them* came the camera crew: two disgruntled guys in greasy coveralls carrying twelve-ounce picocameras with integrated lasers that could light Ms. Burnheart beautifully even in the stygian darkness of a sewer during a power blackout at midnight in the middle of a snowstorm; and her ostensible producer, a young and slimly beautiful black woman recently graduated from the Sorbonne who was the only person at the station naive enough to take on powerhouse Bobbi.

La Burnheart swept a practiced eye across the facade of the courthouse, its graffiti-covered concrete now glaring with police spotlights. Several battalions of New York police, SWAT teams,

FBI agents, and National Guard troops had cordoned off the courthouse.

Bobbi Burnheart, though, daintily hiked her miniskirt up over her hips (revealing nothing except support panty hose) and clambered over the blue sawhorses that the NYPD had set up as a barrier.

"Hey, you can't cross . . ."

Bobbi flashed her dazzling shark's smile at the policeman pointing his stun club at her. "It's all right, Officer. Channel 50."

"My orders . . ."

But Bobbi had already turned to her two cameramen. "Get him on tape. Be sure to get his badge and name tag in focus."

They grumbled but rolled twelve seconds' worth of tape. The police officer, not certain if this was a chance at fame on TV or a warning not to infringe on the First Amendment, forced a smile for the cameras and then turned and ran to find his sergeant.

"Which windows?" Bobbi asked, now that they were in a clear space. She noted, somewhat smugly, that none of the other TV crews had dared to cross the police barricade even though she had. It confirmed her opinion of her supposed competitors. Of course, none of them had doting fathers who owned a chain of TV stations and a couple of U.S. senators.

The black producer consulted a smudged photocopy of the courthouse's floor plan, then pointed to a row of windows on the fourth floor. "Up there—I think."

"Good enough," said Bobbi. "Nobody will know the difference."

For the next several minutes her team of dresser, hair stylist, and makeup man fussed over her while the two cameramen and the producer talked over the best angles to shoot. Finally Bobbi was ready. She looked splendid in her toothpaste-tube ruched and pleated kelly green dress, her golden hair shining in the glow of the police spotlights like a goddess's helmet. The cameramen knelt at her feet to make a dramatic picture of Bobbi against the courthouse facade.

The producer put one hand to the nearly invisible communicator plugged into her left ear, cocking her head slightly to hear the voices from the control center at the station. She held up three fingers of her other hand, then two, one, and finally pointed straight at Bobbi—who instantly put on her dazzling shark's smile.

"Inside the windows you see behind me, a courtroom drama unlike any courtroom drama you've ever seen is being played out against the lives of dozens of men and women."

Staring earnestly into the nearer of the two picocams, she went on, "At approximately three-thirty this afternoon an unknown gunman seized courtroom number two, up there on the fourth floor, and has been holding several dozen people hostage, including the presiding judge, Justice Hanson H. Fish."

The producer was madly scribbling prompting words on a long roll of what looked like toilet paper and holding them up for Bobbi whenever Ms. Burnheart took a breath between lines.

"The case being tried involved the publishing industry. It was not a criminal case. No one knows who the gunman is, or what his demands are. He has released two hostages, the guard and bailiff on duty in the courtroom, but has issued no statement as to his reasons for taking the hostages or what he intends to do with them."

Breath. New set of prompts.

"Shortly after releasing the two men, a fusillade of shots was heard. But no one knows who has been killed, if anyone. The chances are that human bodies are bleeding inside that courtroom, while the police, the FBI, and the National Guard wait outside, trying to avoid further bloodshed, if possible."

Breath. New set of prompts.

"For now, all we can do is wait. And pray."

Turning toward the courthouse, but making certain that her face was dramatically profiled against the spotlighted courthouse facade, Bobbi Burnheart ad-libbed: "Will justice be done in courtroom two?"

TWENTY-SIX

CARL Lewis thought of a line from the Statue of Liberty as he gazed around the courtroom. "The wretched refuse of your teeming shores."

The courtroom looked like the steerage class of an old banana boat. Thirty-eight men and women sat, stood, sprawled in various attitudes of fear, frustration, despair, or exasperation, waiting for some unknown fate at the hands of an obvious lunatic.

The gunman had released the two uniformed men, the bailiff and the overweight guard who was supposed to stand duty at the courtroom's entrance door. Then the news reporters, huddled along the wall opposite the empty jury box, demanded that at least one of them be released too. The gunman had lined them against the wall and then used one of his semiautomatic pistols to shoot each and every one of their laptop computers where they rested on the press table. The reporters cringed. Two of them fainted. When the smoke cleared, they gaped at the wreckage of their precious laptops. And stopped making demands.

Shortly after the shooting, the New York Police Department,

true to its standard operating procedure for hostage situations, had cut off the building's lights, heat, and water. It was not cold in the courtroom, not this early in the evening. And the police spotlights outside threw slanting beams of glaring bright light that bounced off the high ceiling and scattered an eerie harsh illumination across the courtroom. The problem was water. The women were already complaining about toilet facilities. The only one that the gunman would allow them to use was in the judge's chambers, where there was no exit except through the courtroom. At least a half dozen women were lined up there constantly.

Carl sat on the same stiff bench he had been sitting on when the gunman had seized the courtroom. His back hurt and his buttocks were numb. Lori had stretched out on the bench, looking emotionally drained, and fallen into an exhausted sleep half an hour earlier. Carl had taken off his tweed jacket and bundled it into a rough pillow that now rested under Lori's soft cheek.

He gazed down at her, breathing the slow steady rhythm of deep sleep. She looked so beautiful, so desirable. He knew that he loved her, and he would do anything to keep her from harm, even face death itself if he had to.

The gunman was up at the judge's chair, peering out at the windows that glared with police spotlights. He had taken off his shabby topcoat and spread his arsenal of pistols and submachine guns across the top of the judge's banc. Since he had taken over the courtroom nearly three hours earlier, he had spoken hardly a word.

Ralph Malzone and Scarlet Dean had moved toward the rear of the courtroom, where they sat with their arms wrapped protectively around one another. Mr. and Mrs. Bunker were at the defense table, holding hands and speaking in low, earnest whispers. P. T. Junior had moved from the back of the courtroom to sit with his parents. The five defense attorneys were under the table, cowering.

"Well, son, I don't know how long you intend to hold us here," the cowboy lawyer called to the gunman, "but sooner or later you're gonna need a good defense attorney.'' He got up from his chair at the plaintiff's table and reached into the breast pocket of his suede jacket.

The gunman jerked as if a spasm had struck him and grabbed the Uzi submachine gun from the collection spread out before him.

''Sit down!'' he screeched.

The lawyer took a small white oblong from his pocket and held it above his head. ''I just wanna give y'all my card. You're gonna need a lawyer. . . .''

''And you're going to need a mortician if you don't *sit down!*''

The lawyer sat.

''And shut up! Keep your lying goddamned mouth shut!''

Far in the back of the courtroom, Lieutenant Moriarty sat in frustrated silence. He was unarmed, since the hospital personnel had routinely taken his gun, badge, and other possessions from him and stashed them in the hospital's storage center. His unauthorized leavetaking had prevented him from claiming his stuff.

Patience, he told himself. Patience, Jack old boy. This nutcake can't stay awake forever. Sooner or later he'll doze off, and that's when you grab him.

Provided you don't fall asleep yourself, first.

Moriarty studied the lean, lank, scruffy gunman. He can't be the Retiree Murderer. This isn't the same style at all, and therefore not the same man. But the murderer is in this courtroom, I know it. I can feel it. And so is his next intended victim.

He easily identified P. T. Bunker, Jr., up front with his mother and father. But try as he might, he could not find anyone who looked like the man who had tried to kill him. The harsh glow from the reflected searchlights cast strange shadows across faces, making it difficult to see people's eyes.

The murderer sat across the courtroom from Moriarty. He had recognized the police lieutenant shortly after the gunman had taken over, and wondered why Moriarty had not simply shot the maniac between the eyes and gotten this whole ordeal over with. He trusted that his disguise would keep him safe enough; after all, Moriarty hardly got even a moment's glance at him when he had attacked the lieutenant with the poisonous orchid's thorn.

But what was Moriarty doing here, in this courtroom? And why didn't the poison kill him, as it should have? The murderer had taken off his trenchcoat and folded it into a neat little cushion that he now sat on, fairly comfortably. He fingered the slim plastic box in his right jacket pocket. Inside it was another poisonous thorn from the deadly Rita Hayworth orchid.

Should I knock off young Bunker while that police detective is so close? he asked himself. Probably not. Although—if the cops try to break in and grab the idiot up there who's taken us hostage, there's bound to be a lot of shooting. Perhaps I could get to Bunker Junior then and do the job, in all the confusion.

Wait and see, the murderer told himself. Wait and see.

One other man was counseling himself to be patient: Justice Hanson Hapgood Fish. He sat slumped on the witness chair, unwilling to move any farther from his rightful seat of authority. He glowered up at the man who had taken over his chair. The blue veins in his forehead throbbed with unconcealed fury. This mangy bum, this crazed idiot, has taken over my courtroom. My courtroom! He's allowing all sorts of people to use my private toilet. Who knows what kinds of sickies and perverts are pissing in my bowl?

Judge Fish tried to force himself to be calm, without much success. He closed his eyes and imagined himself as the Grand Inquisitor of the good old days in Spain, with this filthy disgusting derelict stretched on the rack. "Boil the oil," Justice Fish muttered to himself. "Heat the branding irons."

He smiled cruelly.

"You people all think I'm crazy, don't you?"

All eyes shifted to the man up at the banc.

"You think I'm just some wild-eyed fruitcake who's gone berserk. I know what you're thinking. I can see it in your faces. Well, I'm not crazy. And even if I am, it's you people who drove me to it." He waved a heavy Colt pistol at the staring audience.

The Writer enjoyed the attention. "You think you're so damned high and mighty. Well, I'm here to tell you that you ain't. I'm here to *show* you that I'm just as good as you are. Maybe better.''

He rambled on for hours, as the night grew colder but not darker, thanks to the spotlights flooding through the windows. People curled up on the hard wooden benches and tried to sleep. Eventually the Writer stopped speaking to them. But he dared not close his eyes.

From time to time the telephone back in Judge Fish's chambers rang, but the Writer would not let anyone answer it.

"I'm not ready to talk to them yet. I still got plenty I want to tell you people.''

But he lapsed into a grudging silence, and the thirty-eight hostages drifted into little knots of twos and threes.

"Do you think we'll get out of this alive?'' Scarlet Dean asked in a small, frightened voice.

"Sure we will,'' said Ralph Malzone with a certainty that he did not feel. He put his arm around Scarlet protectively, and felt her trembling. "We'll be okay, Red. We'll be fine, you'll see.''

"As long as you're with me,'' Scarlet said, fighting back tears of terror. "I can stand anything if you're with me, Ralph.''

"I'm right beside you, baby. All the way.''

Pandro T. Bunker was also comforting his wife as the chill of November began to seep into the unheated courtroom.

"It's all my fault,'' Alba Bunker was saying softly. "If I hadn't pushed you into this Cyberbooks project . . .''

"No, no,'' said P. T. "It's *my* fault. I've hidden myself away from the world for too long, left all the burden of running the business on your shoulders.''

Junior discreetly got up from his chair beside them and started wandering aimlessly down the central aisle of the courtroom. He knew his mother and father wanted to say things to each other that should be said only when they were alone. Briefly he thought about the five lawyers huddled beneath their table. So they hear Mom and Pop coo at each other; they won't understand a word of it. They're lawyers, not human beings.

"That cruise we took this past summer," P. T. was saying. "I've been thinking . . ."

"It was a wonderful cruise," she murmured.

"Wouldn't it be great if we could cruise the seas all the time? Live on a boat. A sailboat. Just sail to anyplace that strikes our fancy—Tahiti, New Zealand, Copenhagen, Greece, Buffalo."

"Buffalo?"

"I've never been to Buffalo. I've never seen Niagara Falls. I've never been *anyplace*. I've always been too damned busy with the company."

"You've had all the responsibilities of business. . . ."

"*We've* had all the responsibilities. For too long a time, dearest. We're not getting any younger."

Alba smiled up into his handsome face. "Oh, I don't know. That cruise took ten years off your age, or more."

Smiling back at her tenderly, P. T. answered, "What I mean, darling, is that we've worked hard all our lives and now we should start to enjoy what we've made."

"Enjoy?"

He nodded. Glancing up at the mumbling, half-drowsing gunman, P. T. said, "If . . . I mean, when we get out of this, you and I are going to buy a yacht and sail it around the world."

"But the business!"

"Let somebody else worry about the business. Why should we kill ourselves over it? Let's enjoy our lives while we can."

Alba blinked with surprise. Let someone else take over Bunker Books? Leave it all and go sailing around the world? A voice in her head warned against it. But in less than a moment it was drowned out by a surge of joy and wonder and gratitude at the marvelous, wise insight that her loving husband had just shared with her.

"Pandro, you're right," Alba heard herself say. "Leave the business to Woody or whoever wants to slave over it. We *deserve* to enjoy the rest of our lives!"

Carl was half-stupefied with the need to sleep. But he refused to let his eyes close. Sooner or later that lunatic up there was going to nod off, and when he did Carl was determined to race up to the banc and disarm the madman.

Beside him, Lori stirred and pulled herself up to a sitting position. "What time is it?" she asked, rubbing her eyes.

Glancing at the glowing digits on his wristwatch/calculator, Carl replied, "Almost midnight."

"The police haven't done anything?"

"Guess they're afraid of starting a bloodbath."

Lori shivered. "It's cold!"

Carl put his jacket over her shoulders and then wrapped his arm around her. She snuggled so close to him that he could feel her body warmth even through the jacket.

"When will it end?" Lori asked.

Carl shrugged, and kept his bleary eyes on the gunman.

The Writer kept on talking because he knew that once he stopped, the temptation to sleep would overwhelm him. He was babbling about his life, spinning out his autobiography for his captive audience.

". . . and I couldn't afford to go to college. Couldn't get a scholarship, even though I had good marks in high school. I wasn't a member of any recognized minority. I thought about changing my religion, or dyeing my skin, or even a sex-change operation. I wondered how come a group of people who make up fifty-one percent of the population could be classified as a minority. But there wasn't a college in the land that would let me in. Not one. . . ."

I ought to ease on up toward the front of the courtroom, thought Lieutenant Moriarty. This boob can't keep droning on like that forever. He's putting everybody to sleep, and sooner or later he's going to doze off himself.

As he got up slowly from the rearmost bench, a stray thought wafted through his mind, about how blind people seem to compensate for their disability by increasing the sensitivity of their other senses.

Now why would I think of that? he asked himself. Good detective that he was, Moriarty knew from experience that the subconscious mind often comes to realizations and understandings long before they are recognized by the conscious mind. What's my subconscious trying to tell me?

A faint whiff of something strange, a cloying pungent odor, like something from a tropical jungle, some strange hybrid flower that was beautiful but deadly—the Rita Hayworth orchid! The doctor at the hospital had told him that the flower produced a strange, powerful scent. Moriarty turned in the eerily lit courtroom and began to follow his nose, like a true bloodhound.

P. Curtis Hawks sat with the news reporters at their table along the far wall of the courtroom. The shambles of their laptops lay strewn across the long table and scattered on the floor around them. Whenever anyone shifted a foot, it crunched on the remains of silicon chips.

The afternoon and evening had been a revelation to Hawks. He realized, with deep shame, that he was a physical coward. When that psycho had started shooting, Hawks's heart had gone into palpitations and his bowels had let loose. Now, smelly and sticky and thoroughly ashamed of himself, he sat with the reporters. To the others, it looked as if he were doing something brave, deliberately sitting with the group that had come closest to death. Actually, Hawks figured that lightning would not strike twice at the same place. The reporters had been cowed into abject silence. One of them was still comatose, stretched out on the floor with his hands folded funereally over his chest.

All he needs is a goddamned lily, Hawks grumbled to himself.

He had worried, when he had drifted over toward the reporters, that they would object to his awful smell. But they never noticed it. Either that, or they were extending him their professional courtesy.

"You think you're so high and mighty," the Writer was rambling from his perch up at the judge's seat. "Well, I'll tell you something. Without the writers you're *nothing*. Your whole damned industry, all of you—editors, publishers, salesmen, every one of you—you'd be *noplace* without your writers. The writers are your gold mine, your oil field, your natural resource. And how do you treat them? Like a dog, that's how. Like a horse or a mule or worse.''

Lori was nodding as she listened to the gunman's increasingly passionate tirade. He must be a writer, she realized. And she found herself agreeing with what he was saying.

"I wrote a book," he went on. "Might not be a very good book, but I wrote it as honest and real as I could. And I sent it to your company. More than a year ago, now. And you never answered me. No letter. Not even a rejection form. You never sent my manuscript back! It was the only copy I had! Now it's lost and it's all your fault and you're going to pay for destroying *Mobile, USA*.''

Carl, groggy and sleepy, shook his head. "Did I hear him right? He just accused you of destroying Mobile, Alabama?"

But Lori was suddenly wide-eyed. She gasped. She clutched at Carl's arm. "*Mobile, USA*! That's the novel I want to publish! He's the writer I've been trying to contact!"

She shot to her feet, breathless with excitement. But before she could say a word there was a sudden scuffle off to one side of the courtroom and the writer, screaming with fearful rage, grabbed the Uzi submachine gun from his desk.

REJECTION SLIPS ▄▄▄

The Usual

Dear Sir or Madam:
  Thank you for submitting your manuscript for our considera-
tion. Unfortunately, we find that it does not suit our needs at the
present time. Naturally, we cannot give individual comments on
each of the many manuscripts we receive.
                          Sincerely,
                          The Editors

The Cruel

Dear Sir or Madam:
  Who are you trying to fool?
                          Disgustedly,
                          The Editors

The Japanese

Most respected author:

We have read your work with inexpressible pleasure. Never in our lives have we seen writing of such sheer genius. We are certain that if we published it, your book would be brought to the attention of the Emperor, who would insist that it serve as a model for all future writings. Since no one could possibly hope to equal your sublime masterpiece, this would put us out of business. Therefore we must return your manuscript to you and lay it at your feet, trembling at the harsh judgment that future generations will have of us.

> Most humbly and sincerely,
> The Editors

TWENTY-SEVEN ━━━━━

P. T. Bunker, Junior, was standing off to one side of the courtroom, by the empty jury box, wondering if he should get in line for the toilet in the judge's chambers or just whiz out the window. He made his way through the shadowy courtroom to one of the long windows and stood on tiptoes to see outside. Squinting against the powerful glare of the police searchlights, Junior saw that the street below was still jammed with TV news crews, cops, soldiers, and hundreds of onlookers.

No whizzing out the window, Junior said to himself. Not unless you want it shown on *Good Morning, America*.

Junior utterly failed to notice the rather tall, bearded man sidling up behind him with one hand in the side pocket of his suit jacket. The bearded man failed to notice the stocky form of Lieutenant Jack Moriarty stealthily stalking him.

It all happened in a flash. Junior turned away from the window and was suddenly confronted by the bearded man, who whipped his hand from his pocket and started to poke at Junior. But Moriarty grabbed the man's arm and yelled, "Get out of the way, kid! He's a killer!"

267

A strangled scream came from the judge's banc, where the gunman leaped to his feet and cocked the submachine gun he had grabbed. Then a woman's voice pierced the courtroom:

"Don't shoot! I want to publish *Mobile, USA!*"

Moriarty wrestled the bearded man to the floor and twisted the thorned stalk of the Rita Hayworth orchid from his hand. The false beard slipped off the man's chin. Even in the shadowy light, Moriarty recognized him from the photographs he had studied in his hospital bed.

"Weldon W. Weldon, you're under arrest for five murders and one attempted murder," he said.

Weldon cackled insanely. "You can't arrest me!" he screamed. "I'm the chairman of the board of Tarantula Enterprises! I can buy and sell your whole police force!"

Across the courtroom, P. Curtis Hawks heard the old man's shrieking voice. "My god!" he gasped. Forgetting the condition of his clothes, he dashed across to where his erstwhile boss was writhing in the grip of the long arm of the law.

"You can walk!" Hawks cried, astonished at the sight of Weldon out of his wheelchair, even though he was stretched on the floor with the solid weight of Lt. Moriarty on his chest.

Weldon glared up at his employee with insane fury flashing in his eyes.

The Writer, meanwhile, stood frozen up at the judge's banc, the Uzi in his hands, cocked and ready to fire.

"You want to publish my novel?" he asked into the midnight air. "Did somebody say they wanted to publish my novel?"

"I do," said Lori, rushing to the foot of the banc. Carl came up beside her, protectively.

"Who're you?" the Writer asked.

"I'm an editor at Bunker Books. I've been trying to contact you for more than six months. I've written half a dozen letters to the address you put on your manuscript, but they were all returned by the post office with a stamp that says you've moved and left no forwarding address."

The Writer put the Uzi down on the desk top. "Uh, yeah, I did move," he mumbled, feeling sheepish.

"I want to publish *Mobile, USA,*" Lori said. "I think it's a great work of art."

The Writer sagged back onto the judge's chair, his mouth hanging open, his arms dangling by his sides. He felt suddenly dizzy, weightless. The room swam before his eyes. Slowly his head came forward and clunked on the desk top. He had passed out.

It took nearly a week to straighten out everything. A week of surprise after surprise.

The following Sunday, however, was one of those brilliant Indian summer days that Washington Irving admired so much. The sun was bright and warm, while the air sparkled with the crisp bite of autumn.

Carl, Lori, Ralph Malzone, and Scarlet Dean were having brunch together at the penthouse restaurant atop the recently re-re-renovated Chrysler Building. The restaurant was small and elegantly decorated in art deco style with bold angular motifs that matched the spire's high, slanting windows.

Despite the stylized crystal flutes before each one of them and the silver bucket that bore a heavy magnum of champagne in the middle of the table, Carl stared morosely out the window nearest their table at the skyscrapers that marched row upon row up the long narrow avenues of Manhattan. Like the windmills of Don Quixote, he thought glumly. And like Don Quixote, I've tilted against them and lost.

For this was a farewell party.

Even so, there was laughter. "The crowning blow came the next morning," Scarlet Dean was saying, "after we all returned to the office and started to sort things out. Mrs. Bee came running into my office, waving a sheet of paper from the law firm that represented us at the trial. The bastards had charged Bunker Books $45,000 for the nine hours those five twerps had spent as hostages!"

Ralph Malzone wiped at his eyes. "That was the last straw. When P. T. heard that he ran right out of the house and bought the yacht."

"And they've already taken off?" Lori asked.

"Yeah. First stop, Bermuda."

"And P. T. has made you the head of Bunker Books while he and Mrs. Bee sail off around the world," Lori said.

Still looking slightly dazed by it all, Ralph ran a hand through his rust-red thatch of hair and replied, "Yeah. I'm now the chief operating officer of Bunker Books. And Scarlet is taking over Mrs. Bee's role as publisher."

Carl had drunk as much champagne as any of them, but he did not feel drunk. Nor happy. He was numb.

Ralph toyed with his fluted glass, gave a sidelong glance to Scarlet, then turned his attention back to Lori. "And I've got some news for you, kid. You're the new editor-in-chief of Bunker Books."

Lori gasped with surprise. "Me? Editor-in-chief?"

"That's right," said Scarlet. "Ralph and I agreed on that right away."

Forcing a smile that he did not feel, Carl raised his champagne glass. "Here's to your success, Lori," he toasted. "You've earned it." With bitterness burning in his gut, he added, "And to yours, Scarlet. And to yours, Ralph."

They sipped, but then Ralph's face grew somber. "My success isn't going to do you any good, pal."

"I know," said Carl. "I understand."

Scarlet put a hand on Carl's arm. "The only way to keep the company from going down the tubes was to make a deal with Woody and the sales staff. We've agreed to drop Cyberbooks."

Carl's lips pressed into a tight, white line. But at last he said, in a low voice, "Lori's been keeping me informed. I guess it's the only thing you could do."

"I didn't want it to end like this," Ralph said.

"It's not your fault," said Carl. "I understand the fix you're in."

Lori tried to brighten things. "At least I get to publish *Mobile, USA.*"

"Now that's something I don't understand," Carl admitted. "You told me that the novel was a work of art, and if you published it, it wouldn't sell enough copies to pay for the ink used to print it.''

"Oh, that was before the author became famous. Taking over the courtroom and holding us hostage has made him a celebrity.''

"But he's in jail, isn't he?''

"We got him released into our custody,'' Scarlet said. "He's doing interviews with all the big news magazines and TV talk shows. We're rushing his novel into print, to take advantage of the publicity.''

Carl took a longer swig of his champagne. "You'd be able to get the book out this week if you'd do it as a Cyberbook.''

Ralph shook his head. "No can do, pal. We made the deal with Woody and his people and we've got to stick with it. Nobody in the whole publishing industry will touch Cyberbooks.''

"It's a damned shame,'' said Scarlet without much feeling.

Carl took a deep breath. "Yeah. A damned shame.''

They finished their brunch in a quiet, subdued mood. Ralph and Scarlet were obviously overjoyed at being handed Bunker Books on a platter, but they could hardly celebrate properly when the price of their good fortune was scuttling Carl's invention.

The four of them took the long elevator ride to the lobby and went out onto the sun-filled street, where Ralph and Scarlet hailed a taxi uptown. Carl and Lori walked toward their apartment building, some twenty short Manhattan blocks downtown.

"What will you do now?'' Lori asked him.

Shrugging, "Go back to MIT. My sabbatical is just about over, anyway.''

"Carl, I'm so damned sorry about all this. . . .''

"It's not your fault,'' he said. Then, looking squarely into her dark, limpid eyes, he worked up the courage to ask, "Lori— would you come to Boston with me? Will you marry me?''

Tears welled up in her eyes. "I can't,'' she said, her voice almost pleading. "I've just gotten the first big break of my career. And with this novel finally coming out, I can't leave now. This is my first real chance. I can't give it up, no matter how much I love you, Carl.''

"You do love me?"

"I do. I love you. Didn't you know?"

"I love you!"

They melted into each other's arms and kissed passionately. Thirty-seven pedestrians, including three married couples accompanied by children and fourteen singles walking their dogs, passed them on the sidewalk before they broke their fervent embrace.

"Stay here in New York, Carl," Lori said eagerly.

"No," he said. "This isn't the town for me."

"But . . ."

He shook his head sadly. "It's not like the romantic novels, Lori. This is real life. True love doesn't always win."

"I don't want to lose you!"

"Then leave the publishing business and come up to Massachusetts with me."

"I can't! You can't expect me to throw away my career, my life. . . ."

With a bitter smile, Carl said, "And I can't stay here and let you support me. I've got a career to think about, too."

They walked in dejected silence back to their apartment building. Once in the elevator, going up, Carl said:

"We'd better say good-bye right here and now, Lori. It'll hurt too much to prolong it."

The elevator stopped at Lori's floor with its usual jolt. The doors slid open. Lori leaned a finger against the button that held them open.

"You mean . . . this is it?"

"I'm going to take the next train to Boston. Today. This afternoon."

"But . . ."

"Good-bye, Lori. I love you and it's tearing my guts apart."

They kissed one last time and she pulled away from him and stepped out of the elevator. Carl stood there, frozen with grief and guilt and doubt, staring at Lori's troubled, teary face. Then the elevator doors slid shut and he could no longer see her at all.

ROOM AT THE TOP ▬▬▬

P. CURTIS Hawks sat at the broad desk in the spacious office on the next-to-the-top floor of the Synthoil Tower. Chairman of the board of Tarantula Enterprises (Ltd.). At last!

He wore a magnificent military uniform of his own special design, heavy with braid and medals. The emergency meeting of the board of directors the previous week had gone extremely well: he had been elected chairman unanimously. Weldon W. Weldon was safely tucked away in a well-guarded private sanitarium far upstate, pretending to be a cripple once again. The Old Man was hopelessly insane and would spend the rest of his days in his powered chair making imaginary deals with phantom associates and tiptoeing around his funny farm at night to slaughter hallucinatory rivals.

It had taken the better part of two weeks to clear away the jungle that the Old Man had created. Just cleaning the rugs had been a Herculean task. But now the office was back the way it should be: sparkling, grand, imposing, even humbling to the lower-caste visitor.

Hawks inhaled deeply and smelled the new leather and high-

273

gloss aroma of power. He sat in his magnificent elevated chair. It's mine, he congratulated himself. All mine!

The desk phone chirped.

"Answer answer," Hawks said crisply.

"Mr. Hawks, sir"—the phone computer's voice was that of a groveling *bhisti*'s singsong—"a certain Mr. MacDonald McDougall requests the honor of your presence in the boardroom of the Synthoil Corporation at eleven o'clock this morning sharply, sir."

Hawks exhaled. The Synthoil board wanted to meet him. The computer was merely reminding him of the appointment in the groveling way it had been programmed.

Hawks took the private elevator up the one flight to the Synthoil offices. While Tarantula was on the next-to-the-top floor of the mighty tower, Synthoil was at the very top.

A slim, dark, curly-haired young man dressed in a jet-black Italian silk suit was waiting for Hawks at the elevator doors. Without a word, he ushered Hawks into the plush and panelled conference room of the Synthoil Corporation.

MacDonald McDougall smiled genially at Hawks. Even though Hawks had never before met the CEO of Synthoil, the Scotsman's bushy red beard and handsome mustache were unmistakable. He wore a bulky tweed business suit, with a plaid sash of the distinctive McDougall tartan slanting beneath his jacket.

"Sit yerself doon, Mr. Hawks," said McDougall, waving his huge hand toward the only empty chair at the long, gleaming conference table.

The chair was at the very foot of the table. All the men on one side of the table were stocky, frozen-faced Orientals, dressed in gray business suits. And every man sitting on the other side was dark of hair, wide of girth, and dressed in jet-black suits of Italian silk. And sunglasses.

Hawks's heart sank as he was introduced to his new masters.

WINTER,
Book IV

RETIRED NAVY OFFICER DIES

Chelsea, MA. Capt. Ronald Reginald Clanker, USN (Ret.), died yesterday in the Army/Navy nursing home where he had spent his final ten years.

Capt. Clanker, last remaining veteran of the Battle of Midway in 1942, was 93. He was the author of *Passion in the Pacific*, a novel published three weeks before his death. According to a spokesperson for the nursing home, Capt. Clanker suffered a fatal heart attack shortly after being informed that his book was no longer available for sale, and all unsold copies had been pulped by the publisher.

There are no survivors.

TWENTY-EIGHT ▀▀▀▀▀

Two things surprised Carl that cold February afternoon.

First had been the telephone call from P. T. Bunker, Junior. Out of the blue, Junior had invited Carl for drinks at the Parker House in downtown Boston.

Second was the snow. The day had dawned frostily clear, and the sky had still been crystalline when Carl had entered his lab building at MIT. He had scooted along the basement tunnels to get to his 2:00 P.M. class, as he usually did. It was quicker and warmer; he didn't need a winter coat. After the class he had returned to his windowless laboratory through the same tunnels.

So when he stepped outside for the first time since early morning, he was surprised that nearly a foot of snow lay on the ground, with more gently sifting down out of a darkened sky.

It took a little longer for the transit train to make the short run from MIT station to Beacon Hill, but Carl reached the cozy bar of the Parker House only a few minutes after four.

Junior was already there, at a little table in the corner, chatting amiably with the cocktail waitress.

They shook hands, Carl took off his snow-wet coat, and settled down onto one of the comfortable easy chairs. He ordered a light beer. Junior was drinking something big and bulbous and frothy, exotic and lethal looking.

Junior looked somehow more mature, more relaxed with himself, than he had a scant few months earlier, the last time Carl had seen him. Maybe it's his clothes, Carl thought. Junior was wearing a conservative beige business suit with an executive's turtleneck shirt of sky blue.

"How've you been?" they asked in unison. Then they laughed.

"You first," Junior insisted.

Carl shrugged. "Doing okay, I guess. Got some bright kids in my classes. Tinkering with some new ideas for electro-optical computers that will link directly to the nerve system. Working with a couple of biologists from Harvard on that one."

Junior nodded. "And the Cyberbooks idea?"

The pang that sliced through him made Carl wince visibly. "That's dead. No publisher wants to touch it."

"Too bad," said Junior.

Carl nodded, thinking more of Lori than his invention.

The waitress brought Carl's beer and smiled prettily at Junior. He grinned back at her. Then, turning to Carl, he said, "I've gotten out of the publishing business, too. With Mom and Dad off sailing around the world and Ralph doing such a good job of running the company, I went out and looked for new worlds to conquer."

"Really?" Carl felt no real curiosity, no interest at all.

"Yup. I'm in the toy business now." Some of the old craftiness seemed to creep back into his expression.

Carl sipped at his beer because he did not know quite what to reply.

Junior went ahead anyway. "Y'know, I've been thinking. The toy industry is a lot different from book publishing. The accent is on innovation, new ideas, new gadgets." He laughed. "You've got to run damned fast to stay ahead of the five-year-olds!"

Carl thought of the nephews and nieces he saw at Christmas-time. "Yes," he agreed. "They can be pretty sharp."

Junior licked his lips and leaned closer to Carl. Lowering his voice, he said, "I was wondering if you could make a Cyberbooks kind of thing for kids. You know, something to help them learn to read. And then they could keep it and go on to *real* books as they get older."

The only sound that Carl could get past his utter surprise was, "Huh?"

Junior explained the idea to him again. And then once more.

"But it's the same device, the exact same thing," Carl blurted, once he was certain he understood what Junior was saying. "The only thing that changes is the content of the books we put on the chips. We'd be doing children's books instead of adult books."

Junior's smile widened. "Right, except that there's one other thing that changes."

"What's that?"

"The distribution system. We distribute Cyberbooks through toy stores, not bookstores. We won't have any trouble with guys like Woody Baloney."

"Won't the toy salesmen . . ."

"They already spend most of their time pushing electronic gadgets for the kids. Cyberbooks will be just another toy, as far as they're concerned."

Sinking back in his soft chair under the realization of what Junior was suggesting, Carl said, "You could create a whole new kind of book publishing industry this way."

"That's right," Junior agreed, looking as if he had just swallowed the most delicious canary in the history of the world. "We start in the toy industry, but we end up taking over the entire publishing industry. It'll be Cyberbooks, just the way you wanted it!"

"Through the back door."

"Right."

Carl thought it over. "It could hurt a lot of people. People we know, like Ralph and the others."

"They can come to work for us, when the time comes."

"I don't know. . . ."

Leaning even closer, Junior said, "We'll have to start out on a shoestring. You and I will be equal partners, we'll share every-thing right down the middle, fifty-fifty. And, of course, you'll have to spend a lot of time in New York. Probably have to come down to the city every week or so."

"Every week?"

A small shrug. "Every week, ten days. Give you a chance to see old friends, huh?"

Lori's phone number flashed through Carl's mind. He thought he had forgotten it, but every digit shone in his thoughts. He stuck his hand out and Junior grabbed it and pumped it hard.

"You've got a deal," Carl said.

EPILOGUE
Fifty Years Later

News Release

WASHINGTON, D.C. The Library of Congress put on display today the last book to be printed on paper in the United States. Carefully protected in a shatterproof glass airtight casing, the book—the fortieth edition of the classic novel, *Mobile, USA*—will remain on public display until the end of the year.

Carl Lewis, Jr., son of the inventor of Cyberbooks, said at the opening ceremony, "My father would have been proud, I'm sure, to see his invention of the electro-optical publishing system totally replace paper books. He was a dedicated ecologist, and he loved both literature and trees."

Mrs. Lori Tashkajian Lewis, the inventor's widow and managing director of Cyberbooks Inc., added, "Back in the old days, when my late husband first invented Cyberbooks, there were fears that electronic publishing would destroy the book industry. History has shown that those fears were groundless."

With tears in her eyes, Mrs. Lewis continued, "I'm proud to

have played a small role in bringing inexpensive literature to the huge masses of poor people all around the world.''

Cyberbooks' latest publication, she revealed, is _Blood of the Virgin,_ by Sheldon Stoker Beta, one of the clones of the late best-selling author.